Joan Aiken and The Murder Room

⟩⟩⟩ This title is part of The Murder Room, our series dedicated to making available out-of-print or hard-to-find titles by classic crime writers.

Crime fiction has always held up a mirror to society. The Victorians were fascinated by sensational murder and the emerging science of detection; now we are obsessed with the forensic detail of violent death. And no other genre has so captivated and enthralled readers.

Vast troves of classic crime writing have for a long time been unavailable to all but the most dedicated frequenters of second-hand bookshops. The advent of digital publishing means that we are now able to bring you the backlists of a huge range of titles by classic and contemporary crime writers, some of which have been out of print for decades.

From the genteel amateur private eyes of the Golden Age and the femmes fatales of pulp fiction, to the morally ambiguous hard-boiled detectives of mid twentieth-century America and their descendants who walk our twenty-first century streets, The Murder Room has it all. **⟩⟩⟩**

The Murder Room
Where Criminal Minds Meet

themurderroom.com

T0352403

Joan Aiken (1924–2004)

Joan Aiken, English-born daughter of American poet Conrad Aiken, began her writing career in the 1950s. Working for *Argosy* magazine as a copy editor but also as the anonymous author of articles and stories to fill up their pages, she was adept at inventing a wealth of characters and fantastic situations, and went on to produce hundreds of stories for *Good Housekeeping, Vogue, Vanity Fair* and many other magazines. Some of those early stories became novels, such as *The Silence of Herondale*, first published fifty years ago in 1964.

Although her first agent famously told her to stick to short stories, saying she would never be able to sustain a full-length novel, Joan Aiken went on to win the *Guardian* Children's Fiction Prize for *The Whispering Mountain*, and the Edgar Alan Poe award for her adult novel *Night Fall*. Her best known children's novel, *The Wolves of Willoughby Chase*, was acclaimed by *Time* magazine as 'a genuine small masterpiece'.

In 1999 she was awarded an MBE for her services to children's literature, and although best known as a children's writer, Joan Aiken wrote many adult novels, both modern and historical, with her trademark wit and verve. Many have a similar gothic flavour to her children's writing, and were much admired by readers and critics alike. As she said 'The only difference I can see is that children's books have happier endings than those for adults.' You have been warned . . .

By Joan Aiken
(Select bibliography of titles published in The Murder Room)

The Silence of Herondale (1964)
The Fortune Hunters (1965)
Trouble With Product X (1966)
Hate Begins at Home (1967)
The Ribs of Death (1967)
Died on a Rainy Sunday (1972)

The Ribs of Death

Joan Aiken

An Orion book

Copyright © Joan Aiken 1967

The right of Joan Aiken to be identified as the author of this work has been
asserted in accordance with the Copyright, Designs and Patents Act 1988.

This edition published by
The Orion Publishing Group Ltd
Orion House
5 Upper St Martin's Lane
London WC2H 9EA

An Hachette UK company
A CIP catalogue record for this book is available from the British Library

ISBN 978 1 4719 1677 9

www.orionbooks.co.uk

Introduction

As well as writing children's books, beloved by generations and still avidly read today, Joan Aiken also quickly established herself in the 1960s as a witty author of adult suspense with the ability to keep readers of all ages on the edge of their seats. Too inventive to stick with a formula she nevertheless revelled in the atmosphere of Gothic parody and was often compared with Mary Stewart. In the tradition of Jane Austen's *Northanger Abbey* Joan gave her long-suffering heroines a set of literary references to support them through their frightful ordeals, and usually a quirky sense of humour, making full use of her own extensive literary background.

In true Gothic style these hapless heroines would become embroiled in a series of events not of their own making, and were usually possessed of many stalwart characteristics – not least a literary education – if not always endowed with obvious physical charms. And they were, of course, always a version of Joan herself: small, slightly gap toothed, and red haired, extremely enterprising, physically intrepid and fearless to the end. She loved to share episodes from her own life, and those who knew her also became accustomed to the dubious pleasure of discovering (albeit disguised) episodes from their own lives in her books – although told with such warmth and humour that she was swiftly forgiven!

What she could also guarantee were indefatigably sinister villains, mounting and finely controlled tension, complex plots, and hair-raising climaxes, often with an unusually high body count. As she confessed, 'I often have more characters than I know what to do with.'

Admired and enjoyed by many of her crime-writing contemporaries such as John Creasey, H.R.F. Keating, Francis Iles and Edmund Crispin, Joan Aiken's adult novels of suspense have lost none of their charm, and their period settings are sure to appeal to a new generation of readers who grew up on her children's books.

Lizza Aiken, October 2014

I was all ear
And took in strains that might
 create a soul
Under the ribs of death

                    MILTON, *Comus*

I

THE TRAIN RUMBLED through the frosty night of Christmas Eve minus two and sitting in it I wept (discreetly and silently, looking out of the black window), oppressed by the sadness of returning home from lighthearted friends to the heavy cares of a love that was beginning to be outgrown.

I had been staying with a large family, all very happy, very musical, whose whole life seemed as gay and full of bounce as a comic opera. The only off-key moment had been when Paul, the eldest brother, the handsome one, in a moment of uncontrollable temper shot the peacock on the terrace because it kept letting out an A-flat squawk when he was playing a violin sonata in C sharp minor, but the peacock was lame in any case; and several of them said it was a merciful release. There they all were, living their separate lives but so friendly and at ease with each other; it seemed like a foretaste of paradise and I was not at all content to be going back to my own life, which had hitherto fitted me snugly enough, but now I thought it would be like creeping into a wet bathing suit, and I wished I could postpone the process.

The Tallents were not given to brooding; their enthusiasms, their grievances, if any, their lightest opinions of each other all came pouring forth in a spate of talk; how easy, how restful it was after the pregnant silences of home! And their talk, though intelligent, was not *significant*; it was not aimed at any particular target; they talked because they enjoyed talking, that was all. I had been for a twelve-mile walk with Paul and his cousin Finn; they were handsome, they were gay, they poured out nonsense all the way; I could easily have fallen in love with either, but somehow, in that household, there seemed no need, really no time, for emotional involvements, the current of cheerful affection sped past that weir. Abandoning myself to the current, I had been immersed and absorbed, I felt I could gladly have lived on those terms for ever, but now, having returned to dry land, I was suddenly invaded by a bleak sense of loss, of opportunities wasted. I had never reflected about freewill before, but, as the train carried me farther and farther south, I suddenly understood that I had been given a chance of launching into a new experience, and had missed it. "Do write, write soon," they all said, Paul among them, and I said yes, but I knew I never would. Scotland was too far. In eight hours from now my old, two-dimensional life would close down on me like a trap.

We had been singing bits of the Christmas Oratorio, and the train began to joggle out the theme from the pastoral symphony, tum-ti-ti, tum-ti-ti, *tum*-ti-ti, tum-ti-ti, and this was too sad to be borne. Life, and my female sex, and this newly apprehended burden of my virginity, weighing on me heavy as an ill-packed rucksack, I took down my coat from the rack, wrapped myself in it, and lay down full length on the seat. Sleep took me quickly and soon I was trying, in a hopeless way, to tidy up the flat in Guilford Square, picking among Maggie's spilt cigarette ash and hairpins, looking in vain for a wastepaper basket.

When the train stopped at Newcastle I became conscious again, for someone clanked into my carriage and slammed the door, but I curled myself up tighter and shut my eyes, hoping that whoever it was would settle down and let me get back to my disagreeable task, but I received a poke in the ribs and then another; this person did not mean to be ignored, and, feeling stiff and chilly, and rather hungry (we had been singing so hard up to the last moment that I'd forgotten to ask the Tallents for some sandwiches) I uncurled and looked at the newcomer.

He was in American airforce uniform, very large, very friendly, with one tooth missing, and he was holding two cups of tea. That is all I remember of his appearance. He had the two mugs of tea in one hand, and had been poking me with the other.

"Have a slug of Scotch in it?" he said.

"No thanks," I replied primly.

"Ah, come on, it's Christmas." And without waiting he fetched a bottle out of his pocket and liberally laced the tea, which he then passed across. It was hot and comforting, so presently I felt more goodwill towards this person who had dragged me out of my oblivion, and in any case I had a suspicion that even in my sleep I must have been calling out for help, or why should he have seen me through the window, nothing but a bundle covered with a coat, and gone back to get a cup of tea for me off the station trolley? There was no point in resisting the help when it came.

2

We sat smiling at each other across the gangway with our knees touching, and he told me his name, which was Wal, and I told him mine, which he said was the craziest name he'd ever heard, and presently the train started again, so he reached down a packet of sandwiches and began passing them across to me, and I wolfed them ravenously. We talked a little, not much, and had some more whisky, as the tea was finished. I began to feel despairingly that I should never get to sleep again, my short spell had refreshed me and thought began pouring down in great cataracts, help, help!

Wal tidied up the paper, tucked the flat bottle back in his pocket, and looked thoughtfully round the empty carriage. We were running through some vast empty stretch of northern England, hill after black uninhabited hill. Wal turned out the seat lights and then came and sat beside me. His embrace gave me the most wonderful feeling of trust and relief, better than having a thorn pulled out, better than finding a secluded spot to be sick in. I once knew an old woman who used to sit, day after day, in her chair, rotating her thumbs round each other. "If I spin them this way," she said, "I can remember the past. If I spin them *this* way, I can foretell the future." "Why not keep them still for a bit?" I asked. She did, and immediately the most blissful, blank smile spread over her face. Well, my future and my past dropped off me in just this way. For a long time we remained immobile, mouth to mouth, chin against unshaven chin, and his buttons printing dents in my angora sweater until I felt like a relief map. It must surely be a fault of memory that makes me think he had his haversack on the whole time but I can clearly recall the square boxlike feel of thick canvas against my wrist.

After what might have been an hour, or only ten minutes, we began gently to rearrange ourselves along the length of the seat, which fortunately was a wide one because this had been a first class compartment in its heyday.

Wal carefully stuffed my coat under my head and began a systematic unbuttoning.

"Hey, hold on!" I protested.

"How d'you mean, hold on?" he said, sounding aggrieved.

"I didn't mean—"

"Ah, now, c'mon, honey, that's not fair. Have a heart. You can't leave a guy halfway!" He seemed so upset and scandalised that I began to fear I couldn't.

"But, truly, Wal, I don't think—"

"Ah, honey. Please. You're a lovely girl. I love you."

I was young and cold-hearted enough to reply "Bosh" to this.

"Why do you say that?" whispered Wal, hurt.

"You needn't feel obliged to say things like that to me. After all we've only just met."

"Well I should like to see more of you," he said with finality, and went on with his unbuttoning. My heart was banging to such an extent that I thought it would bruise itself against his buttons. His last remark struck me as funny, and I smiled at him in the dimness, but he was too seriously intent to notice, and presently his sigh of satisfaction announced that his arrangements for our mutual wellbeing were successfully accomplished. Over his shoulder I could just faintly discern the central ceiling light with its little rosette on each side, and the dark webbed pattern of the rack.

"What are you thinking?" he said at last.

"I'm not sure."

"Come on now—you must be thinking about something?"

I bit his ear gently, to show that I was feeling friendly, and presently said that I was thinking how pleasant it was to add to one's stock of knowledge.

"This your first time, eh?"

"Yes."

"How old are you, honey?"

When I told him he was rather horrified.

"I don't usually cradlesnatch. But there was something about you made me think you were older. What would your Mom say to me?"

This idea tickled me, but I hastened to reassure him. "She's dead—she died when I was five." Which was true, for all practical purposes.

"Say, that's hard. Poor little girl never had no Momma."

"That's right," I said cheerfully, but he insisted on giving me a sentimental hug, because I was a poor orphan, and another slug of whisky, which he administered with great skill, sliding the bottle out of his pocket between us and tipping it against my teeth. Then he had some himself, twisting his neck round, and then we began kissing again. I had never taken much pleasure in kissing before, but now I began for the first time to see the point of it and enjoy myself.

Later on Wal murmured, "I *do* love you, you know."

4

"Please don't keep saying that, Wal. It's not true, and it spoils things."

What a prig I was to be sure.

"But I do," he insisted. "I'd like to marry you. Only we'll have to think of another name for you instead of that goddam awful one you've got. *Aulis*—whoever heard of calling a girl Aulis?"

"Oh, but you couldn't marry me," I said hurriedly. "I'm married already."

"*What?*"

"To a cousin of mine," I continued hastily inventing.

"Well then why—"

"He fell ill, he got polio on our wedding day, so he's been in hospital in an iron lung ever since."

"You must have been married very young."

"Oh I was. I had to get permission from the Lord Chancellor." My conscience did not prick me a bit at telling him all these lies, and I went on gaily elaborating. I was not really doing it in order to deceive him, but to give myself the illusion of another life, full of possibilities lacking in my own, which was at present so frighteningly bounded by the flat in Guilford Square. I felt like the child looking into the glass and saying, "Let's pretend we live in *that* room."

I told Wal all about my cousin Nicholas, to whom I was married in name only, and the strange creature was so tortured by jealousy that he finally told me to shut up. Then he was sorry, gave me some more whisky, and said he'd soon make me forget Nicky, who was probably amusing himself with the nurses anyway.

"Now, are you going to say you love me?"

"I think you're very nice, Wal. I like you very much." I couldn't resist adding, "I can hardly help liking you after all the whisky you've given me, can I?"

At that he suddenly burst out laughing, and our relations became more amicable. After an hour or so Wal went to sleep, and as I was beginning to feel cramped I wriggled out and curled up again on the other side. The train jolted on through endless night, and I began to wonder what of all this I was going to relate to the friend that I loved, and with whom I lived, with whom I had somehow got myself so hopelessly, inextricably entangled. Her name was Maggie and she was a doctor. Even I, in my youthful crudeness and naïveté, feared that she might take this hard, but could I conceal such a major event in my life? I doubted it. The thought of Maggie daunted me dreadfully—her presence suddenly seemed to loom beside me in the carriage like a heavy weight. It is strange how one can love somebody and yet dislike, almost detest, their physical characteristics. I thought furiously, resentfully, of Maggie's largeness, her long, thick black hair, worn in braids on top, the black trousers she generally put on at home, emphasising her wide hips, her habit of breaking into a little dance, incongruous and embarrassing, her untidiness, her carelessness with other people's property, her aura of cigarette smoke. I began to imagine a conversation:

"You mean to say that you let this man make love to you?" Her eyes boring into mine, relentless and intelligent.

"Well—yes."

"Why?"

"Oh, Maggie—you know how hard I find it to refuse people."

No, I must somehow contrive to keep this incident dark. Oppression began to close down again. The train stopped, at some forlorn outpost, and another person entered our carriage, an old woman; I got a dim glimpse of her by the station light before she stowed her luggage about her and subsided, sighing, into a far corner. Almost at once she began to snore, loud, loose, rattling, voluminous snores. It was plain that, however unwilling, I must resign myself to staying awake from now on; after an hour or so I cautiously switched on the little light over my head and amused myself by studying Wal. There was nothing particularly impressive about *his* appearance, asleep, and in some disarray, but his gap-tooth was concealed, which was an advantage, and in any case I felt friendly and at ease with him, very different from the crippling bond of love and obligation which tied me to Maggie because I knew she needed something to cherish. Oh, this desperate anxiety not to hurt people; it has tossed me into more predicaments than all my other failings put together.

I leaned over and tucked up Wal's greatcoat, which was sliding off, but the movement waked him.

"Hiya, cherub," he said grinning, and caught hold of my wrist as I was about to seat myself.

"Go back to sleep. I didn't mean to wake you."

"Don' want to sleep. Waste of time. You come and sit beside me again."

But this conversation had disturbed the old woman in the

opposite corner and she began to stir and mutter, and presently gazed at us out of beady eyes with as little recognition in them as those of a robin. We kept still, hoping she would go off again, but after a while she waked up more and gathered her intelligence.

"I like to be in a carriage where there's company," she said. "It passes the time, doesn't it?"

She pulled out a bag of toffees and offered us each one. I looked at my watch. Ten to four.

The old woman had an extraordinarily hoarse voice, possibly the result of gin or inveterate smoking, or she may just have been suffering from a bad cold. We also discovered that she was nearly stone deaf, and any remark which was to reach her had to be bawled at the tops of our voices. Wal offered her a nip of his whisky and she nodded eagerly and, rather to his chagrin, drained the bottle.

"Never mind—perhaps it'll put the old so-and-so to sleep again," he said, lacing his arm hopefully round me again. But I was rather stiff and unco-operative, as there she sat, wide awake, with her bright eyes disconcertingly fixed on us.

"I've been seeing off my daughter and son-in-law," she whispered hoarsely after a pause. "Flying to Greenland they were—fancy! They were married two days ago. It's the first time she's ever been away from me, she's only seventeen. We sat and cried all day yesterday."

A dreadful lump of woe burst in my heart; I suppose it was the first time I had ever truly sympathised with anybody. Wal said kindly,

"She'll be all right, ma'am, he'll look after her."

Then we began to have a long and intolerably dull conversation about our home lives. I can still remember the vivid picture I formed of Wal's home in Iowa, his married sister with whom he passed his leaves, the hens in the yard, the nieces and nephews, and the old woman's various married children with whom she spent her year, travelling on to the next every three months. Wal wrote down the sister's name and address for me on a bit of paper and said if I ever travelled to the States I was to go there; his sister would think I was cute. The train stopped somewhere, it may have been Doncaster, and the old woman suddenly darted from the carriage.

"Hey, d'you think she's gone and forgotten to take her things?" said Wal hopefully. "I want to kiss you again."

"Well you can do that anyway."

"No—you know what I mean, honey."

"Well I don't. I expect she's gone to get a cup of tea," I said dampingly, but returning his embrace.

"Tea!" said Wal springing up. "By god, couldn't I do with some!" But at that moment the train started, the old woman triumphantly returned with three cups, and there was nothing for it but to continue the conversation. The midland country has never looked so hideously flat and unpromising as it did, unveiling itself by degrees that damp December day. My heart sank into my boots at the thought of King's Cross, the 77 bus, and the short walk to Guilford Square.

Wal was not travelling as far as King's Cross. His unit was established around a mansion at Bishops Langley, and he was getting out there.

"Say! Why don't you come too?" he suddenly exclaimed. "The boys would be tickled to meet you, and you'd get a Christmas dinner. We're having a party. Come on, do! It would be great."

"But I couldn't really, could I?"

"Sure, all of them have girl friends in. You and my colonel would get on like a house afire—you're both kind of serious."

Wal seemed to be on very intimate terms with his colonel, considering he was only a sergeant. The whole unit sounded most unconventional to me, and in the end I agreed to go, partly out of curiosity, and partly to stall off my return to the flat. In any case Maggie hated the festive season and would probably have volunteered to go on double duty at the hospital. I hoped she wouldn't be moved to meet the train.

We said goodbye to the old woman and got out at a dreary little prefab modern station. Waiting for a bus on a wide, ribbon-developed bit of dual-carriageway, I shivered. The day was raw and foggy, with not a soul stirring. I felt stiff, and no wonder; I gave a tremendous yawn and Wal looked at me guiltily.

"You're low on sleep aren't you, honey. Tell you what—I'll tuck you up in my bunk when we get there and you can have a nap while I report myself and see what's cooking. Then you'll be all spry for dinner."

The bus put us off at some park gates and we walked up an interminable drive between beeches and chestnuts. As we neared the mansion there began to be Quonset huts among the trees, and presently Wal branched off towards one of these.

"Here we are, home from home," he remarked. "Wonder if anyone's in."

Nobody was in, and he skilfully wrapped me in blankets on a lower bunk, gave me a friendly pat, and went off saying he'd be back by and by. I sank into sleep like cottonwool and was aware of nothing for a long, motionless time, until a voice roused me, saying just over my head,

"Well, well, look what's here. See what Wal's got in his Christmas stocking."

"Not bad," said another voice. "Not bad at all."

I decided that the best thing for me was to go right on being asleep, which I did. Pretty soon the door opened again, and Wal's voice said,

"Hi, fellers. Manage all right while I was away?"

"*You* seem to have managed all right, anyway."

"Wait a minute till I introduce you. Wake up, honey. It's getting on for dinner time. Had a good nap? That's grand. This is Mike and that's Richard."

"Proud to meet you," they said, grinning. They gave me soap and towel and mirror and I unrolled from my cocoon and tidied myself up. Then we all strolled over to another Quonset hut which was the canteen. The Christmas dinner we had, served from a cafeteria counter on to indented tin trays, was not very exciting.

"Gobble up," Wal whispered to me, "the colonel's invited us in for a drink afterwards." We bolted down our bits of turkey, accompanied by friendly derision from Mike and Richard, who suspected other motives for Wal's hurry, and he then took me with ceremony up to the mansion—only we went in by a back door and along a corridor wide as a canal, with green baize locks, to a room which had probably once been the servants' hall.

"This is my colonel," Wal said, introducing me with pride. "Colonel Fisher, meet Queenie." Why he chose to call me that, heaven knows.

Colonel Fisher was quite bald and very beaming. I have never seen anything so resplendant as his uniform and ribbons, and besides him there were about a dozen other colonels in the room, and several crates of whisky. It was evidently colonels' afternoon off, but why Wal should have been on such cosy terms with them I could not fathom.

"Give the little lady a drink, Wal, make her at home," said

Colonel Fisher, shaking me by the hand for about three minutes. "Can you sing?" he asked me.

Someone put on a record of Bing Crosby dreaming of a white Christmas, and they all joined in. Several of the colonels had tears running down their cheeks. It seemed much more than twenty-four hours since I had been doing the same sort of thing with the Tallents.

Outside, the grey day was turning blue with dusk and I finally said to Wal that I must be going or I should never find my way home. He had absorbed a good deal more whisky in between the singing and was most reluctant to go out in the cold. He kept begging me to stay a little longer.

"Don't go yet, you luscious thing. We haven't had tea yet."

"Tea! I shan't be able to eat for days. No, really, I must go. My friend will be wondering what's become of me." In the course of the day I had revised my life-story to some extent, finding it too complicated to keep up the fiction of my impotent husband.

"Don' like the sound of that friend. Don' like her at all," said Wal, rather darkly, lowering at me. "All right, c'mon then. Where's your traps?"

"We left them at the hut."

He tried to persuade me into the hut when we got there, but I suddenly felt that I had had enough of Wal's company and was most anxious to get back to London.

"I'll come and see you another time," I promised.

"Don' want you another time. I want you *now*."

"Oh, come on Wal, I shall miss the last bus if we don't hurry." He had told me it went at five. He crossly fetched out my bag and we started down the drive. The cold air had made him rather drunker and we had a series of undignified wrestling-matches as he hopefully tried to entice me into inviting bits of shrubbery under the beeches. It was like taking a large dog for a walk in a place teeming with rabbits. But the undergrowth didn't tempt me a bit; there had been a sudden change in the weather which from mild warmth had turned to bone-gripping chill.

"Can't think how you can be so hard-hearted to a poor guy," Wal said sadly.

"Because I want to catch my bus."

"Women," muttered Wal. "They always have an eye to the main chance."

"Yes, when it's catching a bus. You'd better go back—I can find my way to the bus stop from here."

"I wouldn't be so unchival—chivalrous," replied Wal with dignity.

I just caught the bus, by running the last hundred yards, and Wal gave me a warm hug as I swung myself on, which nearly swung me off again, saying that I was a peach of a girl if I *was* a stony-hearted little bitch, and I was to come out again soon, or he'd phone me and we could meet outside Swan and Edgar's. The bus roared off into the dark and I remembered that I had never learned his surname.

II

"A YEAR?" CHARLES SAID. "Just a year?"

He and Eleanor stared at one another across the top of her desk, both very pale.

"I'm afraid so. This is Cardew's diagnosis, you realise, not mine, but he's very—he was very reliable." She slid her fingers restlessly up and down her fountain pen, then looked at her hands as if they were not part of her and placed them side by side in her lap.

Charles stood up and began to move about the room, lingering for a minute by the window, looking out at the Thames which spread in a great sheet of silver outside, absorbing all the light from the winter sky.

How many other patients in similar circumstances had turned to gaze at the river while they struggled to regain composure, to assume an air of calm as if such news were an everyday matter?

"My doctor only gives me a year, so I'm taking my holiday in March . . . giving up the lease . . . not laying down any more port, what's in the cellar will last my time . . ."

Absurdities flew through his head while he tried to adjust to the new, narrow horizon. December. Another autumn then, wet apples lying in tangled grass, the uneasy embarkation manoeuvres of swifts before the journey south. Another Christmas; perhaps; Eleanor had said "a year at best." Certainly one more spring. If he had to die next winter he must at least make the most of this coming spring and summer.

Some people in such circumstances begin travelling, spend

their entire capital on trips to Angkor Wat, Samarkand, Popocatapetl. Charles did not feel inclined for that. Looking at Eleanor's steady eyes appraising him, he knew that she would help him avoid any behaviour that was exaggerated, unruly, over-emotional.

He took out a cigarette and lit it, holding Aunt Julia's little whisky-bottle lighter in a steady hand. Eleanor smiled at him but did not try to break into his thought; she made a couple of hieroglyphic squiggles on a squared chart and rested her hands on either side of it, looking down at them thoughtfully. They were well-shaped hands, rather masculine, white, well-kept, ringless. From her hands Charles's eye travelled up her white-sleeved arm to the smooth fair head bent over the chart; she looked, somehow, like a white point of interrogation in this silent room.

Charles himself had no feeling of curiosity. He was to die soon; well, that was that. The riddle of the meaning of it all he was content to leave unanswered. He strolled back to the window again thinking, must cancel that suit, and : make a will, everything to Eleanor, I suppose, poor girl, this must be hard for her too.

She was looking tired, he thought, strained; well, not surprisingly. Besides, she had been overworking for years, and particularly since her partner had been killed in a car-smash, leaving her a double load of patients as well as the hospital job.

It's a good thing I haven't any children. The idea was like a cold chill at the base of his mind, a little pocket of freezing sorrow. To disperse it he said aloud :

"Just as well poor Zita didn't get landed into this."

Eleanor looked inquiring.

"She'd probably have been just about due for her first baby by now."

Judging from her expression his sister thought this remark in poor taste. She said,

"If Zita had been alive I've a notion this would never have come about. I imagine all that business played its part in worsening your heart condition. The exposure, the shock, the way you went on diving even when it seemed fairly plain there was no hope of recovering her—all the emotional strain of wondering why she'd done it—and quite apart from the physical illness you were near the verge of a mental breakdown yourself."

Charles seemed irritated, started to speak and then checked himself.

"Am I keeping someone—another patient—waiting?" he asked abruptly. "I forgot to scan the dining-room queue."

"No, I purposely put you at the end so we'd have time to talk."

"Thoughtful of you," he grunted, and then, "Sorry, Nell, I'm being boorish. It just takes a bit of getting used to."

"Of course it does," she said calmly. "Sit down and we'll make plans. I'm absolutely at your disposal, Charles, you know that. The practice doesn't matter a rap—I can get rid of it any time—quite glad to, in fact; since Cardew was killed it's been a bit too much for me. And I've been thinking of giving up my job with the Ogham."

He nodded and dropped into an armchair by the fire.

Dusk was beginning to close in, the cold watery lights of the street lamps gleamed along the embankment between the ragged boughs, and the sky was aquamarine, studded with dark segments of slaty cloud. Nell's room, which had seemed severe and impersonal, began to open up a little in the dimmer light, the red carpet glowed, the boxlike shape of the walls softened. A log softly sputtered in the fire and the cat who lay in front of it stretched out his large shape on the rug and rolled on to his back in an abandonment of warmth and comfort.

Out of habit Charles ran a friendly toe along his ribs and, as usual, the cat rolled over and round in a flash, burying teeth and claws in Charles's shoe. Charles looked down at him with a touch of hostility, thinking—he'll live longer than I shall—will he notice when I'm gone?

"I'd better give up the job now, I suppose," he said. "I'd like to spend my last months doing something I really enjoy—while I can. The question is what. What do I enjoy, Nell?"

She raised her brows.

"Gardening? Messing about in boats? Neither is the ideal pursuit for a man in your state of health, but I agree; you might as well enjoy yourself. It can't make any ultimate difference."

Charles winced a little at the absent-minded callousness of her words. Still, she was a doctor, she was bound to view these things in a practical light.

"I should certainly give up the job," she added.

"The American trip would have been fun," he said rather wistfully.

She gave him a swift look. "All the same, you'd be well-advised not to go on with it. A high-pressure business mission like that must be a considerable strain; you have to think of all the nuisance to other people if you suddenly dropped dead—inquests and cremation and carting you back in an urn on the Queen Elizabeth."

He laughed outright. "Good old Nell!"

She looked at him, slightly puzzled.

"What do you suggest, then?" he said.

"Well—" Now she seemed unusually diffident. "You've always wanted to get back to Cornwall in the end, haven't you? Supposing I found a practice down that way somewhere? You could dig into your capital and buy a house—no sense in hanging on to it now—and I could contribute a bit of course. Then you could potter, do a bit of sailing, and I'd be there to keep an eye on you, and Nin to housekeep."

"It sounds fine for me, but what about you?" he said doubtfully. "What about after I was gone?"

"It's only an idea," she said easily. "Nothing hard-and-fast. Think it over, though."

Then she added as an afterthought, "We might go and live somewhere near Aunt Julia. She's as entertaining as ever."

Charles did not answer. He sat staring at the fire, seeing in it a grey west-country house set among trees, approached by deep narrow lanes winding among fern and campion, foxglove and bracken. At least it made a more enticing picture than hospital wards, inquests, funerals, dark clothes, and short notices in the local press. "Mr Charles Foley, recently retired from the City for health reasons—suddenly of a heart-attack—"

Eleanor dropped her hand lightly on his shoulder.

"You know how I feel," she said. "There's nothing I can say. I must be getting along to the hospital. Stay here as long as you like—stay the night if you want. Nin will make you up a bed. I'd turn in pretty soon, that sort of news is a shock. A good night's sleep will help. Take a couple of sleeping pills, I should. You'll find a bottle of Somnil in the bathroom cupboard."

"Oh, that's all right, thanks awfully, Nell," he said. "I think I'll get back to the flat. I must start thinking things over a bit and get in touch with the office. I'll call you tomorrow."

"Do," she said. "And don't lie awake and brood. By the way, of course I'm afraid I go along with poor Cardew's diagnosis, but if you'd like a second opinion, which you're fully entitled to have, I could put you in touch with several very good—"

"Oh no, thanks all the same," he said. "What would be the point?"

"All right." She nodded at him kindly. "Well—see you tomorrow."

The door shut behind her with a soft, decisive click.

Charles sat on staring at the fire, the sleeping cat stretched against his feet.

I hope to goodness, he thought, suddenly rousing, that Nell doesn't tell anyone about this. Should have warned her.

He imagined the faces of friends and acquaintances, pitying, curious, inquisitive. Heard about poor Foley? Less than a year to live. Heart, apparently; bit dismal, eh? Hardly worth living out the year.

"Hardly worth living," he murmured aloud.

The door opened and a spare elderly woman in black with a white apron came in.

"Oh, I didn't know you were still here, Master Charles," she said. "I just looked in to see if the fire was all right. Miss Nell didn't say if you'd be stopping to supper? There's a nice bit of broth and I could make an omelette?"

"No, that's all right, thanks, Nin, I'll go out presently," he said to the old woman, searching her face for any sign of unusual compassion or dreadful knowledge; but no, she looked blessedly normal and was shaking her head over some coaldust on the carpet and a worn place on his cuff.

"That cat! The amount of hair he puts on the rug, I'm sure I don't know. Well, Master Charles, look in again soon, we don't see enough of you these days. You're looking a bit run down, you work too hard."

He managed a smile as she left him and returned to his musing.

Of course I've seen it coming, he imagined people saying, he hasn't been himself ever since the tragedy. Oh, didn't you? Shocking thing, he'd just got engaged, he and this girl were on holiday in Italy with the sister. Zita something, pretty creature, everything seemed paradisial, and then all of a sudden she left a little note with the padrona to say she'd decided she couldn't go on living any more, and went off and drowned herself. No reason given, utterly inexplicable. Old Charles was off fishing; got back at teatime and found the note. She'd gone down to the bay, the woman said, so he rushed down like a lunatic, asking everyone; yes, she'd taken a boat out, hadn't come back; so he went out, found the empty boat, swam, dived, damn nearly drowned himself too. He got pneumonia, Nell only just managed to pull him through, lucky she was along. Funny thing, apparently the girl had complained to her earlier about pains, which Nell easily diagnosed as indigestion from too much antipasto—girl was as sound as a bell physically, but they concluded at the inquest she was a hysterical type who'd imagined they were symptoms of some fell disease. Awful thing for poor old Charles—it would be natural to wonder if it'd been his fault in some way, wouldn't it?

Charles's hands were gripping the arms of his chair, he was sweating, his heart was thumping. Easy now, he admonished himself, but he could smell again the hot, salt smell of the sandy cliff track and the nets spread out to dry, the pale, flat look of the sea in the bay and the infuriatingly blank faces of the people he had asked.

"La Signorina Newman? No, signor—" their flung-out hands as if pitying his stupidity—look, if you wish, but obviously she is not here.

Then the frantic endless search, first in the boat, while the sky grew greener and the rocks blacker, then swimming, desperately, futilely diving, calling "Zita, Zita!" finding the heap of clothes, the last descent into unconsciousness, his rescue by some returning fishermen, who carried him to Nell, just back from a trip to the local monastery.

The weeks after that had been a nightmare of injections, sweating and shivering in the lumpy bed because he could not be moved to hospital, the extraordinarily unpleasant tisanes cooked up by the padrona, Nell's drawn look when he questioned her again and again about Zita. Why, why could she have done it? They would never know. He would never forgive himself for being elsewhere while she was going through her crisis, whatever it was. Surely he could have helped her, made her feel that life was worth living. It must have been a momentary panic, something that a word of sense would have blown away; in the morning when he left she had been gay, full of absurdity and fun. Lovely, irresponsible Zita, her black hair blowing in the harbour wind, as she perched on a coil of rope and waved him off.

"I shall expect you to come back with enough fish for a chowder supper!"—full of mockery, turning for a final carefree wave before she swung off to chatter with the market-women at the flower-stalls.

People said she was unbalanced, over-impulsive, and perhaps it was so. Certainly their mutual love had burst up to fruition with soul-shattering rapidity, from the first breathtaking, tentative kiss to the perfect rapture and security they had so swiftly achieved. Or, he thought they had achieved; that was the dreadful part. He thought her nature was open to him, that she had given herself with complete unreserve, with the abandon that seemed characteristic of her. But what dark impulse, what unknown, terrifying factor had been able to drag her so swiftly from his side?

He would never be any nearer the answer if he lived another hundred years—let alone the miserable pittance of life that remained to him now.

The question that had been lying doggo at the back of his mind all this time here came out and presented itself.

"Is it worth going on at all? For over a year you have been wretchedly trying to bury yourself in work. Is it worth trying to preserve this halfpay existence for another twelve months, with the added disadvantage of possible death at any moment, the inconvenience and horror to friends or strangers, the misery and worry for Nell? Why not anticipate the natural course of events by a short—possibly very short—margin?"

Nell's words suddenly returned : Take a couple of sleeping-pills. Don't lie awake brooding. There's a bottle in the bathroom cupboard.

Moving mechanically he went out of the door, across the passage into Nell's neat, efficient bathroom, and found the bottle. How many? They were not large, it would be easy to swallow the whole bottleful. That ought to do the trick.

Not here, though. That would be an unforgiveable thing to do to poor old Nin, who had taken him in his pram to see the Lanrith regatta, the first thing he clearly remembered. White sails and green water. Wait till you're old enough to go out and sail a boat yourself, Master Charles.

Well, he was old enough now, but he had done little enough sailing with one thing and another—service in the navy, managerial training, pressure of work building up with the firm's success, then working harder still, trying to forget Zita.

"God damn it," he said angrily. "What a rotten way to end."

He thrust the bottle into his pocket and went into the kitchen to find Nin.

"Goodbye, Nin, take care of yourself." He gave the old woman a hug and glanced round the warm room. "You've made it nice here, haven't you." It was a large kitchen, for a flat, and Nin's occupation had transformed it into a rich fragment from another world. Genuine cottage instead of boutique farmhouse. A large cuckoo clock ticked noisily above a fringed mantel, loaded just now with Christmas cards, there was a rag rug and a brass fender. A shell-box on the dresser had "A Present from Lanrith" painted on its largest cockle. He recognised it as a treasure brought from the family home, sold long ago; he had given it to Nin for Christmas when he was ten.

"Nice enough," she said placidly. "But you can't have a proper kitchen upstairs, to my mind. Now, don't you go getting your feet wet, Master Charles, there's a nasty little sleet started." She turned her cheek up calmly to his kiss and then went back to her knitting; he heard the click of the needles begin as he closed the door.

Outside it was, as she had said, beginning to sleet, and he paused irresolutely, looking at the black, flecked surface of the river facing him, the lights reflected in its surface.

A dull weariness and depression overtook him. His mind was made up, but where to do the deed? He had a horror, somehow, of his own flat, dull, cold, and dark. He caught a bus at random, left it, and struck across Piccadilly Circus, ignoring the squeak and hoot of taxis on wet tarmac, the lit, rain-spangled buses curtseying past with a sweep of mud-spattered red skirts.

He went into a pub off St Martin's Lane, a familiar, comfortable place full of red velvet, goldleaf, and chandeliers, suitable antidote to his desolate mood.

"Keep off short drinks," Nell had suggested and he had promised to do so, but now—after all, what did it matter?—he ordered a double rum and took it to a snug, plush-lined alcove in a far corner.

"Why, if it isn't Charles!" exclaimed a pleased voice.

Oh my god, he thought, now who? Of all inopportune moments to meet an acquaintance this is the worst—but then the depth and quality of the voice reached him; only one person sounded like that; and turning round he saw that he was right and said with sincerity:

"Claire! I can't think of anyone but you that I'd want to see."

"That sounds bad. Here, you slide into that corner while I get myself another drink and then we'll have a real gossip. I'm just back from Moscow," she said. "Been covering the women's athletics."

Claire Dean was, as even her best friends would agree, no oil-painting, but there was something about her—a quality of warmth and easiness, an uninhibited eagerness to make friends—that endeared her to an enormous number of people. She was tall, rangy, slapdash as to clothes; her hair was a frizz, her deep eyes looked out from noble but ill-assorted features that were frequently ink-smudged, she was always perfectly serene, whether encouraging children at a local tennis-tournament or helping royalty through a difficult moment at a race meeting. For years she had represented Great Britain on various women's athletic teams, and, when she retired from competing, graduated naturally to writing a Fleet Street sports column. She helped innumerable lame dogs over stiles and generally had some derelict or other in her paper-strewn flat—an alcoholic who was being jockeyed back to normal life, a pregnant refugee looking for a job, a down-and-out actor or penniless writer.

Charles bought her usual large whisky (no drink ever had the slightest effect on Claire) and she said, "So you're feeling low? Well, I sympathise. The sight of all those Moscow mothers tossing the caber and holing in one put me off; I'm thinking of packing in the job and retiring. Getting on for it, anyway." Few people knew Claire's age but she was reputed to be nearing her sixties.

While she spoke she had been studying Charles and now she put one large capable hand over his. "I say, you *are* looking poorly," she said in a totally different tone. "Want to talk about it?"

Surprisingly, Charles found that he did.

All the time he was talking Claire held his hand between her two warm ones and watched him attentively while the smoke from her cigarette drifted wraithlike between them. She did not interrupt and he received a feeling of comfort and warmth just from her air of concentrating on his problem to the exclusion of everything else.

"So you see how it is," he ended.

"I can see why you're knocked all of a heap," she said slowly. "It's no joke, really, is it?" and he was aware of relief.

"But I tell you what!" she exclaimed, her eyes lighting up, "what a marvellous chance!"

"To send back messages from the next world?" he said acidly. But already she was making him feel better.

"No, of course not, you ninny." She dug him in the ribs. "Oh, I shall miss you dreadfully, of course, I don't say I shan't—if you *can* send messages I'll be delighted to receive them. No, what I meant was, now you have the chance to do absolutely what you like without fear of the consequences. Had you thought of that? Publicity, or expense, or danger just don't matter any more. You could take on dotty missions, or put on a West End play—I know several chaps with very good plays looking for backers—or volunteer for a space-craft—"

"You have to have A1 health. And I don't want to do any of those things," said Charles crossly. He felt like a child going off to boarding-school for the first time amid the hypocritical encouragement of his elders—"Aren't you *lucky* to be going to school—" when both he and they knew that he was heading for undiluted hell, no use pretending otherwise.

But Claire was not pretending. Her eyes shone with envy.

"You've always meant to have a boat somewhere and sail, haven't you? And you can write your memoirs, never mind the libel actions."

"They wouldn't be interesting enough." He gave a reluctant smile. "You're the one who ought to do that, Claire."

"Oh, I'd never have the perseverance. Then, think of being able to blue all your money."

"I suppose so," he said without enthusiasm. He got up and carried their glasses to the bar. When he came back he thought for the first time, Claire's ageing. Would she ever acquire that smallholding she'd always yearned for? And if she did, would she really be happy, or would she go mad with loneliness and drink herself to death? He imagined her tramping through mud in sandals, carrying buckets of mash to the animals with a cigarette in one corner of her mouth. People would call her funny old Miss Dean and she'd be very kind to children, inviting them in to her cottage on their way home from school to see the chicks hatching in the bread-oven.

"You look broody," he said. "What's on your mind?"

"I was trying to put things together—wondering if it was the loss of Zita that had caused your illness. Because, oddly enough, I thought you'd recovered from the actual physical shock of that fairly well."

There were some spent matches lying on the table and Charles took a minute or two making them into a Greek key pattern before he answered.

Finally he said, "God knows if I'd be so honest with anyone else, even Eleanor, but I've never had any pretences with you, Claire, and it's too late to start now. A couple of months after Zita died I was trying to stifle an almost incredulous sense of relief—a dreadful feeling that filled me with guilt and horror. Because I'd realised that if Zita and I had married it would have been a great mistake. We weren't really suited; probably in two or three years we would have drifted hopelessly apart. It's not that we weren't in love; we were, even now it makes my throat ache to think of it—but I was too serious for her, she was too careless and irresponsible for me. We'd have driven one another crazy.

"I sometimes wonder, and it's a sort of torture, whether Zita had realised that. Because I'd already begun to see that I didn't need her as she needed me. I never gave her a thought all that day—I was utterly absorbed in what I was doing. I can't help sometimes wondering if this was her way out."

He stopped and looked interrogatively at Claire, who was sitting unmoved.

"Well," she said severely, "that's one of the silliest confessions I've ever listened to. And I've heard plenty. It's a good thing you got that off your chest—you can afford to torture yourself in a puritanical sort of way if you're well, but not if you only have a few months to live. Let's get this clear, Zita would never have killed herself for such a dotty reason. I knew her too, remember. She'd have been upset, I daresay, made a scene—but to go and *drown* herself! The idea's preposterous. She was a bit feckless and impulsive, but not in that way, not at all."

"But then," Charles was back worrying at his problem again, "it was such a frightful thing to discover so clearly and abruptly that we wouldn't have done for each other. It was like walking at night when you get lost for a moment; you see in the dark what looks like a tree and a gate; then suddenly the moon comes out and you see your tree was really an angle-bracket and the gate was three faint strips of light and you realise you are somewhere miles from the place you thought you'd reached."

"I wonder if you've ever really been in love?" Claire said without unkindness.

"I've always had the ridiculous fancy—" his tone was apologetic—"I suppose everybody has it—that somewhere or other I should meet the person who was really meant for me. Zita had all the physical characteristics I'd always imagined my ideal girl would have—small, black hair and blue eyes and that wonderful bubbling laugh—only there was something missing in Zita. Gradually one began to notice an odd blankness, a lack of response—oh, it sounds monstrous to say it about her now. She was sweet, affectionate, gay, but there was a lack of something . . ."

"Yes, there was," Claire said soberly. "Poor Zita."

"Poor Zita," he echoed, but his heart felt curiously light. For the first time his sorrow and pity were unmixed with that crippling load of remorse.

"Cigarette?" Claire appraised him like the surgeon who has completed a successful operation and sewn up the incision.

"Have one of mine." Delving in his pocket he encountered an unfamiliar object and pulled it out, puzzled. "What the devil— oh." He met her eyes over the bottle and there was a pause.

"I'm surprised at you, Charles," she said then, levelly. "I thought you had more quality."

"I hadn't absolutely decided," he said. "I was carrying them for security. Or, no, that's not true. I had decided. But I don't feel so sure now."

"Well I'm glad I met you. If only because I seem to have eased your morbidly sensitive conscience and given you a peaceful deathbed."

With a swift movement she slipped the bottle into her bulging handbag and snapped the catch.

"Come on; that wretched pianist's climbing on to his platform so we shan't be able to hear ourselves talk. Anyway we've said enough. You'd better come home and spend the night with me; I don't quite trust you by yourself just now."

"If you're sure—" he said. The place filled with clattering music and he could not hear her answer but she nodded vigorously and, taking his arm, dragged him out into the sharp night air. The sleet had turned to snow and carpeted St Martin's Lane. They walked in silence, Charles feeling deliciously relaxed as if he had abandoned all responsibility into Claire's hands.

"Anna's in the spare room," she said, "but you can sleep on the divan. It'll be like old times."

They had met ten years before : Charles had been up at Oxford and Claire happened to be there covering Eights Week. They had been literally thrown together when Claire, swerving her car to avoid a mentally deficient child who had run into the

22

road, crashed into a wall and was flung over her windscreen into Charles's arms. In the subsequent taking of the child to hospital for shock, bandaging Claire who was much the more injured party, and compilation of statements for the police, Charles and Claire had discovered some affinity of a fundamental kind. It surprised most of their friends, who could see nothing in common between the untidy, haphazard woman and the self-contained, diffident young man half her age; nevertheless they continued to be excellent friends when he came down from Oxford, and after he had done his naval service and took a City job.

"Lord," said Claire rummaging, "have I forgotten my key? No, all is well." Her flat was in a ramshackle block off Covent Garden. They went up a rather smelly flight of stairs and had to wait again at the top for Claire to locate another key.

"Don't encourage Anna to talk," she hissed ominously. "She's running away from her husband who beats her."

"Probably deserves it," Charles muttered. He felt exceedingly tired, all of a sudden; the thought of Anna and her troubles struck no chord of sympathy in him. Happy thought—he could make his heart condition the excuse for retiring at once: "So sorry, but I might drop dead at any moment, I really think I'd better turn in." Perhaps there was something to be said for Claire's point of view.

However, when she opened the sittingroom door it became plain that they were due for more than a mere tale of woe from Anna. Shrieks and thuds resounded, a chair flew across the doorway and hit the wall.

"What's going on?" Claire said, striding in. Charles looked over her shoulder.

It appeared that Anna's husband had caught up with her. The room was in a considerable state of chaos with cushions and chairs strewn about, an overturned jug of tea and lemons soaking into the carpet, and a trail of broken gramophone records. Someone seemed to have crowned someone else with a picture, for it lay on the floor, a head-sized hole through the middle. Anna, a blondish central-European girl with well-developed calf muscles and the duck-footed stance of a ballerina, was in the far corner, glaring, with disarranged hair, a bruise on one cheekbone, and a considerable cut on her left forearm.

"Look, Claire!" she exclaimed furiously, holding out her arm. "See what the swine has done!"

"It's your own fault, ducky, if you will let him in," Claire said without sympathy. "Just throw him out, will you, Charles dear, while I get this bandaged up."

Charles looked about for the husband and received a shock. Instead of Anna's male counterpart there was a perfect giant of a man breathing heavily behind the door. He was gaunt and haggard, wore a navy blue seaman's sweater, and had a three-day growth of beard. He was leaning negligently on a meat-axe, and looked quite prepared to use it on anyone who crossed him.

Charles's eyes wavered past him to the table, which had survived the general wreckage. There were two plates, two forks, a plate of tomato salad, a french loaf, a chianti bottle; apparently the pair had been enjoying a pleasant domestic evening before some trifle occurred to spoil the harmony. Charles wondered if the man took his meat-axe with him wherever he went, like a walking-stick, or if he had brought it along this evening full of grim purpose? And had he brought it in and left it leaning against the bookshelf while they had their amiable supper and before Anna made her fatally annoying remark—"I do wish you'd shave a bit more, darling," or "Well, *I* like french mustard and if you want the other sort you can just make it yourself," or had he left the axe outside the front door and later stepped outside saying "Excuse me, I just forgot something—"?

All this flashed irrelevantly through Charles's mind in the second or so before he took a cautious step towards the man, who lifted the axe at him menacingly. Charles felt a mad desire to laugh, he thought, "We haven't even been introduced," and then he realised that if the man did split his skull it would be a restfully neat solution.

"Come on, get out, we want to go to bed," he said with brisk authority, seized the man's right arm, swung him round, and propelled him through the door. Puzzled, sheepish, the man obeyed, all his menace gone; he gave Charles an appealing glance as he was shoved out. "After all, if women will run away, what can you do but go after them with a meat-axe?" he seemed to be asking. As Charles shut the door on him he was staring down pathetically at his bright blade; if he had not been so tired Charles had a strong inclination to go out and keep the poor fellow company, walk along the street arm-in-arm with him to cheer his loneliness. "I know, my dear chap, women are full of these infernal whims and fancies, always expecting to be understood—as if anyone could—never there when you want them, always when you don't. Never mind, that Anna looks a perfect fool of a girl. In my opinion you're well rid of her."

He went back in and started rather wearily tidying up the mess. Claire reappeared.

"Well, that's disposed of Anna, I bandaged her and put her to bed. Did you get rid of Boris? Grand. Now you'd better turn in. The divan's made up."

As Charles sank to sleep he thought neither of Zita nor of Eleanor's pills, still in Claire's handbag somewhere among the clutter, nor of his impending death. His last conscious thought was one of pleasure at the way he had handled that great brute with the axe, and then he drifted off into a confused brightness of white sails on green water.

III

HERE, THEN, IS the bereft Maggie—Dr Magda Tassák, M.D. (Gold Medal)—heavy as grief and dark as night, standing at a loss on the platform of King's Cross station at ten in the morning and wondering where her young friend has got to? And when the last trickle of alighting passengers has dispersed, and she has found out that the next train does not arrive till two-thirty, she is even more at a loss and makes, with her ponderous march, for the nearest Espresso, to smoke four cigarettes, drink some black coffee, and beat a vain tattoo on the glassy cool translucent table. Nothing for it now but to get a bus (for Maggie never walks if she can help it) down as far as Russell Square, leave it, and turn eastwards along a passageway into the Georgian cranny of Guilford Square. So up the steep dark stairs of number twelve, and on the third floor she pauses, studying the all-too-plain evidence of full milk bottle and two days' uncollected mail.

There is too much horror, for Maggie, in coming back to an empty flat, so, hearing John's radio on the floor above, she goes up and rings his bell.

"Happy Christmas." A waft of oilpaint and coffee surged out when John opened his door.

"She hasn't come back."

"Who hasn't? Oh, you mean little Twopence hasn't come back? Perhaps the train was late."

"No I met it. She wasn't on it."

"Then she missed it," said John reasonably, setting Maggie by the gasfire with some coffee blacker than the pit. "Don't worry your head about that little goblin. She'll turn up. More's the pity."

But since large tears, to his horror, began rolling down Maggie's cheeks, he hurriedly fetched out brandy and gave her a tot of that, together with buttered toast, which was his specific for all griefs, and not a bad one.

"Look, my dear soul," he presently said, "I have to go out now, to lunch with old Writtstein, but if you'd rather stay in my flat, do : you can hear if Twopence comes back. Make yourself lunch if you want; there's a ham. Did I shave? Damn."

The door slammed behind him, his feet rattled on the stairs, and a moment later she saw him cross the square and vanish into Guilford Passage. She stayed at the window hoping to see a small black-haired figure with suitcase and duffelcoat come from the opposite direction, but none appeared, and she returned to sit brooding by the fire.

The afternoon dragged by.

When the door bell rang Maggie opened it hastily, in despairing hopes, and saw Mrs Nikolaides from the floor below, pale, with a silver teapot in her hand.

"Oh it's you, dear. Isn't Mr Fitzroy in?"

"Not just now. I'm keeping his flat warm for him."

"Well I'll just come in for a minute, if you don't mind. I'm in such a pickle, my husband found out that I'd invited my sister for tea and he'd had a drop too much to drink at dinner so he hit me with the poker, just look at that bruise, dear, and said he'd do me in if any more of my family came round the place, so I popped up here for a bit till things blew over. You don't mind, dear, do you? I know Mr Fitzroy wouldn't, he's so kind."

Maggie was scandalised at the bruise and felt obliged to dress it for Mrs Nikolaides. There seemed no first-aid equipment in John's flat, so she braved the cold darkness of her own, with its unlit Christmas tree, and found bandages and disinfectant.

"That's ever so sweet of you, dear, it's miles better now. I daresay my hubby is over his little tantrum by this time, it doesn't generally last long with him I will say, but I'll stay another half hour just to be on the safe side. I've got some photos of my little nephews and nieces I brought up to show Mr Fitzroy, would you like to see them?"

But Maggie, who had returned with a couple of large medical textbooks under her arm, explained that she had arranged to meet somebody and was obliged to go out.

When the five-thirty had also arrived cargoless she returned to a cafe in Lambs Conduit Street called Mount Athos, where she sat over two leathery sandwiches and tried to work. Before long it was quite dark outside, and dribbles of steam ran down the windows, which were painted with a design of improbable dishes of fruit and cakes and roast chickens at which a repellent chef beamingly pointed. Every time Maggie raised her head from the textbook she caught this apparition's eye. Whenever somebody came in her head jerked up uncontrollably and then she forced her eyes down again.

Seven o'clock struck. The streets were empty and skinned with snow as she walked home, a policeman stood shrouded in mystery by the callboxes, two cats flitted past towards Coram's Fields. She kept her eyes on the ground while crossing Guilford Square, and made a bargain with providence; if I don't look up at the windows there'll be a light, she will be back. But outside the front door she abandoned the bargain and looked up. There was a light in the window.

Shouts of laughter came from behind the Nikolaides' front door; evidently Christmas was getting into orbit, the trouble had been composed. She dug in her pocket for her latchkey, hearing, as she did so, faint sounds from inside the flat as if a mouse were tentatively making itself at home.

She opened the door and stood questing like a bloodhound. Kitchen—no. Bathroom—no. Sittingroom—yes.

IV

WHEN I GOT back to the flat Maggie was out. *That* was a relief. I could make it tidy and warm before she appeared—give myself some sort of ground on which to take a stand. There were cigarette ends everywhere, books lying about, dregs in the coffee-pot but no sign of food having been eaten.

While I was cleaning John came in.

"Oh, it's you," he said, not very friendly. "Maggie's been in a fine state, wondering where you'd got to."

27

"Where is she?"

"Don't know. I daresay she'll be back soon. Why couldn't you come on the train you said you'd take? She was up there at King's Cross to meet you this morning."

"Oh *lord*, was she? I thought she'd be on duty at the Ogham."

"So she was but she fiddled two rotas together. She's been on for thirty-six hours nonstop. Why can't you be a bit more decent to her?"

John's ugly, honest face, his direct, accusing look, hit me the same sort of blow that the wretched old woman in the train had done. I wanted to clasp my hands over my chest and burst out crying like a child, "I have a pain here!"

"It's no use looking at me in that grieved way," said John (his sense of justice must have worked him up to this for it was most unlike him); "you're treating Maggie abominably and you know it. I'm sorry for you—"

"But, John, damn it, this is the *only* time I've been away— and Maggie has dozens of other friends—it's only a crumb of time in comparison—"

"What's a crumb to you is a whole Christmas cake to her," said John. When he smiled his face became suddenly carved with transverse lines. "Maybe it's hard on you, but it's Maggie's interests I'm watching. Think what she's been through already, and yet she's plainly headed right for the top of the medical tree, if things go right for her from now on. I don't want to see all her capacities mucked up by a little twopence-halfpenny like you."

There was no sense in arguing. I knew his views on Maggie's potential and with reluctance, with annoyance just then, I supposed that I shared them.

"Well—" said John. "I must go and work." He glanced approvingly round the warm, tidy room and said, "Make some soup. She doesn't eat enough."

I sat down on a hassock when he had gone and glared at my unopened suitcase. It recalled my night in the train. Why didn't John ever worry about *my* welfare? Maggie was at least twelve years older, she ought to be able to look after herself, why did I have to do it? I remembered the firm friendly touch of Wal, rolling me in the blankets in his bunk. No, that's unfair, Maggie is always doing me little services, or intending to—oh, damn, blast, and hell. Why have I got into this predicament?

I felt sleepy and inert; wished that I could go to bed and postpone the whole affair—explanations with Maggie, life, experience, death, eternity. They seemed to run on in a hideous procession, like a school timetable, with no time allotted for getting from one to the next.

My bed—the folding one, that let down from the wall—was already made up. I unfolded it, to see. But just then I heard steps coming up the stairs—heavy, unmistakable—and hastily swung it up again. Her key scratched and the front door opened.

I was shocked at her face—white, drawn, with deep indentations in the cheeks, and the mouth a heavy crescent of exhaustion. She came and sat on the arm of the sofa and looked at me. A pulse was beating at the side of her neck.

"Where have you been? Why weren't you on the early train? You promised—"

"I'm dreadfully sorry—I didn't think you'd be meeting it—"

"Couldn't you *bear* to drag yourself away from the Tallents?"

"Yes, of course I could—"

"I suppose you were having a wonderful time listening to them all playing their musical instruments," Maggie said bitterly.

Maggie had an odd streak in her make-up about music. She told me once that her father, who had been a talented pianist in Budapest, had abandoned her mother when Maggie was about five. Two years after that (during which time nothing was heard of him) he called at the flat one afternoon when no one was there and left a Christmas present for Maggie—a beautiful record-player, at a time when such things were almost unobtainable, and a stack of records.

Oh well, no use going into that story now, dead and buried in a dead and buried city twenty-five long, cold years ago, but you can't wonder that Maggie kept the scar of it, the child's bewilderment and anguish, the smashed records, the speechless gramophone. Her mother must have been very bitter. Maybe she had cause.

Music was a topic best avoided, therefore. Which was rather a nuisance for me as before Maggie took me under her wing I had enjoyed playing the guitar. But I'd had to give my instrument away; it caused too much trouble.

Now I quickly said no, we had spent most of our time out shooting, and Maggie's lip curled again at these *Country Life* pursuits, so I explained that it was target-shooting at a popinjay that Paul had constructed in the garden, and then began to tell her, snatching words at random, about the long walk through the leafless Scottish oakwoods that we had taken the day before.

"Listen, Maggie, we saw two poor little snakes, little dead ones, silver and sad and tarnished, frozen stiff in the road—wasn't that a queer thing to find in December?"

So I chattered, pouring soup into bowls and buttering a piece of pumpernickel, but Maggie hardly looked at the food, she was not to be put off.

"What train did you catch back, then?"

"The night train, Maggie."

"But that's the one I met. Where have you been all day?"

For a wild moment I toyed with the notion of lying, but I knew it was no use. Maggie was nose down on the trail like some huge pursuing animal, there was no dodge or feint that would throw her off. I could lie only for my own amusement, in a real crisis the truth came shooting out like water from a burst main.

"I made friends with an American airforce sergeant on the train, he invited me to Christmas dinner at his camp, there was a party. It was so amazing, you can't imagine how many colonels were there and we all—" We all sang, I was about to say, but hurriedly changed it to we all drank a lot of whisky. "And then Wal put me on a bus."

"Wal?"

"The sergeant."

And I stifled a grin, thinking of that dusky, chilly walk among the clumps of bushes with Wal so obstinately determined to get me horizontal, and my mind so set on the bus. How many worlds there are, separate, each within the other, Wal and I cherishing our different futures, and this dark intent Maggie, hands on knees, feet apart, staring at me with neck out-thrust. I fidgeted, slid my hand under a cushion, dangled my slipper from my toe and studied it. Maggie had pushed the food to one side and I bustled it on to the tray.

"Have an apple?" I said, knowing she never did.

Maggie did not even answer. Although I had moved, her direct, dark glance went on boring into the spot I had left, inching along my trail. The wheels slowly went round, the levers clicked up and down.

I took my trayload to the kitchen and made coffee. Normally Maggie had to remind me to make coffee, I always forgot it; but now I was out to please, even remembered brown sugar and the top of the milk, nicely poured into a little yellow pitcher.

Silence from the other room.

Oh, Maggie (I feel now), don't be too hurt. I can't bear your sense of loss as you sit staring at the wall and know that your child has been taken from you. But at that time I was not concerned with her feelings, only wondering how to escape from this dreadful moment enclosing me like a prison. And indeed there's not much use in cherishing feelings of sorrow now, my repentance won't help Maggie a scrap as she sits in the wicker chair. We bought those chairs together so happily when we first took the flat, some Victorian conservatory set, and I said they were hideous, but Maggie said they were comfortable and she was not going to sit in any spindle-legged bit of nonsense. So throned she sat now, like Judgment herself.

I poured the coffee and she drank hers at a gulp with no comment.

"What sort of a person is this American?"

"Oh, just an American, you know, big, and friendly, with a tooth missing."

My superficial voice, mincing up these live human beings into squares and triangles. And how had I described Maggie to Wal: "The friend that I live with; oh, she's foreign, escaped from Hungary, studying medicine, a bit temperamental, you know, and possessive."

"Is he educated? Intelligent?"

"No. No, I don't suppose so."

"Well, what did you talk about then?"

"Oh, Maggie, I hardly remember. Where we had been, where we lived."

"Did he kiss you?" said Maggie. First turn of the screw.

"Yes, a bit."

"Rather odd, surely, to kiss someone you've never met before?"

Jenny kissed me, I thought, when we met. Jumping from the chair she sat in. "Is it? Oh, I don't know. Americans seem to feel more friendly than other people. Anyway, it's Christmas."

"When did he kiss you?"

"Oh, on the train, of course. Maggie! Why are you looking at me like that? What do you suspect me of?"

"Fornication," said Maggie, bitterly, wearily, leaning back a moment and passing a hand over her face.

"For heaven's sake, what a word to use! Anyway, how do you

know?" So indignant was I, to have my secret jumped out of me like this, that I lost caution.

"How do I know? Your expression, my dear, the guilty way you've been slinking about, your revolting little smirk when you talk about this man. I'm right, aren't I? Aren't I right?"

"Oh, I suppose so," I said angrily, sulkily. "I don't really know what you're talking about."

"I suppose the next thing will be that you find you're pregnant."

"Oh, come off it, Maggie, for pete's sake!"

"Has this happened before?" said Maggie, suddenly standing up, coming close and threatening. "I can't think why I should care, you're such a little rat that it should make no difference *when* you started coming apart, but I want to know, so tell the truth. Has it?"

Well, I grabbed up my last rags of privacy and wrapped them round me, shut my eyes to my befouled nakedness, and refused to answer. Be damned to her, I thought, she shan't have the consolation of knowing that this is the first time, that I have been virtuous, if this is what virtue consists of, up till today. She's giving me a hell of a time, let her have one. I shut my mouth tight.

She slapped my face twice, front and back of her hand, heavy as a lead-filled stocking. I stood looking at her stupidly with my head tingling, oblivious of the pain, intent on the question: What is happening to us?

"Well?" said Maggie.

I didn't answer that one. There seemed nothing to say.

Maggie lost patience. Her face was distorted by rage, she loomed above me gigantic as St Paul's and I could do nothing to avert what happened next. I heard her voice again and again, repeating "Was that the first time? Was it? Was it?" I felt her hands on my neck, tighter and tighter, throttling and shaking me about like a shred of banana peel, and at last the room went blank on me.

I can't have been out long, only a few minutes I imagine, and then I slowly began waking up again, noticing the lamp-shadow on the cream-washed wall, and droop and drape of dark-green hessian, nearly dragged off the bed. I was lying on the bed, and that was odd, for I'd been standing in the middle of the room. I shifted a little, my head swam, and then I heard Maggie's voice: "John, John! Is she all right?"

A dreadful sound jerked into my ears, the sound of Maggie sobbing.

"Oh, my dear soul! She's not worth it, you know."

The voices faded. He was leading her into the kitchen. Warily I raised myself on one elbow, glanced around, saw my shoes in one corner, my coat in another, where I had flung it down when I came in, and with desperate speed and silence put them on. Still some money in my purse, good, and now I was tiptoeing past the kitchen to the front door, always difficult to close without a bang but I managed it, gently pulling, and down the black precipice of the stairs.

In the street I was vaguely surprised to find that it was snowing quite hard. A white Christmas, I thought, just like Bing Crosby said it was going to be. I buttoned my coat tight, stuffed my hands in my pockets, and began walking eastwards along Guilford Street.

I didn't know where I was going, I was going away, not towards. I still felt very strange, my ears were humming and my breath came in swoops of irregular length, I couldn't get them sorted into equal gulps. All I wanted was to walk a bit and settle my mind, try and find out where I was and what was to become of Maggie and me.

The street lights were a long way apart and the snowflakes came spiralling down out of dark vacancy and flew at my feet, making leaflike shadows before they hit the ground. As I walked on these snow-shadows gradually moved closer and passed me, moved closer and passed me, following the glide of the street-lamps. Looking up I saw the lamps almost veiled by the crazy fluttering, but there was no sound, not the least sound in the world, and it was like walking on felt; I hurried on, faster and faster, trying to leave behind my own horrified thoughts. But they came with me like a swarm of bees; between the bees and the snowflakes I went forward in a dazzle.

I am not sure now, where I went; at one time I looked up and saw the large dark bulk of Mount Pleasant; all silent; then I struck right and wove through a maze of City streets, empty, hollow, and dark. Presently there was the Tower of London, squat at the foot of its slope, and I turned west again. My head ached, my back ached, my feet were icy, my hands were hot, and I didn't know where to go; the thought of Maggie's hatred was like a sharp knife in my chest, I couldn't bear to go back, and yet I walked along, past St Paul's, frosted like a wedding-cake and St Bride's, a musical toy. The snow had stopped falling and Fleet Street was tidy and white, with the vans and hurrying crowds long gone. Up the smooth sweep of Aldwych and now, if I could have done it, I ought to have concentrated on finding somewhere else to go, but I felt too queer to think. One baleful vision possessed me : Maggie outstretched on the kitchen floor, like dying Gerard in *The Cloister and the Hearth*, arms extended, wrists slashed, and ash on her forehead. Kingsway and Southampton Row flashed past me in a hurrying dream. I was counting breaths as the familiar square and trees received me, ninety-one, ninety-two, and the stairs rose up tread by tread, to the dirty green door and ground-glass panes. There was a light. Key, I thought, but it had left my pocket, moved away, no doubt, to a warmer climate, and I pressed the bell, kept my finger on the buzzer till the door flew open and Maggie's indrawn breath was the last sound I heard as I pitched down on the floor.

V

CHARLES THOUGHT HE would lunch with Eleanor next day, and he went round to the Ogham Hospital for Glandular Disease to collect her. He had not been home; after leaving Claire's flat, rather late, he had gone to have a Turkish bath, regardless of its possible effect on his heart, and now, feeling clean, purged, and full of wellbeing, he gazed with pleasure at snowy stretches of park through the hospital waiting-room windows.

Some illustrated papers lay on a severely functional metal table by the window and he leafed through one, skipping past lumpy debutantes in white dresses, pausing at an article on the gracious and lovely home of Lady Thing, who had converted a Devon farmhouse to her own beautiful taste, making the very most of the existing amenities while adding only such modern comforts as would bring the house entirely up to date while still retaining . . . "and only spending twenty or thirty thousand," muttered Charles, scanning the flagged terraces, morning-room-conservatory, all-glass kitchen, and the bedroom which, to judge from the photograph, must be at least eighty feet square. "And I expect it was a pretty place once."

"Charles!"

Eleanor stood in the doorway, her face as white as her coat.

"Why, Nell—what's the matter?" The magazine dropped from his hand.

"That fool of a porter didn't say who it was—just said someone to see me," she jerked out, a little colour beginning to creep back into her cheeks.

"Well, but who were you expecting—Dracula?"

"No, only I've been so worried about you, so terribly worried," she said, sinking on to a webbing chair as if her legs would hold her up no longer. "When I got home this morning I tried to ring your flat and got no answer; your caretaker said you hadn't been home all night. Then I found that bottle of Somnil was gone and I suddenly had an awful fear that—that you might have done something foolish, perhaps taken some of them in a pub or restaurant, not realising how fast they acted. I didn't know what to do; it seemed idiotic to ring the police and I knew you'd be furious if you were all right; on the other hand, if you'd had an attack somewhere—oh well. I'm glad you're all right."

She smiled at him wanly.

"You look all in," said Charles, concerned. "Why, you look more likely to have a heart attack than I do. Do take it easy. You simply mustn't worry about me so much. If it has to happen it will. I'm getting quite used to the idea myself."

"But where were you? And what did you do with those tablets?"

"Oh, they're somewhere about," Charles said vaguely. "I know, they're in Claire's handbag. I spent the night at her place. But I say, can you come out and have lunch? I want to talk."

"You spent the night with *Claire*?" Eleanor said, utterly bewildered, after she had fetched her fur coat and they were descending the slippery, slush-covered steps. "But why?"

"Oh, not with her in any immoral sense," said Charles, remembering belatedly that Eleanor rather disapproved of Claire for some obscure feminine reason—but hang it, he hadn't time any more to step aside for these involved underground complications, they must sort themselves out as best they could—"I just happened to run up against her in a pub."

They picked their way through the mess underfoot to Eleanor's white Ford and Charles, partly to tease her, partly because he liked the memory, gave her a description of the arrival at Claire's flat the night before.

"But why does she bother with these extraordinary people?" asked Eleanor, weaving dexterously between a couple of buses. "I never can understand what you see in Claire."

Under the squirrel she was wearing beautifully cut silvery grey tweeds. Green jade earrings picked up the colour in her well-shaped grey eyes. Her neat profile, with the boyish lock of fair hair, was bent over her gloved hands on the wheel in frowning preoccupation.

Charles reflected that it would be hopeless trying to explain, to break down the barrier of non-comprehension between the well-dressed, well-groomed woman and the unkempt one who nevertheless commanded the respect and friendship of countless men. He wondered what Claire thought of Eleanor; was not sure that he had ever heard her express an opinion on his sister.

"Oh, I'm very fond of old Claire; she's grand, really," he said. "I was feeling pretty grim last night, in fact verging on suicidal; you may have Claire to thank that I'm here now taking you out to lunch. She talked to me like a Dutch aunt and generally knocked some sense into my head."

"Did she?" said Eleanor, turning to glance at him for a moment and then carefully sliding in alongside a parking meter, forestalling a Daimler by hairsbreadth timing. "Well if she has that to her credit I certainly owe her some thanks."

"Oh, I'm sure you'll like her when you know her better." He waited while she locked the car, then took her arm. "Anyway, that's what I want to talk to you about."

They negotiated the swing doors of the restaurant and found a table.

"Claire's decided to retire," he said when they had ordered. "She's going to embark on that long-cherished dream of a small-holding. Oddly enough she was proposing to set off quite soon to do some house-hunting in Cornwall or Devon, and she says she'll look on our behalf at the same time. If you're still sure, that is, that you want to go ahead with this plan of moving down there?"

"You don't mean, share a house with Claire?" Eleanor's look was a little blank.

"No, no." Charles smiled at her. "Even I have that much sense. But I thought it would be fun if we were neighbours, and Claire seems to favour the idea."

"Yes, of course." Eleanor crumbled her roll. "But I have to find a practice, you know. That will condition where we live, rather, I'm afraid."

"Oh, Claire isn't particular. And I'm not, so long as it's within reach of the sea, or a river. I want to do a lot of sailing. You know, Nell, Claire gave me such a talking-to."

He beckoned the wine waiter.

"What about?" Eleanor asked when he had ordered a bottle of Beaune.

"Well, I was in a pretty defeatist mood, as I told you, and she somehow made me see that it's stupid not to make the most of the rest of my life. So that's what I'm going to do."

"How?"

"Keeping livestock," Charles said, ticking them off on his fingers, "gardening; reading the books I've never had time for, like Meredith and Voltaire; astronomy—"

"It sounds a bit of a hermit's life," Eleanor smiled faintly.

"No, I was just coming to that. You know, Nell," Charles said, leaning forward and speaking with the earnestness of a younger brother, "all my life I've somehow been scared of personal relationships. I've felt there was a sort of barrier between me and other people that I couldn't—didn't dare risk breaking down. I've no close friends. And the only time I fancied I was in love—"

"Yes, I know—"

"Well! I'm going to change all that. What you told me yesterday gives me a kind of immunity. I'm not going to be scared any more of how people can affect me; in this last year I'm going all out to get to know people. In fact I've *been* living a hermit's life but now I'm going to come out."

Eleanor was staring down at her knife and fork.

"Do you think that's wise?" she said. "I know it's your life, but don't you think you may lay yourself open to misunderstanding and trouble?"

"How do you mean, Nell?"

"Well—if you make new friends, for instance." She was speaking with difficulty. "I feel it's hardly fair, in a way, to embark on new relationships that are bound to be so—so short-lived. If you encourage people to become fond of you—"

She seemed so troubled that Charles thought, cursing his own obtuseness, that she was minding all this far more than she wished him to know. Beneath her collected, medical exterior she was, after all, his sister; he was her only relative in the world, apart from old Aunt Julia. It was not to be expected that she could enter into his plans for a self-indulgent last year with much enthusiasm when the end of it would leave her to go on alone.

"I'm sorry, Nell," he said, "I expect it all sounds a bit selfish and childish."

He had a sense of deflation. How often Eleanor made him feel this, when he came to her bubbling over with some hopeful scheme.

"Of course it's not," she said kindly. "We'll have a lovely year." She looked at her watch. "I ought to fly, my dear. There's a private call I promised to make before I go back to the Ogham. Can I drop you anywhere? I'm going up to Bloomsbury."

"I'll come with you," he said. "I wouldn't mind a stroll round the British Museum. Haven't been there since God knows when. Who's the patient?"

"I had a call from a friend of mine, Magda Tassák," Eleanor said, when she had started the car and moved out into the traffic. "I don't think you've met her. She shares a clinic with me at the Ogham, she's an extremely gifted doctor. The girl she lives with went into a faint or something; hysterical, I suspect, from the sound; she's a lot younger than Magda and a little fool by all accounts. But Magda's worried about her so I said I'd call round and see what I thought." She drove a few more blocks in preoccupied silence and then said, "Would you like to come up and meet Magda?"

"No, I think not just now, Nell, thanks all the same. I'm not sure that she and her friend sound quite my cup of tea."

"This is where they live, Guilford Square," Eleanor said, pulling up. "I'd take you to the museum, but I'm running a bit late as it is—"

"That's all right, it's only five minutes walk. Well, thanks for the ride, be seeing you—"

She offered her cheek for his kiss.

An elderly flower-seller had her pitch on the corner of the square. With a gesture which, as soon as he made it, Charles knew that Eleanor would consider deplorably sentimental, he bought a great bunch of forced, scentless daffodils and put them in her arms.

"Really, Charles," she said as he had known she would, "what an extravagance." She looked as if she hardly knew what to do with them.

"Oh well," he said, "it isn't every day that—"

He never finished. A small object, hurtling down from above, struck the bouquet such a violent blow that half the heads were smashed; Eleanor started back but Charles was just in time to catch the flowers as she dropped them; embedded in a green-and-yellow gluey mess in the middle he found a small carved bird.

VI

WAKING UP WAS terrible. It would have been better in sheltering dark but morning had come long ago. I must have slept nine or ten hours solid. I shut my eyes again, wished I could fall back into unconsciousness but it was no use; the loathsome day had to be faced. And *how* loathsome : even the black-and-blue pattern on the carpet seemed menacing, the wormeaten wickerwork was squalid, so were the coffeecups and ash on the table. Heartbreak hung in the room like a sour smell.

I could see that one time had ended for me, and another was due to begin, and of course, having precipitated the change, I didn't like it, wanted to cry, "Take me back! Help me out of the boat, mother!" only, unfortunately, there was nobody to help. What chiefly appalled me just then was the fact that *I* was responsible for Maggie's anguish—it wouldn't have been so bad if it were somebody else's fault.

A hump of blanket cut off the light; presently I made out that it was Maggie sleeping on the sofa. I was occupying her bed; why she couldn't have pulled mine down heaven knows. It seemed pretty stupid to spend a cramped night, insufficiently covered by the bearskin rug, but that was Maggie all over; if I went out for an evening and left her a fully-cooked meal it could grow mildew while she ate cocktail wafers and drank black tea.

The humped shape stirred, groaning, and rolled to its feet. I hastily shut my eyes again. In normal circumstances I was the one who got up and made coffee, but today I meant to lie doggo till I'd gauged the temperature. Let her fend for herself a bit longer.

All the same, as I heard her fumbling progress about the

kitchen and followed every clink and clank with intimate topographical knowledge I longed to shout, "Put the kettle on first, you fool, *then* grind the coffee."

I hate simple things done badly.

Maggie was the coming doctor of her generation I think—in fact I know she was—but it's different living with these people. I bet Marie Curie was a trial in the home.

So I lay in bed vilifying Maggie, thinking how crass she was, how intolerant, how uncivilised, brutal, uncouth, inconsiderate; she gave away a whole boxful of my clothes to some hard-up girl at her clinic, she abused me for not liking her friends, she never made the slightest effort to like mine, she ignored all my dearest interests, she was content to live in squalor—

At this point Maggie came in with a tray which she thumped down beside me on the bed.

As she ignored my pretence of sleep I had to abandon it and sit up. I was naked, and she angrily threw me a robe which I put on. The silence prolonged itself while I looked at the breakfast tray.

From somewhere Maggie had procured an embroidered pillowcase which she was using as a traycloth—an unheard-of innovation in our menage. Half the time she wouldn't even trouble to find a tray, just brought things in one by one, or on the breadboard.

Pots of coffee and hot milk stood side by side, the cup and saucer actually matched, on a plate lay ten little bits of toast, scraped, with the crusts cut off; I had heard her scraping away and knew the kitchen floor would be knee-deep in crusts and charcoal. Maggie never could make toast without burning it.

On the plate, among the toast, was a little crystal bird, a Chinese crow. It was Maggie's dearest possession, had belonged to her mother who vanished in November 1955 and was never heard of again. Sometimes, in certain lights, it picked up a spark and shone, but on this grey morning it sat among the toastcrumbs like a beautifully shaped lump of slushy snow.

I looked my question.

"It's for you," said Maggie. Her tone was gruff, her expression noncommittal.

"But, Maggie—it's yours. It's your precious thing."

I could have wept. The little bird was pretty, but it meant nothing to me. I should probably drop it or lose it—my belongings never stayed with me very long. Whereas for Maggie it represented the last link with childhood.

"Even I myself am not a link any more," she said to me once. "People undergo complete bodily change every seven years. I am not the same person at all. The little crow was once in Budapast; I never was. I have no past."

She had the bird in her pocket, nothing else, when she came out.

"I can't take it, Maggie," I said.

"I want you to have it."

"I don't want it."

The bird lived like a charming stranger among her functional possessions; for me it would simply be one of a dozen other sweet oddments. It had no value for me—except the weighty one of obligation. Maggie was giving it to me as a token—of what? Her repentance? My amendment?

"Why do you want to give it to me?" I asked.

"Because I was stupid and I am sorry for it. If I give you this I shall remember and perhaps you will remember too."

"Remember what?"

"That I feel responsible for you. That I love you."

Maggie was sitting in the wicker armchair, a little turned away from me, in her usual position, hands on knees. After she had spoken a heavy sort of tranquillity seemed to settle on the room. There, said the silence, lying over me like a quilt of lead, now see what you have let yourself in for.

"I know that, Maggie," I said, clearing my throat. "You don't have to give me the bird to prove it. I'm sorry for—for yesterday. I won't—"

"Don't talk about it," she said grimly. She picked up the bird and tucked it into my dressing-gown pocket with the clumsy, unpractised movement of one who seldom makes personal gestures. "There—it's yours."

"But, Maggie—" I didn't know how to say it so as to make it earnest enough, my voice almost cracked with effort—"*I don't want it.*"

"If you don't accept it," said Maggie coldly, heavily, "I shall throw it out of the window. Are you going to take it or not?"

I felt like a puppy having its nose rubbed in a puddle.

"No." I put it back in her hand. She hurled it through the window, which was open at the top, and went out, slamming the door.

I lay back on the pillow feeling, now I came to think of it, quite peculiarly weak. I was sweating and shivering; my breath emerged in odd short gasps.

About three minutes later the doorbell rang. No sound from Maggie, though I knew her to be in the kitchen. Let it ring, I thought, let it ring. Why should I always be the one to scurry round clearing up the scraps, tidying after Maggie's little haphazardries? I'm ill, she's up. I'm staying in bed.

The bell rang again, peremptory. Cursing, I got up, buttoned my dressing-gown, and paddled barefoot into the front hall. It would be a cop, no doubt, complaining about missiles from the window, and then what? I certainly wasn't going to be chivalrous and say I'd thrown it.

There was icy grit on the floor, and wind seeped up my bare legs making the robe as much use as an inverted icecream cone, so I tugged open the front door irritably. Behind my back, behind the closed kitchen door, I could feel Maggie, black and broken, a half-discharged thunderstorm, waiting.

It wasn't a policeman, it was that cold female salmon, so spick and span, Eleanor Foley, Maggie's workmate at the Ogham clinic, not a blonde hair on her head out of place. There was a man with her, brown eyes, nice, harmless looking, and I noticed from the corner of my eye that he was holding Maggie's crystal bird. Oh well fielded, sir, well held indeed, and bang goes poor Maggie's gesture, but isn't that life for you, and in particular the sort of trick it serves out on Maggie; the only time she ever decided to throw herself under a train they started a rail strike that very evening and she sat for two hours on Bishop's Stortford station platform before somebody told her why things were so quiet.

"Oh, hallo," I said with hauteur; I could feel Eleanor's eyes hard at work cutting my toenails. "Maggie's in the kitchen if you want her. I'll just hop back to bed if you'll excuse me, otherwise I'm likely to faint."

And I hopped, shutting the sittingroom door firmly behind me, thinking, Aspic, that's what that woman is, smooth and tough and firm and shining and tasteless. But why should I care, let Maggie make friends with all the prawns in the British Medical Association, thank god I am not responsible for her any more. And comforting myself with this delusion I roped myself round in tangled sheet and lay staring at the cracks in the plaster, which seemed to be swinging about a good deal, whether because I was really ill, or merely over-excited, or because the house was due to fall down, I couldn't be bothered to pronounce.

The kitchen door opened. I heard Aspic's voice, Maggie's voice, man's voice, and wondered what account Maggie was giving of the bird's exit from the window—"Just practising long-hops; you know I hope to make the hospital second eleven next summer."

Goodbyes were said, the front door opened and closed, and as I could still hear Aspic and Maggie talking in the passage I concluded that Male Voice had not liked my bare feet and the toast crusts in the kitchen. Lucky lad, off to his club no doubt, and didn't I wish I had somewhere to sneak off to likewise, that the bookshop where I worked wasn't shut for Christmas week. Even the public library would be preferable to home.

The ceiling had slipped a bit farther away and I wondered if eating breakfast would make me feel less sick, but it looked repulsive by now, with a sort of crocodile skin over the milk and the toast sunk in on itself. Anyway at this moment the door opened and in came Maggie and Aspic.

One can't glare very well from a horizontal plane, but I did my best to convey with a look that their entry was unwelcome. Maggie didn't even try to meet my eye.

"Eleanor's kindly come to examine you," she said staring out of the window.

"Why? What do you think I've got? Leprosy?" I knew it was childish but I couldn't just lie there saying nothing. I sat up angrily and Aspic jabbed me all over with a stethoscope till my back must have looked like a bar counter with beer rings. She also took my temperature and told Maggie she'd fix up for some X-rays, both of them talking over my head in that terse, upper-sixth, medical way, as if I were both deaf and mentally defective.

What the devil is all this? I thought, I've got flu, maybe, but I'm not as ill as all that, and then I realised that for Maggie my illness was a let-out, a blanket excuse for my unaccountable and licentious behaviour. We could put the whole affair down to delirium and bury it deep. "That explains it all," I could imagine Maggie saying; she was a great one for attributing people's faults to psychosomatic causes and thereby excusing them from guilt. A little of this goes a long way with me; I'd sooner bear my own guilt and feel free to blame other people for theirs.

"Half past four?" Eleanor was saying on the telephone to the X-ray department. "All right, you'll send an ambulance? You know where Dr Tassák lives, twelve Guilford Square? They'll be here in about ten minutes," she said, ringing off and turning to Maggie, "and they'll bring her back afterwards."

Be damned to that, I thought, as they returned to the kitchen for another prefects' meeting, why should I let myself be carted about like so much offal? I'm getting out of here.

I rolled off the bed, dug a pair of warm corduroys out of my case, and pulled them on. I'd just got into a sweater when the telephone rang and I pounced on it, hoping it was the X-ray department to say they'd had a fire and all the machines were burnt out. But a familiar voice, as American as molasses, came warmly into my ear.

"That you, honeychick?"

"Wal?" I said, incredulous, rather horrified. "How did you know my number?"

"Went through your pocketbook, of course, while you were asleep. It's great I caught you in. Listen, can you meet me at Piccadilly in fifteen minutes?"

"You're in London? But how? I thought you weren't expecting any free time for a fortnight?"

"You don't sound very pleased, sugarlily. I came up special to see you. Wal's AWOL, ha ha, get it?"

"But, Wal, you'll be in trouble, what will the colonel say?"

"Oh, he doesn't mind, bless your boots. He thinks it's a great joke, sent his love. He thought you were cute. Now hustle up, put on them red silken pantalettes, and I'll be seeing you."

"Wal—"

"Don't begin making excuses now," he said, sounding aggrieved in advance.

I had been going to do just that, but suddenly I changed my mind and said,

"Have you got the car with you?" He had told me the colonel often lent him a car when he went AWOL.

"Sure."

"Could you come and pick me up here?"

"Right away," he said. I gave him the address, rang off, and began feverishly doing my hair. Then I grabbed a coat and a toothbrush, let myself quietly out of the front door, and went upstairs to John's. I didn't dare risk going along to our bathroom, which was beyond the kitchen, and there wasn't much

44

risk of John being in at this time. When I'd brushed my teeth in his bathroom I put on the coat because I felt shivery and sat in his studio keeping an eye out of the window for Wal with the car.

Although of course I hadn't said so to Maggie, privately, I'd regarded the Wal episode as closed, and hadn't the least intention or expectation of seeing him again. But now in the midst of all this rumpus the thought of him was as comforting as a hot drink on a cold day. It was easier not to think in Wal's company, he was a kind of antidote against it.

A huge, pancake-shaped car, smothered in stars and stripes, drew up outside our house, just in front of an ambulance.

"Oh, oh," I thought, "this is where I have to be nippy," and I scooted out of John's front door and down the stairs, passing the ambulance attendants on the way up. Wal had stayed in his limousine and was sitting with one elbow on the horn, cradling a posy of shocking-pink carnations. But when he saw me he leapt out and gave me a tremendous hug, right there on the snowy pavement.

"That's my sweetheart," he yelled. "Ready on the tick. I didn't like to come up in case that friend of yours that I don't like the sound of was anywhere about."

Looking past his elbow I saw that Maggie had come out of the tobacconist's on the corner and was standing staring at us, a packet of Gauloises in her hand.

VII

CHARLES SOON BECAME impatient with the complicated and slow-moving negotiations by which Eleanor disposed of her London practice and secured another one. Through an unusual stroke of luck, though, it turned out that an elderly GP would shortly be retiring in Lanrith, the small fishing-port three miles from where Aunt Julia lived, and Claire was therefore house-hunting in that area. As soon as Charles had let his flat and arranged for a successor in his job he went down to join her.

Claire met him off the train. Because Lanrith lay deep in a sort of fjord the station for it had to be nearly a mile away, on the opposite hilltop; from here the railway crossed the Lan

River on a viaduct built by Isambard Kingdom Brunel in his most impressive period. There was no road bridge; cars had to cross by the ferry. This was a ramshackle raft, approached down a one-in-three incline, very prone to come unhitched from its escorting tug and drift perilously downstream. Charles greeted it with pleasure.

"I'd forgotten all the incidental delights of living in Cornwall," he said, as they made the leisurely trip across. "Life here is lived at a Mediterranean pace, isn't it?"

"You're not too tired after the journey?" Claire inquired, when they had gone in to the Ferry Inn for a resuscitator. "It's a hell of a way in the train—I half expected to see you borne out on a stretcher and carted straight off to the cemetery."

"In a way all this seems rather a comic waste of effort."

"That's thinking lazy. And not true. No effort resulting in a week here would be wasted. It's paradisial."

"Wait till the winter," he said, "when it hasn't stopped raining for three weeks and the west wind never lets up and everything's covered with mildew and a thin layer of salt." But he looked out affectionately at the green harbour water and the intricate tangle of little granite houses, jammed around the quay and fitting like a jigsaw puzzle.

"I was brought up in the country too," said Claire, "and not your snobbish nanny-to-amuse-you and stay-indoors-when-it-rains circumstances. I had to cycle five miles over Northumberland moors to school."

"Tough as an old hickory-root," said Charles applaudingly. "Can we get a meal at this pub? And will you drive me to see houses? I've decided that my driving isn't a fair risk to other road-users, and sold my car; I shall stride about with my shirt collar open to the waist sniffing in great snorts of country air."

"You look a bit peaked; I daresay walking won't hurt if you go easy on the hills. You'll want to put in a funicular if you buy Watertown, though."

"Tell me about this place."

She had sent a grubby enthusiastic postcard: Eden rediscovered and no serpents ascertainable so far.

"It's down-river from here, in what they call a Pill, a little deep valley running into the main river, completely on its own."

"Can I keep a boat?"

"Oh sure, a flotilla."

"Where's the house situated?"

"About halfway down the side of the valley. Farm cottage at the bottom. Barns and sheds and old mill building in between. The place looks like a whole village, but it isn't, it's all yours if you buy it. Two orchards and a walled garden and a couple of fields."

"And you? Is the cottage empty? Would it do for you?"

"Well——" said Claire slowly. She pushed her whisky about the table. "It would do, all right, but I think I won't commit myself yet. I'm not dead certain that your sister is very keen to have me there."

"That's bloody nonsense," Charles said, but he said it with unnecessary emphasis. "Bloody nonsense," he repeated. "Of course she'll be delighted to have you in the cottage, and so shall I. Now, what about some food? And when can we go to see your Eden?"

Claire looked round; the gnomish old bar-tender was digging her in the back with the edge of a loaded tin tray.

"Your chicken's just done to a turn, my lover, so don't be lingering over that Highland Maiden any longer or Mrs Varco'll have the ears off me."

"Oh, thank you, Sam," Claire said. "Come on, Charles, drink up. We eat in the parlour."

It was characteristic of Claire that she arrived at christian-name and mutual-service terms as soon as she had known people twenty-four hours. Before they went into the parlour Charles heard her arranging to drive Sam's wife to a hospital outpatient department next day and accepting an invitation to sing in the Matthew Passion produced by the town choral society. It was comforting to know that, even if she was chary of living in Watertown cottage, at least she seemed to be in process of putting down roots in the neighbourhood.

Charles looked out of the parlour window in great content as Sam dumped enormous platefuls of chicken in front of them, meanwhile telling a long and complicated story about someone called Alfie Button who had apparently driven off the end of the car ferry while under the influence of drink.

It was dusk outside, too late to go and look at Watertown today, perhaps, but the parlour window gave on to Lanrith harbour and he could still see the great expanse of pale green crisscrossed with spars; gulls were crying and settling and the Marlin lighthouse out on the opposite point had switched on its cartwheeling beam, which scythed across the water every two minutes and picked out the white faces of cottages on the far shore.

"And so there 'e were and if 'e 'adn't been too merry to shut the car door 'e'd be nibbled to a skeleton by now," said old Sam. "Laugh! 'Tis going to cost Council nigh on five 'undred pound to shift that car out, right in the channel 'er be."

VIII

M AGGIE HAD THE idea that country air would put me on my feet. There was something in it, no doubt, but she hadn't worked it out carefully. For one thing it was always I who did the paperwork in our moves, cancelled the milk at one end and sent a telegram to the cows to expect us, saw that if there was no soap, at least we were equipped with a half brick for scouring. Maggie acted as if such things didn't matter.

Well, this occasion turned out even wilder than usual because the cottage contained no amenities at all, no half-brick, not even torn-up pages of the *Radio Times*.

It wasn't actually raining, so I went out into the garden with a chopper—naturally the first thing I did was to ladder the nylons Wal had sent me—and chopped up some twigs so that we could light a fire in the kitchen grate. The chopper was a sort of stone-age axe we had found in the outside privy. I could hardly lift it and as I staggered back indoors (it had begun to rain by this time) I sniffed in breaths of raw, wet air that smelt as if it had been kept fresh and chilled on rocks, and thought, I'm on my feet now, all right.

While I was upstairs getting tissue-paper out of suitcases I heard voices—Maggie's, exclaiming in pleasure and astonishment, and a man's voice. Whoever it is, I thought, I hope he's brought some firelighters and a cold chicken and won't stay too long.

I hadn't much hope of the latter though, because when Maggie did make a friend the merrymaking tended to go on nonstop till people's offices rang up to ask what had become of them. I once sat through *Gone With The Wind* three times round while she argued with one of her thoroughgoing friends about whether the British national intelligence was declining.

When I came down the narrow wormeaten stairs with my little handful of tissue-paper I saw a stocky man in a cloth cap and dungarees carrying one of those carpenters' holdalls. Wood shavings dangled from him like cobwebs, and he had a smiling, mysterious cat's face.

Maggie, to my surprise, turned to him and rattled off a long string of Hungarian to which he replied in kind, and then he swept off his cap, dumped the toolbag on the floor, and made me a low bow.

"Pleased to meet you!" His s's came out thick and soft, so that *pleased* sounded like feast. "Tomorrow I fix this door so he will shut," he said, looking with scorn at the warped front door which perpetually swung inwards to admit a fine mist on to our box of books.

"This is Matyas Kormendi," Maggie said to me, her eyes shining. "Imagine meeting another Hungarian down here. He came to England in 1944 and he's been here ever since. He's the master carpenter at Noble and Rowse, who are doing up the Foleys' house, and he lives in the cottage at the top of the hill."

She and Kormendi burst into another torrent of Hungarian at each other and it was plain that if anyone unpacked and made supper it would not be Maggie, so giving the carpenter an uphill smile I went over to the range and began digging out sodden ash, decayed birdsnests, and showers of rust.

"Please!" said Kormendi, and he shoved me aside, removed a few of his festooned shavings, and with them and my paper and sticks had a fire going in no time. "Coal in shed," he said. "Miss Foley order." Good for Eleanor, I thought, going with a bucket and finding a substantial mountain, butter our paws and we'll stay the course. Why she is so keen to have us down here in this mist-sodden end of nowhere cybernetics alone can explain, but she certainly appears to understand that if Maggie is to stay anywhere she must be kept warm.

With the fire going, and the luggage dragged upstairs, and the beds made, life began to look more possible. There wasn't any furniture downstairs except for our book cartons and the built-in dresser in the kitchen, so we sat on the boxes and ate supper off the dresser. Kormendi had brought half a dozen eggs, extraordinary eggs so brown they might have been polished with Kiwi.

"Do you feed your hens on mahogany chips?" I asked him.

His face crinkled into its Cheshire smile. "My hens ver' good hens," he told us, and went on to explain how Hungarian hens have plenty of character-training and are regarded as part of the family, whereas in England hens are neglected and ignored, treated as mere egg-laying dependants, consequently their eggs can't help being pale-shelled and anaemic. Of course he stayed to supper and shared the eggs and a tin of pork lunch meat that I'd brought, and of course Maggie told him that she'd just become a Member of the Royal College of Physicians and we were celebrating with a month in the country. He saluted her achievement with another sweeping bow and cycled back to his cottage to fetch a bottle of Tokay which, apparently, he always kept by him for emergencies such as this, so our first evening in Cornwall passed off more gaily than might have been expected.

I was feeling tired and my legs were beginning to buckle, so shelving the question of how we were to wash up without water or sink or soap I crawled upstairs and slumped gratefully into the hummocky comfort of the old cottage bed that Eleanor had picked up at a sale. Downstairs the voices ran quietly on, outside through deep silence I could hear the hushing of three separate streams, and the water dripped comfortably off the eaves. The fresh, cold, primitive smell was here, too, seeping through ill-fitting windows and cracks in the roof. What will Maggie make of this place, I thought, has she ever been in the country before? But I am glad, at least, that she has found a friend.

I ought, I suppose, to have been feeling miserably rebellious; certainly Maggie expected it. When she remembered, she treated me like something small and fragile and explosive, but that was partly a habit left over from the pneumonia through which she had nursed me with such self-discipline and devotion. (Discipline for me too.) How she managed, during the same six weeks, to finish working for and pass her Membership exam, god knows, but that gives an example of Maggie's calibre. She read text-books while she sat and waited for my breathing to stop, every now and then prodding me into having another try at keeping alive. While she was out doing her papers John came and invigilated me, treating me with kind, grave disapproval. He hated fuss and public scenes; he had been shocked to the core by my running out on Maggie and then collapsing on the pavement. Wal, too, had been disconcerted by this episode. At the time, deciding there was nothing to be done, he had laid the pink carnations down beside me and then beaten a hasty retreat, leaving Maggie and the ambulance men to cart me back to bed.

Coward! Skunk! I cried silently in my mind at Wal, but really it was the simplest course.

When he sent me some grapes and a Get Well card, and Maggie said curtly, "You understand there's to be no more seeing *him*," I felt no particular wish to rebel, because I was still so weak. Soon after, however, Wal rang up and asked me out. Maggie took the call.

"Yes, she's here." Her face set like cement. "No, I'm afraid that's not possible. Yes, you may speak to her."

"Hullo, Wal," I said under Maggie's Gorgon stare. "Yes, a bit better, thank you . . . no, no, I'm afraid I can't. Yes, of course I'll soon be all right. No, *no*, nothing like that. What?—I can't tell you. No, I'm not. Yes, she is.—Oh, thank you, that's very sweet of you . . . So do I." I glanced out of the corners of my eyes at Maggie. "No, I must stop now, I'm still only up for five minutes at a time. Do you? Oh—I don't think I should be much good at that. I'd love to, sometime. Well, goodbye, be seeing you."

"And give a raspberry from me to that granite bitch," said Wal's voice in my ear, just before I put back the receiver.

It was after this call that Maggie accepted Eleanor's invitation to Cornwall. She'd won a Fulkinge Award for exceptionally high marks, and I'd sold a short story, so we had a little money in hand, and Maggie wanted to rough herself out a ten-year-plan of research into the thyroid gland, which was her chief interest. Aspic, with her brother Charles, the one who appeared that day with Maggie's crystal bird, had bought a farmhouse near Lanrith. Eleanor had taken over a practice there and the brother was retiring due to ill-health. We were invited to spend a month in the pertaining cottage. Maggie jumped at the suggestion. Lord knows why she was so keen on Aspic; perhaps because she was so efficient; one always felt that Eleanor had her whole existence under control down to the whereabouts of the last pin, and that her patients recovered in double-quick time out of sheer cowed obedience. Maggie admired that.

So here we were.

By next morning the rain had stopped. When I went to get water (from a spring a hundred yards up the road, a charming stone basin all fringed about with ferns) everything was damp and glittering. The birds were singing like lunatics. Maggie came out to take a look at it all, blinked, and went back indoors where she had established a screened-off Maggie's-nest by the glowing range, with a broken-down rocking-chair from the barn, a tin coffee-pot, her medical books, and a blanket of cigarette ash.

"We must have Eleanor and Charles to tea this afternoon," she said when I had found an enamel basin in the hedge and done the washing-up.

"For god's sake, Maggie, why?"

"It's very kind of them to lend us their cottage—"

"I don't dispute it, though I wish there were a bit more furniture—"

"Eleanor told me last night she'd bought some more at a sale. It's coming today. So the least we can do is ask them to a meal."

"Yes, okay, but why today? For one thing, there's no food."

"You can make a cake. I would like them to receive a good impression; I think they picked up the idea that we lead rather a Bohemian life, and of course that is frowned on in the English country," Maggie said knowledgeably.

I grinned, remembering Charles and Eleanor at the flat door, dignified as two sarsen stones, with the crystal bird. But Maggie went on, very earnest,

"You can make a cake, and there's watercress in the stream outside our front door, Matyas told me. Watercress sandwiches, very English, very respectable—"

"I could make a cake if I had flour, milk, eggs, sugar, a pudding basin, and a baking-tin. And I could make sandwiches if I had some butter. Also we've nearly finished the loaf I brought."

"Well, make a list and go into Lanrith and get them. Or, no," Maggie said, remembering and looking at me appraisingly, "you make the list and I will go in. You aren't strong enough yet for the walk both ways, and somebody has to stay here to receive the furniture."

She found an envelope and a stub of pencil and started writing on her knee.

"Eggs, you say—what about the eggs Matyas brought?"

"We ate them for supper, remember. All but one, and I can't find it anywhere."

"I ate it in the middle of the night. Yes, then, eggs, flour, sugar, butter—"

"Pudding-basin, cake-tin."

"How shall I know what sort?" Maggie said, looking daunted. "I think you had better go after all."

"Oh, just the ordinary sort, Maggie. There won't be much choice in Lanrith."

There were two ways to Lanrith; by road, three miles, and by the cliff path, one mile. The road followed the course of our little valley up to meet the main Lanrith-Truro highway. But the path climbed steeply over our left-hand headland and so back in a left sweep along the Lan river cliffs and down about a thousand steps to the port. The path also commanded a fine view of the main-line railway, which crossed the Lan river on a twenty-span viaduct, nipped through the nose of our left-hand headland in a cutting, and crossed our little valley on another six arches of viaduct. Maggie had grumbled that we'd never get any peace, with trains crossing at all hours, but I thought the viaduct added a stately touch to the wild scene, and the trains were undoubtedly useful for telling the time.

I gave Maggie my rucksack to carry the groceries in.

"Why don't you ask Aspic to take you in her car?"

"Good heavens no," Maggie said looking scandalised. "We can't bother her like that. Besides she's probably gone already; I think she has a surgery in Lanrith at nine. And don't call her by that name, please; it's not kind."

She swung on the empty rucksack, looked dubiously again at the list, and walked off down the footpath. "Oh, by the way," she said, turning back, "would you be a—a chicken and look out some respectable clothes for me?"

I stared with amazement after her broad retreating back. Maggie, of all people in the world, to be making social gestures, asking people to tea and cake, trying to look respectable! Above all, to be voluntarily walking a mile along a rugged cliff path— two miles there and back—Maggie who in no circumstances walked farther than the nearest bus stop. What did it all portend?

I tidied the cottage so far as I could, mopped the flagged floors and draped an old curtain over the book boxes. Then, honour satisfied, I went out into the sun. I felt very much alone.

A narrow strip of walled garden ran the length of the cottage in front, tangled with damson, japonica, and roses coming into leaf. Daffodils in lavish clumps were beginning to wither. I crossed the little bridge, one large stone slab, over the stream that ran in front of the cottage, and followed the path Maggie had taken, longing for a sight of the sea. It was not far away, though in this sheltered valley you'd never guess it.

The path shot up, and in a moment, looking back, I could see Watertown, the Foleys' house, which was hidden from the cottage by an orchard. It was white and square, with a shallow roof and round-arched windows, a simple stone box set snugly among trees. A pleasant-looking house.

The sun struck hot on my back, and was drawing steam from the stones in the path ahead. In a moment I rounded the corner of the hill and felt a wallop as the wind hit me, and another wallop as my dazed eyes took in the fierce brilliant aquamarine of the water which mooched and creamed round black rocks a good long way below. The tide was in, evidently, up to high-water-mark on the cliffs that faced me across the estuary. A couple of fishing-boats were putting out, follow-my-leader, through the middle arch of the viaduct. A line of china-clay wagons clanked across above, their diesel engine letting out a toot of greeting to the boats. It was all very gay and colourful.

But soon I began to shiver up there with no coat, and remembered that Maggie had asked me to unpack some clothes. I went back to the cottage rather reluctantly. From the outside it was a pretty little house, tucked against the hill, a stone's throw from the viaduct, but one never wanted to go indoors; too like climbing into a coffin. Outside seemed the natural place to be, down there.

I found the woollen dress Maggie had worn for her viva, which presumably would do for entertaining the Foleys. Stockings, shoes. In a sudden mood of devotion to duty I decided that her shoes could do with a shine, and remembered that among my own stuff I had a tin of shoe-polish. It must have been months since I used any, though, for when I opened it I found it had turned hard as rock and refused to come off on to the cloth except in chunks or discouraging rubbery smears.

Heat, I thought. I'll melt it. I took it downstairs and left it on the hob while I went to pick watercress in our moat-like stream.

When I came back, blowing on my damp and frozen hands, with the cress in an old coffee-tin, I found that the shoe-polish had melted all right: it was now completely liquescent, had overflowed from the tin, and was just on the point of trickling from the hob into the fire. Matter expands when heated; how to increase your supply of shoe-polish in one easy lesson. I picked up the tin and of course it was nearly red hot, so I dropped it back on the hob, upside down. There was a sort of explosion and for a minute or two all that side of the kitchen appeared lapped in flame.

Water, I thought. There's a little in the kettle. Or would water crack the iron range? A bucket of earth might put out the fire but then, what a mess. And I haven't a spade. Also, to get earth out of that garden would mean cutting down three feet of vegetation first. Properly regulated households have fire-extinguishers that spray out a sort of foam; I must remember to put one on the next shopping-list.

Well, then, a fire can be stifled by depriving it of its supply of air; if the front door would shut and the window were not broken that might be a possibility. But stopping up the chimney would be difficult. Of course I could smother the fire with blankets but they belong to Eleanor. And there isn't a carpet. We must get a hearth-rug; I'll put that on the shopping-list too.

Having decided that the only way to deal with the fire was to apply very small quantities of water, I was about to put this plan into operation when a voice from the doorway interrupted my calculations. It said drily,

"Are you having any trouble?"

Charles Foley was there, standing with his hands in his jacket pockets looking like a naval officer.

Oh dear, I thought, this isn't going to lay a very firm foundation for the good impression Maggie wants us to make.

IX

WHEN ELEANOR HAD driven off to her surgery Charles walked out into the fresh morning with feelings of delight slightly impaired by frustration. It was four weeks since they had moved into Watertown; only four weeks, yet already he felt as if he had been there a lifetime. Sometimes the sheer physical ecstasy of living in such a beautiful place almost over-threw him. It was difficult to remember he was ill; he made no effort to remember it. He felt transfigured; if this was due to his illness he did not want to think about it.

From time to time Eleanor said, "Do take it easy, Charles; remember the least exertion may be too much." He paid little attention. His only thought, like a host making ready for guests, was to see how much he could do before death stepped in and put an end to this enchanting new existence. But changes were achieved so slowly; he scowled, now, looking at his watch, since it was plain that the builders were not coming today. They tended to turn up spasmodically, two or three days at a time, and then vanish away on to other jobs until by a series of increasingly irate telephone calls he managed to marshal them back again.

This morning it was particularly provoking. Charles was impatient to get some livestock on to the place. Eleanor had gently ridiculed the notion, saying that she for one had no time to look after animals, that Nin was too old, that the work would almost certainly be too heavy for Charles, and what would happen if he died? In the end they compromised. Charles agreed to give up his idea of a dairy herd which, he admitted, had been rather high-flown, and settled for some Rhode Island Reds, which were due to arrive tomorrow. And their home was not yet ready for them. Charles proposed to keep them in an enclosed henyard, and had its structure carefully planned. The walls of the disused shippen and cowshed were to form two sides of the yard, and posts had been driven into the ground to support the other two walls, but the corrugated iron sheets were not yet in position. They were still, in fact, forming the roof of a ram-shackle pighouse which Charles intended to pull down. Mr Rowse the builder had faithfully promised to send two men along today to finish this job.

Enraged, Charles finally strode indoors. Thank heaven the telephone had at least been connected.

"Mr Rowse? Well, can you find him?"

Fuming with impatience, he waited. The telephone was in an arched window, halfway up the stairs; outside, the sunshine flashed tantalisingly on clean-washed leaves and pale stone. The road ran sharply uphill past the front door, veering round in a gravity-defying corkscrew.

"Oh, is that you, Mr Rowse? Why aren't your men here?"

"But they weren't coming *today,* Mr Foley," Mr Rowse's agreeable, fruity voice came singing over the wire. "Oh, no, I thought that was quite understood. Tomorrow and Saturday morning they're coming, certain sure. Oh, no, not today—"

He listened deprecatingly to Charles's comments.

"I'm sorry, Mr Foley, I really am, but even if they *had* a' been coming today I couldn't send them now; called off, they've been, to a rush job in Lanrith; there's been a fall of cliff above the harbour with all that rain and we have to shore it up, you see ..." He was quite imperturbable.

Charles recognised defeat and rang off. Damn it, he would do the job himself. Eleanor was not there to dissuade him; anyway, if he had to die, this was a fine morning to die on.

Collecting a light aluminium fruit ladder he set off for the pig-house but realised, after five minutes, that it was a two-man job. He needed somebody down below to receive the galvanised sheets as he clawed out the nails and dropped them; otherwise they crashed down and buckled themselves on the cobbled yard beneath. Also the frail and rotten timbers of the roof were not up to his weight. If Eleanor were at home—

He looked at his watch. But it was only eleven.

Then he remembered Nell's friends in the cottage. Maybe one of them wouldn't mind lending a hand; they were on holiday after all. They were supposed to have arrived yesterday; there could be no harm, anyway, in strolling down to see if they were settling in all right.

He swivelled round cautiously on his perch. From here it should be possible to see smoke coming from the cottage chimney or other signs of life.

What he saw made him drop his claw-hammer and slither as fast as possible down the steep slope of the roof. He missed the ladder and dropped, landing on hands and knees, forgetting that he was supposed to be taking care of himself. A thick dark plume of greasy-looking smoke was pouring from the cottage chimney, and as he ran down the road he saw that it was emerging from the cracked windows and open door as well. What were the women doing? Trying to cure a ham?

When he reached the door and looked inside a good deal of the smoke got into his eyes and blinded him for a moment. Then he saw that the range was a mass of flame, and that a girl was standing motionless before it, apparently lost in thought. He couldn't help smiling, as he pictured how efficiently Eleanor would have been darting about in similar circumstances. This creature seemed content, like a child, to gaze at the spectacle of the flames. Perhaps she *was* only a child? Then, as his eyes became more accustomed to the smoke, he recognised the girl who had answered the door on that day when he had caught the crystal bird.

"Are you having any trouble?" he asked mildly.

She turned in apparent relief. "I was just trying to decide on the best way to put it out. I should think a little water, shouldn't you?"

Charles saw that the blaze was not, in fact, very serious. He fetched a wateringcan from the garage, filled it at the stream, and with a couple of canfuls had the whole fire completely extinguished.

"I don't want to seem ungrateful," the girl said, "but now you've put out my cooking-fire and I'm supposed to make a cake when Maggie comes back."

"Have you any kindling?" Charles said. "Right; I'll be back in a minute."

Muttering inward maledictions against all women he went back to the garage and returned carrying an implement that looked like a blunderbuss.

"Good grief, what's that?" the girl said, gazing at it with respect.

"An electric firelighter. Oh, you've got the grate cleared out, splendid. You just pile up wood and coal, switch this thing on, it sends out a beam of ten-kilowatt hot air—*don't* put your hand in the way—and in no time at all it'll set fire to almost anything."

"What a horribly efficient weapon. Who makes it?"

"It's called a Diabolino; I got it in Italy. It runs off a battery, so you can keep it charging up when not in use."

"Just the job for down here," she said, as the pile of fuel burst into flame.

"I suppose you were trying to light the fire with paraffin?"

She grinned, wiping back a strand of dark hair with a sooty hand. "Far worse than that. I was warming up the shoe-polish. And all in order to make a good impression on you and your sister. It doesn't pay to try these gestures."

"No it doesn't," Charles agreed. "We'd soon have found out what you were really like. Arsonists. I don't quite understand about the shoe-polish, but let it pass."

"We were going to invite you to tea."

"Shoe-polish sandwiches?"

She burst out laughing. "Oh, goodness, it's a shame to laugh, but I was just thinking of my friend and the sandwiches—so English, so respectable—"

"Is she about, Dr Tassák?" Charles said, looking round the bare room.

"No, gone into Lanrith to buy a cake-tin and flour."

"Damn," said Charles, "I was hoping she'd lend a hand with some corrugated iron sheets."

"I'll help. I certainly owe you a good deed."

"You look a bit small for the job."

"I'm strong," she said.

"Well—I suppose," Charles said, "come to think, you needn't do any actual lifting, if you wouldn't mind sitting up on the roof and passing them down to me. Here, come along and I'll show you."

Swept away by the urgency of his desire to get the job done, Charles put the Diabolino back in the garage and almost dragged her up the hill.

"There, you see—the roof's not so steep as it looks from here. You'll find each sheet is held in position by six large nails. All you have to do is claw the nails out with the hammer, or here's a chisel for the ones that are rusted in, and pass the sheets down to me. The roof should take your weight all right—anyway it's an earth floor inside if you do fall."

She was amused. "All right; what do I do with the nails?"

"Put them in your pocket."

He passed her the hammer and chisel when she had climbed up and called, "Let me know when you're ready to drop one."

The angle of the roof cut her out of his line of vision, but he could hear her tapping and scraping. Presently she called,

"One coming now."

"Right. Standing by!" With a tooth-jarring rasp of metal on metal the large sheet grated over the edge and into his waiting hands.

"It's nice up here in the sun," she said, tapping away. "You get a good view." There was a pause. "Another one coming."

This was most satisfactory. At such a rate they'd have the roof dismantled by lunch, and he could put up the henyard walls during the afternoon.

"Damn! Watch out!" A third sheet came rattling down the roof and hurtled over the edge. He just managed to break its fall.

"Sorry," she called. "They are a weight, aren't they? Are you all right?"

"Quite okay." Then he thought he ought to warn her. He

climbed up the ladder and stuck his head over the edge of the roof. "By the way I think I should tell you that I've got a heart condition which makes me liable to drop dead any time. I wouldn't want you to think you were responsible if it happened."

She was sitting sideways below the gap she had made in the roof, with her legs tucked under her and an elbow hitched over a decayed-looking beam. She turned from chipping at a nail and surveyed him ironically.

"I see. It's nice of you to warn me. What should I do? Just stroll off and leave the body?"

"If you like," said Charles cheerfully. "*I* shouldn't mind." Then he was attacked by compunction. Perhaps it was rather a gruesome communication to make to a comparative stranger. "Would you rather leave off doing this? I hadn't thought; it's not very considerate of me."

"You're really serious?"

"I don't make that kind of joke," he said, slightly stiff.

"Sorry."

"My fault. I'm used to the idea now."

"In that case," she said matter-of-factly, "let's get on with the job. It seems silly to waste time." And she wriggled round and went on with her chipping. Charles sorted the sheets as she passed them down into two heaps, good and bad.

"Knock off for a cigarette?" he called presently.

"Thank you. I'll have mine up here, though. Once I get off this beam I don't think I should be able to climb back, now most of the roof's gone."

He passed a lighted cigarette across the gap, and remained perched on the edge of the roof, companionably puffing.

"I'm ashamed to say that I haven't learned your name yet."

"Oh well. Maggie always calls me Tuesday."

"Why?"

"There's a story attached to it. Rather a boring story." She seemed anxious to change the subject so he said, "And your real name?"

When she told him he exclaimed, "Good heavens, didn't you write that book—"

"Yes I did," she said. He noticed that she was blushing a deep pink.

"I read it last year. I forget its name."

"*Mayhem in Miniature.*" She stubbed out her cigarette and, turning away, industriously prised out a nail.

"But you must have been very young when you wrote it?"

"I was seventeen. I have a lively imagination," she said, screwing her head round and looking at him defensively.

"You must have. But didn't it make you rather notor— quite a celebrity, I mean?"

"Well, yes, but it didn't affect me much. I don't know many people and quite a few of the ones I do didn't connect me with the book. Look, here's another sheet ready."

She's rather elusive, he thought, catching the strip as it slithered down. He tried another approach.

"You and your friend—Dr Tassák—seem extremely different. How did you come to set up together?"

"We met at a publisher's party. I'd gone along hoping to see my mother who isn't often in England but said she might come to it—in the end it turned out she was in the south of France—and Maggie had been brought by a friend of hers who writes best-selling books on psychiatry and who knew me slightly; he introduced us and—and we just took to one another. Is that your sister coming now?"

In fact he saw Eleanor's car. Ten to one. How the morning had flown, but they had finished the job.

Eleanor got out and came up the grass slope, followed by another woman.

"Hullo," Eleanor said rather disapprovingly. "I thought we agreed you were to leave that job for the men?"

"Yes, but blasted Rowse chooses today to take his men off—"

He was interrupted by an indrawn breath of horror as the other woman, Dr Tassák, strode past them staring over Charles's shoulder at the roof.

"What *do* you think you're doing up there?" she shouted. "Those beams don't look at all safe. And you're still convalescent, you shouldn't be doing anything like that—"

"Convalescent?" Charles looked guilty. "Is she? She didn't say—" Then he remembered that there was something about one of them having been ill—or was it working for a medical exam?

"Look out!" There came a sudden cry from above, a violent rattling, a clang, and one of the corrugated sheets hurtled past Charles's face, missing him by perhaps an inch, landed on its side, and stuck upright between two rows of cobbles, quivering like a knife-thrower's blade.

"Are you all right?" The girl from the roof tumbled herself

61

over the edge, and dropped down among them. "I'm most terribly sorry—that one was such a weight that it pulled out of my hands. —What a relief," she said, looking in awe at the still vibrating sheet of iron. "I was afraid I might have killed somebody."

The dark-haired woman, Dr Tassák, burst out into a storm of indignant scolding.

"Damned stupid thing to do! You shouldn't have been up there at all. But if you were you should have been more careful; you might easily have killed Mr Foley. Well, come on now, it's time we went home and made that cake—and I don't suppose you've done a thing about the furniture—"

Hardly taking leave of the other two she hustled the girl away.

Treats her like a child, Charles thought. Turning to Eleanor he began, "Why don't we—" and then stopped, horrified by the expression on her face. She was staring after the girl with a look of cold fury, almost hate.

"Eleanor—Nell! What is it?"

She started, and turned to him. "It's just that—well, just that! She nearly killed you."

It was not until they were indoors that Charles saw the illogicality of this and began to laugh.

X

MAGGIE DIDN'T SAY anything as we walked downhill back to the cottage. She looked pretty thunderous, so I chattered feverishly.

"What a bit of luck you had a lift back with Eleanor. Did you get the things all right? Are the shops in Lanrith quite good?"

Hell, I thought, if it's going to be like this whenever I have half an hour's conversation with a man from now on, I might as well go into a convent and have done with it. I felt righteously indignant. Charles's announcement about his illness had removed him from the category in my mind marked Male, and transferred him to one marked Caution, Special Treatment. I felt he was like a war memorial, covered in poppies, railed off by an iron chain, and inscribed Sacred. I considered explaining this to Maggie, but didn't; he had made the confidence to me, not to her, and it seemed ghoulish to retail it. Anyway I wasn't going to begin defending myself till she attacked.

"I thought I told you to stay in the cottage and receive the furniture?" she growled.

"Oh it won't have come yet," I said airily.

Unfortunately it had. Left to themselves the removal men had gone so far as to take the stuff inside, very thoughtful of them, but they had then pursued a system of grouping by categories. In the kitchen were four chests of drawers, in the scullery were three wardrobes. The tables were upstairs in one bedroom, and chairs in the other. I couldn't help it—I laughed till I had hiccups while Maggie looked at me in angry bafflement.

"I'll go up after lunch and ask your friend Kormendi to help us shift them. If we shove all these chests together it won't be so bad for now. Let's get this blasted cake made."

Mercifully Maggie didn't notice the traces of my fire. She sogged down in her armchair, boiled up the remains of the breakfast coffee, and was at once absorbed in *Wheeler on Pituitary Disorders,* while I skirmished around her. The oven did smell a bit of shoe polish but Maggie put it down to long disuse.

In the afternoon I left the cake cooling (it filled the cottage with a warm domestic smell that hung oddly among the forlorn clutter) and walked up the road to Kormendi's cottage at the top of the hill. It had been whitewashed and trimmed with the ferocious tidiness of the refugee. Not a grass was out of place in the tiny garden. Two fat pigs snuffled at me through a wire-netting fence, but there was no answer to my knock.

I thought of calling in Charles and Eleanor but suspected this would come into conflict with one of Maggie's bits of convention, which stuck up here and there like coral reefs; normally she'd ask anyone for help, but Eleanor as our landlady apparently came under diplomatic immunity, while Charles, male *and* landlord, was both immune and suspect. Better to hail the first passing car and ask for assistance with the wardrobes; the only difficulty being that cars very rarely used this road, as it led nowhere.

Walking dispiritedly down the hill again I heard voices ahead, and found a pickup truck and a group of men; Charles was there, looking impatient, and Kormendi, and several others with tools and ladders.

"Nice afternoon!" Kormendi said, giving me a beaming grin. I asked if he could come and lend us a hand for five minutes. "In a little minute, yes, I come."

The others turned curious eyes on me; not hostile but reserved, withholding judgment; I felt like a rare animal under scrutiny.

Charles was engaged in a brisk discussion with a little tubby man in a pork-pie hat. "Well, but, Mr Rowse, you say the men *vote* about working on Friday, is that right?"

"Union rule, you see, Mr Foley. It's a bank holiday, so they decide for themselves; then if they work they get paid overtime."

"Well, vote then, and get it over," Charles said shortly.

"I didn't think we'd even be able to come here this afternoon," Mr Rowse reproved him. "That cliff's only shored up temporary. We'll have to go back later and finish her off."

"Yes all right; only vote about Friday so I know where I am, and then I'll be extremely grateful if you'll get my henyard finished and the trough shifted."

"Who wants to work on Friday, then?" Mr Rowse said, looking round the circle with little twinkling eyes. Three hands were lifted, Kormendi's among them. The other three men stared straight ahead as if they were deaf.

"Who *don't* want to work?" The other three hands went up.

"Equal vote," Mr Rowse said.

"Peter Lannick ain't here yet," someone pointed out.

"Trust Peter to be late."

"Here he is now." A clattering bicycle scraped to a standstill beside us, and another man got off, greeted by an ironic chorus from his mates.

"Well, come on Peter, casting vote, man! How about it then? Work on Friday or not?"

Peter was younger than most of them, very thin, and handsome in an angry, miserable-looking way. He did not share in the amusement at his fortuitous importance but said at once shortly that he was not turning out on any damned bank holiday, overtime or no; and that apparently settled the matter. Charles swung sharply round on his heel and disappeared into the Watertown garden; the men dispersed towards the henyard, and Kormendi turned down the hill with me.

"Is a bad workman, that Peter," he said. "Spoiled boy. Too many in England like that; always stop for cup of tea, stop for holiday, stop for crib; work never gets done that way. Some of these men are not bad, but that Peter he's a pain; always is everything wrong for him, nothing but a grumbling."

I said something sympathetic, thinking privately, what a stupid system; why couldn't the men who wanted to work come, and the others stay away?

As we shoved the furniture about, I noticed Charles coming towards the front door and went out to meet him.

"Do you want any more help?" I asked.

"Oh, thank you; no, it's not that. I wonder if you'd mind coming out here a moment." He seemed embarrassed.

There was a sandy patch of gravel beyond the stream, where cars could turn when they discovered that our road was a cul-de-sac. I joined him on it.

"You know what I told you this morning, about my illness, I mean?"

"Yes?"

"I—I'd be very grateful if you wouldn't mention it to anyone. Eleanor seems to feel that it's unfair to tell people, and it does make me feel rather like an exhibit—"

"Of course I won't; I shouldn't dream of it." He still looked uncomfortable; I wondered if Aspic had been angry when she heard that I'd been told. "It'll be easy to forget all about it," I added. "You look so well."

He smiled at that, relieved. "Oh, and another thing: Eleanor says it's terribly kind of you both to invite us to tea, but won't you come up for a drink instead, as you must be at sixes and sevens? It would really suit us better, as Nell doesn't get back from her rounds till about half past five."

Too proud to receive our humble hospitality? I wondered, when I had accepted and he had gone.

Maggie was annoyed.

She didn't mind that the cake had been made for nothing—since neither of us ever ate cake; but she hated being asked out for drinks. She very rarely touched alcohol and when she did it nearly knocked her flat; consequently she disapproved of it.

"Stupid habit, this drinks! Why can't they ask us for a meal if they want to see us? When do we go, when do we leave? I should be ashamed just to invite people in for an hour or so. Do they think we aren't worth more?"

"Don't be silly," I said. "Anyway they're only settling in themselves. And do, *please*, leave when I make a face at you. I don't want to have to keep kicking your shins all evening while their supper goes dry in the oven."

But of course that was just what happened. Maggie had no feeling for the snippets and snappets that go to make up the average social occasion; she liked a good, solid discussion, and when she met an intelligent person she plunged in like a whale in a grove of plankton; she and Charles were enjoying an argument about sleep-conditioning and she didn't see what harm that was doing anybody; why couldn't they argue all night if they wanted to? Let Eleanor go and eat her supper if she was hungry. Unfortunately Maggie was sitting across the room from me so that I couldn't attract her short-sighted attention unless I picked up one of Eleanor's bits of Swedish glass and threw it.

Aspic's self control was beautiful to watch. She didn't even look at the clock. She just sat stiller and stiller and calmer and calmer.

"So you really believe," Maggie said, "that if I tell you a hundred times every night that you can fly, in the end you will grow wings? You think a patient with an advanced case of cancer can be cured in this way? Fairy tales!"

"There are such cures," Charles said cheerfully. I could see—which Maggie couldn't—that he was arguing for the fun of it, and to draw her out. "How about Lourdes?"

"Talking about Lourdes," said Eleanor aimiably—she turned to me—"Weren't you living near there when you wrote your book? Did you know she had written *Mayhem in Miniature*?" she said to Charles, hoping, I suspect, to reduce his opinion of me.

It had been a mistake, I now knew, to publish that book; one of those tiresome mistakes that dog one with repercussions for years after. Writing it was highly enjoyable and diverting—the sort of exercise which at seventeen seems easily worth the trouble. Having made a careful study of the language of sexual innuendo in pop songs I had decided that this could be applied to novels too. With dedicated fervour and total detachment I ploughed right through a dictionary of sex behaviour, noting down interesting examples, wove them all into an Alice Through the Looking Glass situation, and wrote the whole thing out in elegant, euphemistic, eighteenth century language. *Double entendres* were packed tighter than sardines in a tin, but externally it was just a modest little fantasy, a suitable Christmas gift for anyone's great aunt, guaranteed not to bring a blush to the primmest cheek. It sold like hot cakes. Consequently, when I moved on to a Conrad craze next year and produced a serious, gloomy, Conrad-type novel, nobody would take it. They wanted me to write another *Mayhem*. I had no ambition to go on producing bathroom reading for the rest of my life; I tore up the Conrad novel—which deserved it—and went into hibernation, except for a few short stories, until the fuss died down.

Now I made some evasive answer to Eleanor.

Maggie scowled at me. Such was her veneration for the art of writing English that her attitude towards my authorship was that of a disciple who sees a saint with miraculous powers using them to win prizes on a fruit-machine. It was all of a piece with my ruinous frivolity and she couldn't help wishing, quite without malice, that the faculty had been more sensibly and economically bestowed on her.

"Are you writing another book now?" Eleanor pursued socially. "It must be delightful."

I tried to think what her tone recalled, and then remembered my mother, on one of her rare visits to England, talking with fascinated distaste to a member of the Women's Institute. "And so you make dolls' furniture out of apple pips? That must be most interesting."

"Yes," I agreed with Eleanor.

"Amazing," said Eleanor at large. "Imagine just being able to write a book out of one's head. No documentation, no research—"

She gave me a cold, indulgent smile, and I felt good and furious. All right, Gelatine, perhaps I haven't passed all those great big exams, perhaps I haven't spent my life cutting out people's innards and learning symptoms by heart out of textbooks, but so what? I'm still a human citizen. And if you think it's not hard work scraping out your thoughts from inside you and putting them on paper, that just shows how crass you are. Why, I've sat and held my breath over the typewriter till my head was damp with sweat and my diaphragm ached, you superior smugfaced bitch, you, and written two and a half pages in four hours and thought myself damned lucky.

But then I remembered that I hadn't actually written anything for well over a year. Would I ever be able to again? Somehow it was difficult in Maggie's company. Although she wanted me to be useful and creative, her magnetic field was too powerful, or she breathed up too much of the air. What I needed for writing was solitude and peace and quiet and blankness. Perhaps.

"You do get a beautiful view from here," I said, copying Aspic's social tone, and crossed to the window, scowling at Maggie. At last she got the message and rose cumbrously like a walrus coming up for fish. She said we should be off, like a child reciting its piece, and Charles, who seemed to be enjoying himself, looked put out and said, "No, don't go yet. Stay to supper. There's enough food, isn't there, Nell?"

"There are only three chops—" Eleanor looked daggers at her brother.

"Oh, can't you leave them for tomorrow? Nin can make an omelette—" "I don't like meat, I'm happy with just vegetables—" Charles and Maggie said simultaneously.

So Eleanor asked us to stay, and I grinned to myself as I thought of the recriminations there'd be afterwards between her and Charles and me and Maggie. But really I was fed up with the whole situation and I wanted above all things to escape from the sound of their voices. I never have liked groups much, they wear me out, one person at a time is enough, and now I was feeling tired to death—the two gins I'd had didn't help—and wished myself in a cool smooth pillowed coffin.

Ever since the pneumonia I'd had these stupid spells when I'd suddenly feel the need to burst out crying in the street or at the hairdresser's or anywhere at all. Old damn Nature's way of relieving tension. I could feel the hydraulic pressure building up inside me now, like the water behind the dam at Frejus, and I knew that unless I could get away, or somebody said something bloody funny, we were all in for a most embarrassing cataract. So I got up and nipped to the door, murmuring to Aspic,

"Kormendi said this house has a beautiful staircase, may I go and look at it?"

My exit coincided with hers. "Yes, it's charming, do," she said in an irritable, preoccupied tone, "I'm just going to ask Nin about the egg supply," and Maggie threw herself into motion once more and said, "Let me do something," to which Aspic graciously acquiesced, though Maggie would be about as much help in a kitchen as a caber tossed in a colander.

So they passed me as I grimly concentrated on some nondescript sporting prints hung round the charming little spiral staircase Kormendi had mentioned. I took three or four calming deep breaths and felt better, though still mad at Maggie for saddling me with another two hours in this uncongenial house. Aspic's taste was too chintzy for me.

Halfway up the stairs there was an agreeable round-arched window, with similar alcoves on either side, and in the lower one hung a guitar; it struck me as oddly out of place here. I felt sore enough with Maggie not to care what I did, so I went up and flipped a finger over the strings. Out of tune but nice.

"You play?" Charles said.

I hadn't heard him come out to the hall.

"Used to, up till last year. Do you?"

I hadn't yet concentrated much on what Charles looked like. At first there had been other distractions, the bird, and the bonfire; and once I knew about his short expectation of life I had tended to avoid meeting his eye. Now I took a look, thinking, well, it has to be done sometime.

He wasn't a bit like sister Aspic; brown eyes instead of grey, and something undecided about his appearance. People with hazel-brown eyes tend to look slightly worried when they have thick, straight eyebrows, so I couldn't tell whether this look on Charles meant a permanent anxiety about his impending mortality, or fear that I was going to scratch my initials on his guitar, or was just the way he looked. He had thick ruffled fairish brown hair, which made him appear younger than his probable age, and a decent mouth, not one of your Trappist mouths but one with a bit of give-and-take to it, allowance made for more than good morning, nice to meet you. In fact, I thought, standing there with a finger on the guitar strings, it seemed a pity that Charles had to die so soon. Waste of good material.

"No," he said. "My mother used to play."

A sort of zero touch in the atmosphere ought to have warned me, but when I'm on the verge of one of these crying monsoons I'm a bit slow-witted. As he turned his head I was already saying,

"Does she still? Can I meet her?"

"She died fifteen years ago," he said constrainedly.

"Charles," Eleanor cut in—she must have been standing right beside him, but out of my view round the curve of the stairs— "will you go up to Kormendi's and see if he can let us have any eggs?"

Oh, oh, I thought, now we have put our foot in it. Sacred

Mum, not to be profaned by promiscuous, non-graduate, egg-devouring, American-consorting trash like me. What do I do now? Descend the stairs on my knees, breaking an egg over my head at every step?

"Of course." Charles looked harassed and apologetic. Aspic came into sight and gave me the cross smile that was getting to be her trade-mark for me—and suddenly in view of the penitential evening that she was about to endure, I felt quite cheered up. I beamed at Charles and said, "Let me come with you."

He beamed back, and perhaps it was this establishment of naughty rapport, complicity against the prefects, that led to his declaration of independence later, after we had champed our way through the scrambled eggs.

He got up, left the room, returned with the guitar, handed it to me, and in the startled silence that fell, said,

"Won't you play us something?"

XI

THE BUILDER'S MEN usually arrived at eight in the morning, but Eleanor was always awake long before that. She rose at six, did her sleek heavy fair hair, made tea, wrote notes on the previous day's cases, and roamed about the house in a masculine silk dressing-gown and leather slippers, surveying the work yet to be done. At this time a ghost accompanied her, the imaginary presence of a young man called Karl. By breakfast time Karl—who had a real-life existence as a consulting psychiatrist in Munich—was laid for the day. But at night, or in the small hours, or in the thin morning hours, he came back to haunt her. So vivid were her recollections of him that she could almost fancy she was able to see him, leaning against the door with a mocking smile, or hear him flopping heavily downstairs on sandalled feet, whistling loudly.

They had worked in the same hospital ten years before, had had a six-month affair, light-hearted on Karl's part. He really preferred nurses, and never pretended to Eleanor that a pair of trim black-silk-stockinged ankles couldn't win him away from her bed for a night. He was three years younger than she, intellectually more brilliant by far, in temperament wildly unstable.

When his career led him back to Munich there was no question, for him, of affection holding them together; only Eleanor knew the almost physical torture, akin to the pain of an amputation, which the parting had cost her. She could still remember, word for word, their last conversation in his dismantled flat. He was wandering about, making darts out of old examination papers and flicking them out of the window, while Eleanor packed for him.

"Well—it's been a long honeymoon, hasn't it? We've been good in bed together these six months, yes? Shall you miss me?"

"Certainly I shall," she said briskly. "Look—do you want these socks or shall I throw them away?"

"Oh, throw, throw. In Germany the socks are much better. I shall miss you too, Eleanor. You have taught me a lot. But, you know, you were wrong."

"Wrong, how?"

"You said it would be a friendly thing to bed together. It has not been friendly, has it?"

"How do you mean?"

But he picked up an armful of books.

"I am leaving all these—would you like them? My name is in them. When I return to London in twenty years' time driving my Mercedes, you will be able to say you once knew me and sell them for large sums, after the TV interview. Face to Face. First Jung, then me. Heavens, look at the time. I promised to have coffee with Nurse Phillips at eleven, I must run. You did say you'd drive me to the airport, didn't you, dear Eleanor? Then I'll see you back here in two hours' time."

And so her last sight of him had been blowing absent-minded kisses over the shoulders of two stout elderly ladies through a glass partition before she turned to face the coming weeks of savage secret pain. It took time before she could transfer to another hospital, another flat, where his memory could not obtrude on her quite so scarifyingly. Her only comfort was that no one suspected the plight she was in, due to her extreme secretiveness. Hospital acquaintances were convinced that she had no time for the male sex; and, with this brief violent exception, they were right.

Karl's doppelganger smiled at her now from the doorway, said, "Working hard, good girl? That's right," and vanished, as Charles came yawning downstairs and the builder's truck could be heard disgorging its crew of workmen outside.

Eleanor smiled at Charles, hating him because he was brown-haired, instead of fair with gold eyes, because he was her brother, because he was English in his thirties instead of German in his twenties.

She stood up, stretched, and went to put on the kettle.

"I thought we might go and call on Aunt Julia after breakfast," she suggested. "I've no surgery this morning and no private patients till twelve. I can take you over."

"Yes I'd like that. It's awful that I haven't been to visit her yet."

"Still, you're wise not to drive," Eleanor said smoothly. "And as she's not on the phone—"

"Still won't use any invention later than William Morris?"

"She certainly cooks on an oil-stove and uses candles."

Khartoum Cottage, where old Miss Foley lived, lay across the Lan river, out on the headland towards the Marlin lighthouse. In fact it could be seen from the hill above Watertown as a white speck on the hillside, not far from the east end of the viaduct, but the distance by road and ferry was over six miles, and since old Miss Foley would not keep a car, and never accepted invitations, she tended to lead a fairly reclusive existence.

Charles had not, in fact, been to see Aunt Julia since his parents died, but as soon as he stepped inside her door the smell of the house breathed memory into his mind, of childhood visits and long-forgotten occasions.

There was dry-rot in the smell, and damp thatch, the flavour of old carpets, and furniture polish, coat after coat; old books, old velvet curtains, lingering smoke from fifty years of wood fires, scent of apples stored in attics, dampness of earth trodden on to stone floors from gardening shoes, faint dusty fragrance of lavender and the stronger smell from hanks of gardening raffia.

Although the front door was open, only silence greeted them when they went in, and faint crisp rustlings from the log fire in the study, for Aunt Julia kept a fire burning summer and winter alike.

"I'll see if she's upstairs."

Eleanor went up so purposefully that Charles wondered if she wanted a private word with her aunt. In any case he had no wish to follow, he preferred to stay in the rich, silent, dusty room, dark with the weight of trees outside its windows, and listen to the past lapping round him.

The walls, what could be seen of them behind gold-framed pictures, miniatures, silhouettes, and woodcut rhyme-sheets dating from the eighteen-nineties, were covered with a William Morris wallpaper, leaves and berries. Mantel, piano, shelves, and Morris dresser held china, photographs, relics from Bayreuth and Florence, bunches of seedpods and everlasting flowers... He found several things that he remembered from childhood, a paperweight of Sahara sand, a small ivory box of spillikins, a musical thrush, moulting feathers, which played a selection from *San Toy*.

Eleanor came back, looking vexed. "I can't think where she's got to. She's never been out of earshot when I called before."

"Have you been often?" Charles was curious. "I never realised—"

"Oh, two or three times. Didn't I mention? —She really ought to have help in the house. Look at the dust on this piano."

Charles played a chord softly and was aware that for some reason Eleanor disliked his doing so.

"Doesn't she have any help at all?"

"There's a slightly simple girl who comes and does scrubbing. And that young man, Peter Lannick, does a bit of garden work. But I shouldn't think *he's* much use..."

Eleanor looked restlessly out of the window, but Charles was quite content; he wandered into Aunt Julia's study, where she wrote monumentally dry critical reappraisals of nineteenth-century poets. Stacks of Browning lay on the floor and reams of notes on the desk, in Miss Foley's beautiful austere script; it was evident that Browning was now undergoing the treatment.

"Good strong thick stupefying incense-smoke!" Charles read at random from an open volume.

> "For, as I lie here, hours of the dead night
> Dying in state and by such slow degrees,
> I fold my arms—"

"Don't!" said Eleanor sharply.

"Sorry, Nell! I wonder who reads the old girl's books. I suppose they're all bought by university libraries."

He sat down on a hammocky brown velvet sofa. It sagged beneath him, directing the angle of his gaze upward to the Hokusai waterfall print on the wall. Another vignette from the past slipped into his mind: he and Nell, as children, learning to play mahjongg in this room. Charles had never been much good at the game, he was too pleased by the curved, satiny bamboo pieces themselves, with their little magic pictures of dragons, bamboos, winds, and the coloured dice, the little black counters. Nell had been indignant that he wouldn't stir himself to become a better opponent.

"It's no use, Eleanor," said Aunt Julia with her Mona Lisa smile—even in those days she had resembled a sorceress, what could she be like now?—"you just can't rouse ambition in some people, and Charles is one. Your father used to feel the same about me. Never mind, I'll leave you the mahjongg when I die, with your half of my belongings; you'll be able to find someone to play with by that time."

"Who gets the other half of your things?" inquired Nell—he remembered her throwing back the long straight fair hair first from one side of her face and then the other, as she stacked the clicking bamboo tiles.

"Charles, of course. You two are my only descendants. What would you like, Charles, to match the mahjongg?"

Charles let his eyes wander round the room.

"That," he said, pointing to the Hokusai. "I don't want anything else. Nell can have all your other things."

"Certainly not," Aunt Julia said. "Strict fairness is my motto, no favouritism." She spoke briskly, but in an odd way he felt she was pleased with him, and that his sister was not.

"Silly little prig!" she had said afterwards—she must have been about twelve at this time and he eight—"what made you tell such a lie?"

"It wasn't a lie. I don't want her things."

"But Aunt Julia's rich! And she's got lots of treasures—what about the stereoscopic viewer, you'd like that, you've often said so."

"Well, I've changed my mind. If we had her things they'd just be ordinary. They ought to stay with her. Besides I hate people dying and other people taking their belongings."

Charles smiled, remembering this conversation. It amused him to realise how little, now, he minded the prospect of his own death. For the last few weeks, indeed, he had hardly thought about death at all. Accustomed to the idea of its imminence he had, as it were, laid it on an upper shelf of his mind like a spool of fuse wire and then, feeling, That's taken care of, had turned his attention to the hens, and the narcissus and anemone crops, and the installation of some glasshouses. He was, he realised it now consciously for the first time, happy; happier than he had been for years. Was it the prospect of death that made him happy? Almost he felt that it was. Before, life had seemed to stretch out in an anxious, aimless unplanned vista; other people shaped their lives, laid projects, organised themselves; Charles merely lived, did his job, met his friends, and sometimes had a faint twinge of unease as if, presented with a large blank canvas, he had painted in a few tentative dabs with no clear vision of what the full design should be Eleanor, he thought, despised him a little; by her creed what he did was not enough; there should be some sense of purpose to give meaning to the whole. And Charles felt guiltily that she must be right.

But now, happily, he was free from the need for planning or vocation; death itself was vocation enough. And, perversely, within the compass of this new, small, manageable future, he found himself enjoying plans, seriously debating the choice of anemones for the high field, going into the different types of greenhouse as if it were all of immense importance. He found himself often now whistling as he strolled about the yards or garden at Watertown—whistling odd fragments of Tuesday's Kentucky ballads or music by Roncalli or Granados—and was sometimes conscious of Eleanor's surprised gaze on him. Was it natural to be so happy about dying? He was impatient with her solicitude, and sometimes afraid that he had affronted her a little.

Eleanor looked at her watch.

"We can't stay much longer," she said discontentedly, and pushed open the french window that led on to Aunt Julia's tufted, moss-grown lawn.

Charles turned idly to the books that lined the study walls: endless brown-leather-covered sets. Lord Lytton—did anyone ever read them now? Matthew Arnold, Thackeray. Oblivious of the car that drew up in front of the house he raised a hand to take one down.

"Charles!" said his aunt briskly from the doorway. "You ought to remember from your childhood that *nobody* is allowed to touch my books!"

"Oh, good lord, Aunt Julia," Charles said, unabashed, "I never heard you come in. What an intolerant rule, anyway!" And an unnecessary one, he thought; nobody was likely to make off with volumes from this library. He kissed the old woman and then, impulsively, remembering the brandysnap and medlar-jelly teas of childhood, gave her a hug; god, she is ugly, he thought with affection, I remember her witchlike but this is Endor in person.

Miss Foley was rather squat, from the shrinkage of old age; her yellowish grey hair hung in elf-locks; two intensely bright, shrewd eyes glinted diamond-bright in a face that was pouched, wrinkled, and blotched like a toad's, or like some strange fungoidal growth. Two small skinny hands, equally blotched, hung like claws from the sleeves of the four cardigans she wore over a skirt which seemed to be made of brown burlap, much spotted, and snagged by brambles. She carried a sort of carpet-bag, made from garishly striped woven material, which contained sheets of paper covered with notes and quotations, books, knitting full of dropped stitches, and loose five-pound notes.

"You should have—moved back to Cornwall sooner, my boy. Then you wouldn't—have come to this pretty pass."

She wheezed heavily; Charles remembered that she had always had trouble with her breathing; it seemed in no way to affect her health.

"Nell told you, then?" Charles was faintly annoyed. It was for him, he thought, to tell or not to tell—particularly as Eleanor herself had suggested keeping the news of his illness to themselves. Still, Aunt Julia was their only relative . . .

Her old eyes, watching him, were keen and kind.

"It must—have been a bit of a pill to swallow," she wheezed. "Still—I can see—you're used to the idea now. You and I—my dear boy—will be able to keep each other company in—the next world. I wonder—which of us—will get there first?"

"Shall we have a bet on it?" he suggested. Then, over Aunt Julia's shoulder, he saw a familiar weatherbeaten face. "Why, Claire! I thought you were over looking at a cottage in Herodsfoot?"

"It was no good. All prettied up and they were asking the earth for it," Claire said. She looked very much at home, walking into Aunt Julia's front hall in her dirty old slacks, carrying a large flat basket of seedlings. "I knew it was no use waiting for you to emerge from your anemones and introduce me to your aunt—" she gave Charles a sardonic, good-tempered nod— "so I came and called, and got invited to stay indefinitely."

"I'm glad," Charles said, not at all surprised. They would suit, he saw at once; they would have ideas to exchange.

"I'm taking charge of the garden," Claire explained.

"And a very—good scheme—" Aunt Julia wheezed. "She grows—the vegetables and I—teach her—how to cook them."

"Patrick," Claire called through the open front door, "dump the seed potatoes in the shed, would you?"

"Yair," a voice called back.

Even more than by the sight of Claire, Charles was startled at the trio who now appeared in Miss Foley's front garden. Two men carried a sack round the corner of the house. One had a beard and long uncut black ringlets, the other's shock of straight blond hair was sheared round his head like Henry V; both wore windbreakers, jeans, and sandals. They were followed by a girl in a bulky sweater over skintight trews; her soft, straight hair was caught in an elastic band at the back of her small head; she was barefoot and wore no lipstick but her eyes were heavily made up. She followed the two men, carrying a large bag of groceries.

"Who are those beats?" Charles inquired.

"They're Australians: Patrick, Chad, and Kuniang. They were kicked out of Lanrith by the town council, who won't have people sleeping on the beach, so Miss Foley said they could live in her barn for a week; they've got a job picking flowers at Lannivet."

"I warn you, Aunt Julia," Charles said laughing, "you'll never be without protégés if you have Claire in your house."

"I don't mind," Aunt Julia wheezed, "they're interesting—creatures, not at all—uneducated. Though I wish—that poor girl—knew which of them—had been the—baby's father."

"She has a *baby*?"

"It died, poor thing." Claire's kind face clouded. "While they were making their way here from London. It was only a few weeks old, I gather. In a way she hardly feels its loss."

"Consciously, that is," corrected Aunt Julia. "It is the unconscious repercussions—we have to watch for."

Eleanor suddenly came in through the french window. "There you are, Aunt Julia!" she exclaimed. "I've been right up to the top of the hill looking for you. Who *are* those extraordinary characters you have in your garden? Oh, good morning, Claire. I suppose they came with you. Aunt Julia, I'm so sorry—we came to call, but I must be going now, I have a patient. Charles, we must be off."

She spoke with some acidity.

"Claire's—been taking me—shopping in Lanrith," Aunt Julia said easily. "But don't rush off—Nell—surely you can stay ten minutes? I had—something to say to you and Charles."

Eleanor's brows lifted; evidently she thought the venue rather public for any disclosure of a confidential nature. Claire, without comment, carried some parcels into the kitchen and closed the door.

"Having regard—to what you told me, Nell—about Charles's health," Aunt Julia said without beating about the bush, "I have decided—my dears—to alter my will and leave everything—to Eleanor. I was going to divide between the two of you—but as things are—"

"Very practical, Aunt Ju," said Charles quickly and warmly. "No sense in leaving anything to me. Only makes for extra death duties or a legal muddle if I predecease you."

Eleanor flashed him a swift smile of gratitude for easing the awkward moment.

"Just so—" Aunt Julia pursued, "but I don't want—you—to seem quite neglected—Charles—so I'm leaving you—my library. And the Hokusai, of course."

"It's very sweet of you, Aunt Julia. I know the store you set by those books," he said. "I'll read them all. If I have time."

"They stay here till I die, though!" She wagged a finger at him.

"Aunt Julia—well, you can guess how I feel." Eleanor looked grateful, embarrassed, and put out. She kissed her aunt quickly and said, "Charles, we *must* go."

"Charles—need not," Aunt Julia puffed. "Claire—can drive him home later."

"Of course," Charles agreed. "I'll just walk Nell to the gate."

He could see his sister was still ruffled, perhaps by her morning's plans having gone awry, perhaps by Aunt Julia's abrupt disclosure. She seemed still more annoyed at seeing, behind her own carefully tended secondhand Anglia, Claire's large battered Jaguar, relic of palmy days in Fleet Street.

"What a car!" she said irritably. "Honestly! So unsuitable for down here." She gave Charles a cross smile and drove off. It occurred to him that she would be still more annoyed when she learned that Claire was actually living with Aunt Julia. Then he remembered Eleanor's apparent wish to see Aunt Julia in private. To warn her against disclosing the fact that she had been told Charles was dying?

"Nell—seemed upset." Aunt Julia had limped out and was snipping off dead narcissus heads. "Perhaps—I shouldn't—have mentioned my will?"

"Oh, it's just that she hates meeting strangers. And she doesn't care for big, fast cars," Charles said at random.

"Natural—considering—how your father died."

"How did he die?" inquired Claire, joining them. She was without false delicacy; when she wanted to find out something, she asked.

Charles said, "He was a doctor like Nell, but ambition went sour in him; he was bored down here and took to drink. Fast driving was the only thing he enjoyed. That wouldn't have been so bad but he insisted on my mother going out with him, and she was terrified to death at anything over fifty miles an hour. So in the end he went round a corner too fast and they were both killed. Apparently he had a dicky heart—I suppose it's a hereditary thing—the coroner thought that might have caused the accident. Of course he shouldn't have been driving at all. Nell took it pretty hard; she adored our mother and couldn't stand father; they used to have endless rows."

"What a mess people make of each other, don't they?" Claire said pityingly. "Charles, can you stay to lunch, I came to ask? Good, then I'll chivvy those children to pick a bit of watercress." She strode off, her shirt tail flapping behind her.

"And now, dear boy," said Aunt Julia, "come in and—tell me—about yourself."

"Nothing to tell, really, Aunt Julia," he said. "Except that I'm happy," and he followed her, whistling a phrase from Tuesday's guitar.

XII

MAGGIE WAS LIKE a kid over the fact that we had "a place in the country" that we could ask people to—the dilapidation of the place, the lack of beds, didn't worry her a whit, she at once began casting round for someone to invite. Mercifully most of her friends were too hard-working to be able to leave London, but she rang up John—Maggie never wrote letters—and persuaded him to come for a weekend. He proposed to travel down by a milk-train from Paddington—don't ask me why milk-trains should depart for the country in the small hours, you'd think it would be the other way round—which reached Lanrith at 6 a.m. Maggie, full of enthusiasm, said we would get up early and walk to meet him.

When it came to the point, of course, as I had expected, it was quite impossible to rouse her. Maggie asleep was like something sunk on the sea-bed, full fathom five; the only thing that could pierce her unconsciousness was a call from the hospital, otherwise you might as well save your breath, shouts or thumps had no more effect than whispering passages from the *Times* Fourth Leader.

So at five on this fine cool Saturday I got up and started off along the path to Lanrith.

By now I was familiar with every yard of the way, since it was our shopping route, and after her first gesture with the cake tin Maggie had slumped back into letting me do the housekeeping; air and exercise was what I'd come to the country for, she said. Anyway I liked the walk—it gave me a chance to get my mind smoothed out two or three times a week.

The bridle-path followed the mile of cliff along the Lan river, crossing some cowy cliffside fields, and met a cinder-track above the little town's handkerchief-sized musical-comedy park and toy gasworks where you could carry away sacks of coke for a shilling.

Tide was out, and wreaths of mist were curling over the river mudflats. The heron stood where he always did, meditating on the end of the spit where our tributary stream ran in to the river. On the far shore the wooded cliffs were still in shadow except for the very tops of trees which shone pinkish. Underfoot the mud was still crisp from a late frost. One or two birds were calling, letting out long gargling cries, maybe gulls or curlews. I felt gay and free, happy to be on my own with nobody else awake. Life down here wasn't bad, really. We didn't see much of Aspic, thank goodness—she was off on her calls, or cultivating the social possibilities of the neighbourhood, for she had lots of county connections left from Mum's day, bless her true British heart. Maggie had settled into her usual routine of sleep, eat, work, smoke; and Charles and I were striking up a tentative friendship.

Maggie had been so doom-ridden and thundercharged about this at first that in the end I gave the whole business an airing.

"Look, Maggie, I wish you'd rid yourself of the idea that I'm trying my Clytemnestra ways on Charles. Honestly, all the poor sod wants is a little cheerful company, someone to chat with and pass the time of day, and that's all I'm providing."

"Eleanor can't get over your playing her mother's guitar," Maggie said heavily.

"Well, for heaven's sake! Charles asked me to. If she thinks of it as a holy relic she shouldn't leave it about."

"It was a great emotional shock to her."

I'll bet, I thought. The sort of shock you'd give to a lorry tyre by beating on it with a teaspoon.

However, I didn't tell Maggie that Charles and I had fallen into the habit of half hours with the guitar in the barn over our elevenses. Eleanor was out on her rounds at this time, Maggie wasn't up yet; what the ear didn't hear the heart didn't grieve over.

"Damn it all, Maggie, he's ill. Someone has to cheer him up."

Apparently Eleanor had told Maggie he had a troublesome heart condition but not how bad it was; she'd have to tell her something, of course, for Maggie was no fool, and a marvellous diagnostician; put her finger on your skin and she'd tell you every physical thing you'd had wrong with you since teething-rash.

"Well, all right," she said grudgingly. "But be sensible, will you?"

"No rough games, not too many sweets..."

I grinned as I thought of Charles, the object of all this solicitude, tucked up in bed at the moment, no doubt, with his dreams of his boats and his hens, safe enough from me, poor devil, if Maggie did but know it. I supposed that a lot of her anxiety about him was really directed towards the preservation of her beautiful friendship with Eleanor.

It was with a feeling of relief that I vaulted the stile beyond the last field. Three weeks in the country had taught me that cows in right-of-way fields were not bulls, but this was still more theory than belief. From here the cinder-track connected with flights of steps zig-zagging down into the town. When I reached the quay I saw another early riser leaning on the rail of the pier, where it ran out into deep water, with a fishing-rod propped against his shoulder and a comfortable curl of cigarette smoke over his head. It was Peter Lannick, the workman who had voted against coming on bank holiday Friday. I had noticed since then that he generally seemed to be in trouble of one kind or another, particularly with Mat Kormendi, who detested him.

He was staring angrily at the water as if even the fish had contributed to his persecution by arranging to ignore him. I thought it was a pity to look so cross on such a cool, free, peaceful morning.

"Hullo," I called across the empty quay. "Any luck?"

He turned round. The corner of his handsome sullen mouth lifted in a reluctant smile.

He gave me a sawn-off, sideways nod.

"Early up, ain't you?"

"Meeting the ferry from the six-o'clock train. Do you have the time on you?"

"Quarter to," he said. "Ferry's only five minutes from here."

"I can have a breather, then. I've been hurrying."

I leaned on the rail beside him and looked down into the water, which was clear as limejuice. The sun was up now, hot on my back.

"Shall I disturb the fish?"

"They're not biting anyway," said Peter. "Want a smoke?"

"Thanks."

We propped ourselves on our elbows in silence. I felt warm and exercised and sleepy.

"Like it down here?" said Peter.

"Very much. I like not knowing anybody. It's nice and quiet after London."

"It's too bloody quiet," he said violently. "It's a hell-hole. Full of gossiping bloody old besoms pulling everyone's character to bits. I used to be in the navy, see, got about the world a bit, but I had to come home on account of my mum's health. She's a widow, my dad's dead."

"That's a shame." I felt sorry for him; I could imagine how cramping the place might seem to a local boy who had managed to escape.

"Coming back to a dump like this—it fair gets you down." He threw a bit of stone savagely into the water and the light reflections from it chased each other across his handsome miserable face.

"Poor Peter. I hope your mother better."

"Not her. She'll go on till she dies, beery old soak. And that won't be till I've grown fungus."

I hated to see him so unhappy and at odds with the world.

Being for some reason just then full of misplaced confidence in my dealings with the male sex I leaned sideways and kissed him, saying,

"Cheer up, maybe she'll marry again."

He recoiled, looking rather astonished, and stared at me as if I had bitten him. I said, "It's time I met that ferry," and walked on along the quay, wondering if it had been wise to kiss him. I hadn't liked the look in his black wasp's eyes.

But I soon forgot him, for over the harbour was a big new Swedish ship loading china clay, and some dinghies bounced along the jewel-coloured water, and the ferry was working its way across; I caught a glimpse of John standing among the other passengers and waved to him. He looked dazed, but seemed relieved to see me, if not particularly pleased. When I told him we were faced with three-quarters of an hour's walk he was horrified.

"Can we have a sit-down somewhere first? I'm not properly awake. Isn't there a café?"

"Nothing that's open at this hour, that's a dead cert. I've got a flask of coffee, though, if you like to sit on the harbour wall and drink it."

"I suppose that's better than nothing."

For John this was surly; even if he didn't like me he was always polite. But I could see he was very tired; his face was all crags and hollows, black with growth of beard, furrowed and rutted like a coal tip.

The coffee cheered him, though. He fished out a half-bottle of whisky from his rucksack and we both had some; I chuckled, thinking of Wal, and wondered what he was doing now; living it up, painting the town red along with his colonel no doubt.

"I hate early morning," John said. "Never get up at this time if I can help it."

"Why?"

"Too quiet. Nothing happening. You have to think. Later in the day people talk, events trundle on, there's always some distraction."

I was interested to find somebody else who wanted to avoid thought.

"What do you think about when you do think, John?"

"My wife," he said, holding up the half-empty bottle and looking at it. He must have put away quite a lot, for I'd only had half a beakerful.

"How long ago did she die, John?" I knew that Maggie had looked after her in hospital and kept an eye on John ever since.

"Two years ago. In a way it was my fault. I tell myself, if only I'd nagged her into going to a doctor when she first noticed the pain, she needn't have died. It's not a nice death, cancer."

"No." Maggie had told me a good deal about it. "Do you miss her all the time?"

"All the time. You know those statues?"

"Which statues?"

He made a wide gesture, and nearly knocked his rucksack into the water.

"You must know. Barbara Hepworth. Big, with a hole through the middle. That's what it's like. A hole right through here." He dug inwards at his heart.

My lovely clear morning had turned black, like a negative, with harsh white round the edges. Everyone is unhappy, everywhere. Everyone is lonely. Why can't we do something about each other?

The tide was coming in fast, slapping at the stone ramp of the car ferry with a series of sharp wallops, like a wet cloth against a wall.

"But, John," I said, appalled, "what's the point in living if you feel like that?"

"I often ask myself. When I'm painting it's not so bad. Or drinking or talking. And Maggie keeps me up to the mark—she's full of high ideals. But mainly I suppose the reason why I don't jump under a bus is sheer inertia." He swigged down a bit more whisky and added, "I shan't talk this way later in the day. This is just my early-morning spiel. I get to thinking of Nina at this time and it brings out the Irish in me. Sorry, Twopence, you should have stopped me before I got launched." He held up the bottle, stared at it with surprise, and tossed it into the water.

We climbed the interminable steps and walked along the cinder-track to the gas-works. The sky was covered in clouds now and a cold wind gnawed our ankles. The day's pristine privacy had ebbed, and with the arrival of milk-floats and early workers Lanrith was no longer mine, but a going concern, grey and gritty and nasty. We walked away as fast as possible.

"Who was that you waved to on the quay?" John asked.

"A man called Peter Lannick—one of the men who's working

on the Foleys' house. I talked to him before you arrived. He has a drunken mum."

"You shouldn't repeat people's confidences, Twopence," said John gravely.

Oh hell, I thought, then why do people *tell* me things? My new-found confidence shrivelled.

"Here, you go on, John," I said. "You'll see the cottage just round the corner of that next hillside. Make yourself at home, the kettle should be about boiling and your bed's made up in the downstairs back room. I'll be along in a minute."

"What's the matter, you're all white, do you feel sick," he said looking at me curiously. "Did I give you too much whisky?"

"No, it's not that. Oh, do go on for heaven's sake," I snapped. "I just want to have a good cry."

John shrugged and gave it up. He walked on and disappeared round the hill. I took some deep breaths, sat down on a damp rock, and stared at the grey, ruffled sea.

What is life, I thought, but a slap in the face with a wet towel? I thought of the tide, slopping and chopping up the slipway. Blue and green, all prettied up to deceive you into thinking it's a warm bath and then, zonk! you're soaked and shivering. Here we are, quite a small group of people, nothing special about us, all miserable as hell, John about his wife, Charles about his health, Peter about his drunk mum, Kormendi an exile, Maggie in a permanent state of worry because her dear friend has turned out to be a little slut who is slipping through her fingers, and Eleanor—what secret cares gnaw at her vitals?

Aspic's okay, I decided, it's the rubberskins like her, life's Upper Sixth, who get on all right in this world, trampling over everyone else's susceptibilities. And it's up to the highly developed consciousnesses like me to try to stop them from doing it. Even if I can't right the woes of John and Peter and Charles by means of a sisterly kiss, I can be a proper thorn in Aspic's flesh.

This idea pleased me and as I'd finished crying for the time and my bare feet were nearly frozen I jumped up and went down to the cottage to fry bacon and eggs for breakfast.

XIII

ELEANOR SLIPPED OFF the handbrake and let her car roll downhill in neutral to the gravel turning-patch in front of Watertown cottage. The car moved so quietly that the girl kneeling on the grass verge never heard it. What was she doing? She looked like a gutter-brat, rough-haired, barefoot, in jeans, with her hands full of the common red-and-yellow mimulus that grew down by the stream. How easy it would be to turn the steering-wheel a fraction to the left and knock her down into the deep little brook ... She might easily hit her head on a rock and drown. People often died of such trivial accidents. And yet this frail-looking creature must have a tenacious grip on life. She might survive to remember that she had been pushed.

Shocked by the indiscretion and lack of discipline in her train of thought, Eleanor vigorously revved the engine, swung the Ford round, and started up the hill again. Tuesday, whom she now passed for the second time, stood up with a reluctant smile; Eleanor gave her a brisk nod and drove on towards Lanrith.

Death, she thought. Such a simple remedy, so easily administered. Any doctor knows how easily. Death is the difference between one pill and another, between tying a cut artery or leaving it for five minutes. I must take care not to get too matter-of-fact about death. Patients soon begin to sense that what is the end-all to them is merely another symptom to you. Patients don't care to be regarded as so many fragments of clinical material.

In any case death should be administered with finesse; by remote control, at long range, not in mess and dust at the roadside.

Zita's death had been a classically neat piece of manipulation. At the time, Eleanor had acted on impulse, she thought, but reconsidering the matter in the succeeding months she had come to the conclusion that this was not quite so; her act had sprung from a profound assessment of the girl's character.

Such a simple affair it had been : the three of them on holiday, she herself more or less good-temperedly playing duenna, elder sister, mother-confessor, friend, to the engaged couple. Zita had come to her asking advice and remedies for a little pain; a trivial harmless little pain. It was so easy to make a few tests, look grave, pretend a pretence of reassurance. Zita hadn't even waited to learn more. Fatally unbalanced, terrified as Eleanor knew by the very thought of illness, she hadn't dared wait... And Eleanor had added another piece of knowledge to her stock.

It still surprised her that even such a featherbrain as Zita should have fallen in love with Charles; one might as well, she thought, fall in love with a tree or telegraph post. But most women seemed to function in this irrational way; look at the girl in Lanrith who loved a crusader on a tomb and put a wreath of flowers round his dog every Saturday. Thank god she, Eleanor, had been briefly exposed to the passing infection, had been immunised, and was safe from a second attack. Love, she thought harshly, was a dysentery of the mind, a purposeless draining-away of energy.

In the surgery waiting-room she saw the usual hopeful, chatty, muddy-booted queue. The paraffin heater hissed and Eleanor dealt methodically with lumbago and colds, a little boy's badly cut hand, an obvious case of measles—why hadn't the stupid woman the wits to keep her child at home when it was covered with a rash like that—patients who wanted free cough medicine, patients who wanted an excuse to stay away from work. The final one despatched, she looked at her list of calls and planned out a route.

Acacia Cottages were that dismal little row near the gasworks on the edge of the town. She might as well start there and work outwards to the more distant farms. Acacia Cottages. The name seemed familiar: Mrs Lannick.

"Her son Peter works for Rowse the builder," Bridie, the secretary said, handing Eleanor a thick white cup of villainous coffee.

"Peter Lannick, of course; he's the bad-tempered-looking boy." Eleanor sipped at the coffee and pushed it aside.

"He's got enough to make him bad-tempered, Dr Foley," Bridie said earnestly, "with that mother and her slummocky ways; proper old tippler she is. It's a shame, really, for Peter; he'd got a decent life in the navy and then he had to come home on compassionate discharge to look after her, and take a job as a builder's labourer."

"Surely he could do better than that?"

"Not round here, Doctor; the young men have to take what they can get."

A hellish phrase, Eleanor thought in a rage, backing her car out fast into the narrow little street and skinning past a dried-milk lorry. Take what you can get. Find your own level. Fit in where you can, have the corners rubbed off. Want must be your master. How she had always hated those smug catchwords, coined by people who hadn't the guts to do other than conform. People who from laziness—only they called it respectability—would never bestir themselves to prevent suffering or injustice. "It wasn't my affair, was it?" People who let their pets die of neglect and their sewage discharge into the sea because they didn't care.

The road to Acacia Cottages was a no-parking area. Nevertheless Eleanor planted her car firmly on a double yellow line and rapped on the open door of number four. A smell of cold cabbage and sour rags came out and enveloped her.

"Anyone in?" she called.

Hearing a faint sound from above, she went up the steep, dark little trap of a staircase which led straight from the front door to the two bedrooms. She noticed a squashed packet of margarine halfway up the stairs, and a bottle of tomato ketchup which had rolled from top to bottom, spilling half its contents. Someone seemed to have been picnicking extensively in the first of the bedrooms she entered; in the second she found Mrs Lannick.

Peter came home just as she finished her examination.

"That you, Doctor?" he called, and she went down to him. He deposited a bagful of groceries in the kitchen before hastily shutting the door on its frightful squalor and steering Eleanor into the front room. This was neat but dreary and almost bare : two red chairs, a table covered by a worn red chenille cloth and some picture postcards on the overmantel above the black grate were its sole furnishings.

"How is she?" Peter said.

"Oh, she'll be all right," Eleanor told him. "A bit bruised and cut about—falling right down the stairs at her age is no joke—but she hasn't broken anything and she isn't even concussed—she must have a head like a rock. She's pretty sorry for herself, of course, but that's mainly on account of her hangover."

Peter dropped his eyes quickly, but not before she had seen the angry shame in them.

"Does she want any medicine," he muttered.

"I'll put you down for some dressings for the cuts," Eleanor said, scribbling, "otherwise she doesn't need a thing—except to stop drinking." Ignoring his evident furious wish to avoid further discussion of his mother's habits she went on, "I'd better get her into a home, hadn't I? It's a preposterous state of affairs that you should waste your life looking after her, doing a dead-end job in Lanrith. I'll write off today and see what can be done."

"You won't do anything of the sort!" Peter shouted at her.

Eleanor glanced up from her pad in surprise. He had gone a dark dusky red and was staring at her with narrowed eyes and lips pressed together, breathing hard.

"And have the neighbours say I'd asked you to have her put away? Not on your nelly! There's enough talk as it is."

"But you can't go on like this," Eleanor said calmly. "The house is like a pigsty and one of these days you'll come home to find she's burned it down, or tumbled off the harbour wall."

"Not she," he interjected. "No such luck."

"What sort of a life is that? But if I get her into a home they may be able to cure her—she hasn't always been an alcoholic has she?"

"No, only the last two years since my father died."

"There you are, then. Why not be sensible about it?"

"Look!" Peter cried. "Will you just leave us alone? Why should she be cured? She drinks so's she can forget my Dad, don't she? She used to slave her guts out, keeping the place nice when he was alive, only he never took a bit of notice because he was a proper old swine. Now he's gone she just don't care any more, all she wants to do is go to the pictures and get boozed up. Why shouldn't she? If you did get her cured what could she do? At her age? She might just as well be dead, and the sooner the better. But you needn't think I pushed her down the stairs because I didn't," he ended savagely. "And anyway I know how they treat them in those council homes, knocking them about and half starving them—I'd sooner die than have any kin of mine go in there. Why there was a case in the paper about a boy put in with a lot of grown men, the things they did made even the attendants sick, and they must be tough enough, god knows, to take on the job."

He stopped for breath and a thin, whining voice from behind Eleanor said, "Don't you let them take me away, Peter boy, don't you! I'll never forgive you if you do, you know that. I knew she was up to summat the minute she came in the door, I knew she was a cold-blooded scheming bitch. Old Dr Pengelly wouldn't never have suggested any such a thing. Ah, 'tis hard when your own childer plots agen you."

Mrs Lannick had put on a man's pyjama jacket over the skirt which she had not taken off last night, and had dragged a grey blanket round her shoulders. She was an unappetising object, and as she had no teeth her words were largely incomprehensible, but their animosity towards Eleanor was plain enough.

"All right, all right, mother, don't carry on; get back to bed for Jesus sake and let me tidy up some of this mess," Peter said irritably. "I ought to have been at Rowse's yard two hours ago." He pushed his mother towards the foot of the stairs, pointedly ignoring Eleanor.

She shrugged, and walked out towards her car.

"Think over what I said," she called back. "I'll come again on Friday to dress your mother's head and we'll have another talk."

Dead silence was her only answer, and she got into the Ford and drove away, surprised to find herself so angry that it gave her a sharp physical pain in her chest; normally she was able to take patients' reactions with clinical detachment. At the top of the hill she stopped for a cigarette and to calm down; her hands were shaking and she could feel a staccato pulse-beat in her right temple. Bad, very bad. Why should the Lannick family have roused such emotion? She decided that she was probably identifying herself with Peter, since it was not until her father's death, indirectly from drink, that she had felt free to leave home. And the return to Cornwall had brought back some of the constricting emotions of those days.

Irritably she took a tube from her pocket, shook out a couple of tablets, and swallowed them; her heartbeats slowed. She stubbed out the cigarette—her hands were steadier now—and, putting the whole incident firmly out of her mind, drove on towards a farm called Santewan and a poisoned finger.

XIV

MAGGIE WAS HAPPY at having John with us. To someone who did not know her this would hardly have been obvious. When I have a friend staying I like to *be* with them, do things with them, sit on the edge of the bath chatting, go for walks together, so as not to miss a minute of their company. God knows, most of one's time is spent with people for whom one feels indifference or dislike; it seems the height of stupidity to waste a real friend. True, Maggie and John had known one another a long time, and she saw quite a lot of him in London; but somehow down here he seemed more important, because until he came we had been dependent on the Foleys for society.

Maggie, however, was not demonstrative about him. She still kept to her regime : sleep till noon, read and work in a cloud of smoke all afternoon, emerge, yawning, at dusk, for food and conversation. Then of course she wanted to talk all night.

We were having a spell of hot, dry spring weather. John had become enthusiastic about the place. Characteristically, having at first said that he couldn't stay more than two days, he had fallen in love with the landscape and persuaded Charles's friend Claire to drive him into Truro for paints and canvases. Now he had three pictures going at once to use the different lights, an early-morning one of the ruined drystone wall with liverwort growing from it; midday, the twisted, blasted trees straggling down the cliff to St Monack church; and an evening scene of our cottage with the musk flowers in the stream, Maggie reading the medical dictionary outside the front door, and Brunel's viaduct like a gigantic key-signature in the background.

Eleanor had invited Maggie to stay a bit longer; Maggie had agreed provided I would stay too; I had raised no objection. Our day had fallen into a routine by which I revolved round each of three planets in turn : Charles and his guitar till noon, while John painted the liverwort; then I walked over to St Monack with John and a picnic lunch. I'd swim a little in the cold spring sea, and sunbathe while he painted the trees. Occasionally I'd toy with the idea of starting another book. We tried to persuade Maggie to join us but it was bootless; she stayed in her smoky nest, cellar-white, immersed in the pituitary system, while John went brown and I went freckled. Sometimes John swam to keep me company but he really hated getting undressed and walking into the sea, regarded it as a kind if indignity. He looked odd, too, when he swam; one of nature's grownups, not intended to be seen playing. Charles now kept a dinghy in the creek and once in a way John would crew for him, but the two men had little in common; John, who was highly rational when he could be bothered, quickly became impatient with Charles's shy inarticulacy, with an existence that was so largely pursued on the physical plane. Charles tentatively suggested I should go sailing, but I turned that one aside, telling him that small boats bored me; which was both diplomatic and true.

At about five we'd trail home, salt and sandy and sleepy, along the cliff path, to find Maggie warming up some witch's brew of black coffee, her hair dusty with cigarette ash. While John got her outside and set her into her pose I'd make a meal which we'd later eat by the stream in front of the cottage.

At first John suffered badly from lack of drink. As Maggie never needed alcohol herself she couldn't understand anyone else's need for it, and since she loved and respected John that was all the more reason why in her opinion he'd be better without it. John endured for two days, since the nearest pub was two miles' walk there and back; after that he arranged with Claire to keep him topped up when she came to visit Charles.

This kind of dangling dependent life suited me well enough. I enjoyed having no decisions to make, just waiting to swing into someone else's orbit. I've always liked looking at things, but there had been no stimulation in doing that with Maggie, who wasn't in the least interested in appearances, unless they were symptoms. John was different. He had an eye like a lynx, and prodded me on to be more observant, pointing out things I'd never noticed, the way the sun came in stripes through the row of cedars above Watertown, the difference in texture of stone when it sweats, the stream's change to tea-colour after rain, the fact that all the wild flowers in May seem to be pink or white or blue. The lanes that month were smothered in pink campion and bluebells; even Maggie noticed them at last and put some in a jam-jar, where they looked highly incongruous and forlorn. We lived on cheese and watercress and fresh air; sometimes Kormendi brought us down half a dozen of his bootpolish eggs and stayed for a convivial evening.

I've always hated Saturday afternoons. I wonder why? I like to feel that everyone's at work, that the world is revolving; I hate the dead atmosphere of semi-shutness with half the population watching football matches and the other half at cinemas, and unthreaded children sculling about like beads on the suburban roads; there's nothing more heartrendingly dreary than a place like Barnet or Uxbridge at 4 p.m. on a Saturday. Even at

Watertown you'd know what day it was, because the builders knocked off at lunchtime and the Co-op van called in the middle of the afternoon, smelling fustily of wrapped cut bread and factory cake and breakfast cereals. I stocked up with a load of starch and Maggie bought a hundred cigarettes.

I'd stayed home to be sure of catching the van, and presently John came back from St Monack, saying that he'd finished his beach picture and suggested we all walk in to the flicks at Lanrith. They were showing *Richard III*. Maggie demurred; she had done that walk once and once was enough.

"Here comes Matyas," she said. "Perhaps he'd ride us in on his tractor."

Kormendi had saved up enough to rent a couple of fields behind his cottage and was buying a tractor on the never-never so that he could plough them and grow pig-food. Primarily, though, he used the tractor for transport; you could never be sure of being able to walk up the lane past Watertown without having to flatten yourself against the bank while Mat roared past like a Roman charioteer, beaming all over his pussycat face. He gave me a lift into Lanrith once, but by the time we got there I felt as if each one of my bones had been separately dragged out and used as a rolling-pin; also the benefit of having the groceries carried home was not worth the effort of sustaining an hour's conversation with Mat above the noise of the tractor. I preferred my long brooding walks over the cliff.

"You ask him if you want," I said, "while I make some lemon tea." There had been lemons on the Co-op van.

It was a hot, sultry afternoon, very dry and still for May; the sky was a pale hazy blue and when the van went up the hill it left a trail of dust in the air, which slowly settled on the pink campions. Even the birds, who had been shouting their heads off for the last week, seemed tired out, or perhaps they too were all off at a match.

I made the tea and poured it into a jug and took it outside with some cups. There was mint growing in the stream; I stuck a sprig in the jug. Maggie and Mat were exchanging torrents of Hungarian through the ceaseless chug-chug of the tractor; I thought how alike they were, big and square and formidable like the tractor because without noticing it they might simply mow down anything that stood in their way. Having given them cups of lemon tea I turned to look for John. He had climbed the bank of the lane opposite the cottage and was sitting on top.

93

Once somebody had tried to make a garden up there, and a few little gooseberry bushes remained, dragged down by a jungle of climbing weeds. I lay down beside John; the ground was baked knobbly from drought, but the May grass was so thick and sweet and shiny that it was like lying on a bed of rushes. Down below the chug of the tractor and the two voices ran on interminably, a two-violin concerto with the tractor taking the orchestra part, until I was dreaming of a hospital ward with Maggie or my mother asking me why I had not done some essential thing and an Indian sitting on my bed inviting me to join his trade union. Then I was properly asleep, lulled by the tractor. At last Mat switched it off and I woke, but slowly and comfortably, with the smell of grass in my nostrils. Without opening my eyes I said,

"What are we going to do?"

"We are spared the need for decision," John's voice said, somewhere near my head. "Maggie and Matyas are still discussing the evils of the world."

"That's good. Then we can stay where we are."

"I doubt it. There's a car coming down the road and Mat will have to shift."

In fact with a clattering roar Kormendi started up and pulled to the side of the road. I sat up to see who was in the car; it was Claire's Jaguar with a full freight of passengers, Charles in front, and a Chelseaish trio at the back, two men and a girl in sweaters and jeans. I was thinking how odd they looked in these surroundings when it suddenly occurred to me that I must look the same; no wonder Aspic gave me such old-fashioned glances when she met me picking watercress.

Once I would have welcomed some urban company but now I thought, oh hell, who's Claire bringing to disturb our peace and quiet?

The road was full of people.

"Like Brighton beach," John said. Claire saw us and waved, and came along with a carrier-bag full of Haig.

"Thanks, Claire. What would I do without you?"

"Go back to London, I suppose," said Claire. She climbed up and sat beside us.

"Have a nip?" said John.

"I don't mind if I do." She pushed the short grey hair off her forehead. "I've been planting potatoes all afternoon." She drank lemon-tea and Haig from a cup.

"Charles?"

He was standing on the road beneath us, like a well-brought-up but bashful child. Claire extended a long arm and hauled him up.

He seemed amused at the daring innovation of Scotch drunk from teacups at four in the afternoon and accepted a cup with a shy grin, hesitantly, as if he weren't sure he wanted it, but too polite to say no.

Down below Kormendi, who seemed to know Claire's friends, was introducing them to Maggie, whose doctor's eyes were sizing up the girl, taking in her waiflike, frail, not-long-for-this-world look. One of the men was, or had been, a medical student; in no time wafts of technical conversation began coming up the bank, gastrectomies, hysterectomies, something about the Munchausen syndrome . . .

"There ought to be an operation called the Polytectomy," I said yawning, "a sort of insurance against future operations. You just have everything out."

Charles suddenly exploded with laughter as if a catch had been released in him, gulped his drink, and lay back weakly heaving among the gooseberries while John and I began inventing names for new medical treatments and diseases, each sillier than the last, Onassis of the liver, sisterectomy, insecurettage; that's what Saturday afternoon does to you.

"Sheep get something called pulpy kidney, did you know?" Claire murmured dreamily. "Old Sam at the Ferry told me."

"It sounds like a disease you'd get from reading too many doctor-nurse romances; that and softening of the frontal lobes."

The conversation drifted into silence; comfortable background noises of the brook made themselves heard, and the lazy, yawning, gossiping cluck of a hen up the hill somewhere who had found a dustbath and was slowly working herself deeper and deeper into it. I realised that the group in the road had gone; up the hill, apparently, to look at Mat's pigs. Showing his pigs was a mark of esteem.

"Well," Claire said at last, stretching, "I'd better take them along, I suppose; they're supposed to be going to lift carrots at Treadno. So long." She nodded goodbye and the Jaguar slipped uphill between the steep banks; its last whisper was drowned by the row of cypresses.

"What about this film, then?" I asked. John merely grunted; he was nine parts asleep.

"Shouldn't he be covered?" Charles said.

I was tickled, and rather touched. "Anyone can see you were brought up by a good nanny. 'Don't sit on the wet grass, dear, or you'll get piles.'"

"Well I can't help it," he said defensively, but grinning. "I *was* brought up by a good nanny." He collected the cups tidily, went into the cottage, and came back with John's extraordinary full-skirted overcoat which looked as if he'd got it secondhand from an Armenian refugee.

"Anyway Nin would never have been so indelicate as to mention piles," he said laying it over John. "That nasty disease, she would have said. People look defenceless when they're asleep, don't they?" he added. It was a trite enough observation but it seemed to have struck him for the first time.

"Some do even when they're awake." I spoke without thinking and was annoyed to feel myself blush furiously; I squatted down by the stream and pinched a sprig of peppermint for its pungent scent.

"I suppose I've not looked at many people sleeping," Charles said as if to himself; he didn't seem to have heard my remark. He went on quite simply, without noticing the break in his train of thought, "Isn't it peaceful here when they all go off? Let's stroll down to the river."

I knew Maggie wouldn't be pleased, when she came back, but I couldn't think of any excuse. I didn't want to make any excuse. I went with him in silence. My shoes were left behind on the bank, and the leafmould of the river path was damp and cool under my bare feet. We walked down to the little landing-stage with its boathouse and low stone wall and leaned there, and watched a cormorant fishing from a sandbar near the other shore. The woods on the far side of the river were heavy and green and quiet.

Charles suddenly said, "What day is it?" and when I told him Saturday he seemed quite astonished.

"Are you sure? This week seems to have gone so fast."

"Saturday," I said patiently. "The builders have all gone, hadn't you noticed?"

"So they have. How extraordinary."

"What's extraordinary?" I said it to fill the gap and then I wished I hadn't, because he answered simply,

"Why, that they'd gone and I hadn't noticed. I don't care for Saturdays as a rule..." and suddenly a great fear and darkness came down over me, the warmth and peace seemed insubstantial and dangerous as the skin of a bog, and I thought, Hell, hell, how am I going to get out of here? How important is this Charles going to become? What am I going to do about him?

XV

ELEANOR FELT MOST concentratedly herself in early morning. The long dark calm of night had reassembled her molecules in order, stroking them into a serene and beautiful pattern, allowing the alien particles to sink out of sight. The day's burden of jar and grind against other, stubborn personalities would stir up the sediment again, blacken the clarity; she was accustomed to this and no longer struggled against it, even found a kind of pleasure in abandoning control. But the early hours, the ordered morning routine ready to unwind again gave her a taste of early childhood's peace, the state in which there is no sin that will not be forgiven in advance.

Cool in her heavy silk dressing-gown she carried out her morning tasks in the regular sequence, progressing steadily from one to the next, letting her body follow the ritual while her spirit moved in its own course, separate but controlling. There was a kind of ecstasy about this process. She arranged her clothes and toilet articles in precise order, and then moved into her bathroom, which was kept immaculately neat.

She delighted in this room. Charles, because of his heart condition, had a bedroom and bathroom on the ground floor, converted from the old farm dairy, and Nin, who preferred a hip-bath, kept one in her room, so Eleanor had uncontested possession of the upstairs bathroom. It was large, had once been a child's bedroom, perhaps, but remained always rather dark because immediately outside the window a massive yew tree absorbed all the light and let in only a green filtered dimness. Besides the bath and shower there was room for a white-painted rocking-chair and a large marble-topped table on which Eleanor kept medical journals. Here she sat drying her hair, which she washed every morning, while she read about a case of poisoning by amanita phalloides. Satisfied, her hair once more shining and sleekly coiled, she returned the dryer to its case, washed her brush and comb, polished the taps, and sorted the contents of her medicine cabinet. Noticing that there were two bottles of aspirin she took one down to Charles's bathroom, kindly tidied the contents of *his* bathroom cabinet—which was in its usual dusty and sticky muddle—washed and wiped each article, and arranged the rest in a rational manner. Then she peeled off the rubber gloves she had worn throughout, rubbed her hands with scentless lotion, and went into the kitchen where old Nin, punctual as Eleanor herself, had set the table and made a pot of coffee. A kettle was still boiling on the Aga, clouding the room with steam through which the morning sunlight swam in hazy radiance. Eleanor picked up the kettle but Nin's voice from the other door said, "Charles hasn't had his tea yet," so she contented herself with moving it to the cooler side of the stove. The room was warm; she opened a window, sniffed, and said,

"You've been putting disinfectant down the drain again. It's not necessary to do it every day."

"Oh well," said Nin comfortably, "they tell you it kills every known germ, so it can't do any harm, can it? Here's your coffee."

"It's wasteful. This is a house, not a hospital. And I don't like the smell."

"You're too fussy about smells," Nin said, passing the cream. Eleanor shook her head.

"No cream, now? What's all this, then? Not slimming, are you?"

"It's a luxury. I've decided to give it up. Charles would be better without it too. We eat lots of things we'd be better without."

"Well I'm not giving it up," Nin said firmly, putting a dollop on her porridge. "Foolishness I call it, just when we've come down here where cream *is* cream."

Eleanor wrinkled her nose a little as she passed the old woman's chair: Nin, speckless as she kept herself, had the faintly fusty smell of old age, of clean but well-worn clothes, clean but flabby flesh, old woollens, old shoes.

"It's time you had some new dresses, Nin."

"These'll do me a good while yet." The old woman was unaffronted, calmly going on with her breakfast.

"I'll get you two for your birthday, in Truro."

"I'd rather you spent the money on a transistor. I can get me own dresses when I see fit."

Eleanor wasted no time in argument but resolved to get the

dresses none the less and, if possible, dispose of Nin's present ones when the old woman was out.

A truck passed the kitchen window and almost immediately afterwards Kormendi's tractor clamoured by and halted at the farmyard gate; there were voices, shouted commands, a rattle of chain as the truck's rear ramp was lowered and then a loud angry squealing.

"Charles is up already?" Eleanor said, hearing his voice. "What's going on?"

"That'll be his pig arriving I daresay." Nin placidly took her dishes to the sink and began to wash them.

"Pig? He's not getting a pig."

"Sounds different to me. Kormendi was getting it for him."

"Who told you?"

"Why, Charles did."

"But we agreed a pig would be too much work for him," Eleanor said sharply.

"Well, dear, I expect Kormendi will help him look after it. Very capable and obliging he seems; we're lucky to have him for a neighbour."

"It's crazy! He'll be encouraging Charles to do far more than he ought."

Nin paused a moment, dishmop in hand. Her faded blue eyes were calm and steady as she looked at Eleanor. "He might as well enjoy himself," she observed.

"Oh well, I daresay he'll soon get bored by it." Eleanor laughed angrily, pushing back her chair.

"You've hardly touched your breakfast."

"I've had plenty." Eleanor swallowed a couple of tablets.

"Pills, pills," the old woman grumbled. "First it's pep pills, then tranquillisers. You'd be better without all that muck. Wouldn't get *me* touching them—plain milk of magnesia's all I ever needed or ever will."

"Oh, for heaven's sake!" Eleanor swung on her heel and left the room. However by the time, ten minutes later, that she strolled into the road, hands in the pockets of her leopardskin-silk raincoat, there was nothing but a calm interest on her face.

The new pig had given trouble, had escaped from the rather inexpert handling of Charles and the truck driver and fled off downhill to the cottage where John Fitzroy had his easel in the middle of the road. John, alerted by shouts from the top of the hill, had leapt, too late, to intercept the pig, which had knocked over the easel and darted into the cottage garden; there it had been recaptured by the three men with the help of Matyas. Now it was back in one of the old farm pigstyes, until Charles had time to put up an electric fence which Mat had found him secondhand. The men, wild-haired and cheerful after their chase, were leaning against the pigsty wall and discussing the siting of the fence—all except for John who, apparently exhausted, was stretched out full length on the concrete lay-by in front of the house.

"Good morning," Eleanor said with a cold smile as she passed him, and was startled by the look of fear and recognition and anguish that he gave her. She glanced over the pigsty wall at its new inmate.

"Well!" she remarked brightly to Charles. "This is a surprise! I didn't know you had decided to go in for pigs after all."

Charles seemed quite untroubled, showing none of the guilt that she had expected at this flagrant rejection of her advice. He answered in a mild tone,

"One pig is hardly 'going in' for them; and you must admit that she is handsome, Nell! Pure Landrace, and she's due to farrow in a month."

"I see you're quite an expert already; I'm afraid her beauties are wasted on me; I hardly know one end of a pig from the other. Don't they become very neurotic at farrowing-time and turn on their accoucheurs? Are you sure you will be competent to cope?"

"Oh, Matyas will help me, he knows all about it," Charles said easily.

"Many and many a sow have I helped at this time," Mat confirmed. "In Hungary is much pigs, is an often thing."

"And we have a month to get acquainted," Charles went on, leaning over to scratch his new acquisition's back with a pea-stick. She responded with a groan of ecstasy, sinking heavily to the ground and stretching out like a slug. "She is going to be very soothing company, you can see."

"Is a ver' fine pig," Mat said supportingly with a flash of white teeth.

"I can't really take to pigs, I'm afraid. Heavens, look at the time; I should be halfway to Lanrith by now."

She moved towards her car and the men were instantly absorbed in the pig again, but John, still prone on the ground, startled them by bursting into song:

"If I do this for thy sake,
    Honey, said she,
Speak, pig, or my heart will break!
    Hunk! said he."

"I wonder if you'd mind moving to one side?" Eleanor said coolly. "You're rather in the way of my car."

John stood up and bowed to her gravely. Then he pulled a bottle out of his pocket and drank, a long swig; recapped it, put it back, walked down the hill—weaving slightly—to where his easel lay; reassembled easel and picture, with a good deal of difficulty, dropping both several times; stared at the final result for a moment and then, with a shrug expressing resignation and despair, entered the cottage.

"Well," commented Eleanor lightly, "to be drunk at eight in the morning suggests a wonderful constitution which one can only admire, but it's slightly inconsiderate to leave his easel bang in the middle of the road. What about the milk lorry?"

"I will move it," said Kormendi. He roared off downhill in his tractor, followed by the truck.

"Nin told me to say your breakfast is ready," Eleanor called to Charles, starting her car. He nodded, continuing to lean on the pigsty wall.

How like a man, Eleanor thought, to loiter there comfortably admiring the pig in that sordid little pen, instead of getting on with the job of putting up the fence so that at least she has a decent field to live in.

A mile up the road she stopped at the farm called Santewan to look at Mrs Prothero's poisoned finger, which was progressing as well as could be expected in view of the fact that it was almost constantly in contact with grease or earth or coal or dirty water.

Mrs Prothero bore Eleanor's ministrations patiently, as if the finger were no affair of hers and her mind were elsewhere. When it was over she said,

"Was it you reported our cat to the Prevention, Doctor?"

Eleanor had hoped to remain anonymous in this affair, but she despised a cowardly lie and so answered curtly,

"Yes I did. The cat should never have been allowed to go on living in that condition. If you keep pets you should look after them properly."

She had noticed it on her last two visits: a miserable, hobbling creature, one-eyed, its ears in ribbons, only a few tufts of fur left on its scabby sides. Furious, sick with angry pity, she had telephoned the local RSPCA inspector.

"Well you'd no business to do it!" flashed Mrs Prothero. "Nothing ailed Tibbie but old age, she was as happy as you or I! Why, she used to follow my husband up and down the field when he went ploughing, she was as faithful as a dog. The inspector came and took her away and put her down like—like she was an animal! The children nearly broke their hearts when they came home from school, and my husband was just as bad. We'll thank you to mind your own affairs in future, or we'll get Dr Trevelyan to look after us."

"Suit yourselves," Eleanor said, snapping her case. "But Dr Trevelyan isn't taking night calls any more. In the meantime I'll be round on Tuesday to look at that finger."

Eleanor saw Charles in Lanrith later that day. By now she was regretting her morning irritation with him; she crossed the road and said,

"Hullo. How did you get here?"

"Hitched a lift on the milk lorry. I wanted to get some things for Bland."

"Bland?"

"The pig."

"Oh. Would you like me to take them back in the car?"

"It's all right, thanks. The Co-op van's going to drop them. Come and have a sandwich in the Ferry Inn."

Eleanor agreed rather reluctantly. Over lunch she said,

"It's a pity John Fitzroy is staying on so long. It rather spoils the peace of the neighbourhood having him around."

"He's Maggie's friend," Charles said noncommittally.

"It's probably more that other creature he comes to see. I'd expect *her* to have odd acquaintances."

"Oh no," Charles said definitely. "He's Maggie's friend. I gather there's quite a mutual dislike between him and Tuesday —or was till he came down here."

"Really? How do you come to know that?"

"Tuesday told me."

"Oh? How extraordinary. Not that I'd place much credit in anything *she* said; attention at all costs seems to be her motto."

"Why ask them here if you don't like them?" Charles said mildly.

"Because I'm fond of Magda and would like to help her. I wish the others would go, though; I've a good mind to drop a hint."

Charles opened his mouth to make some comment, changed his mind, and said,

"Aren't you eating? They're very good ham sandwiches."

"No, I'm not hungry. I'll have another tomato juice."

When he came back with it Charles said,

"I wouldn't bother John, if I were you. He's a very unhappy man."

"Have you been talking to him too?"

"You don't have to talk to him to see it. And he's sensitive—he's in that skin-missing state of misery where everything jars."

"Dear me! You've evidently been studying him. What afflicts him, then?"

"I gather Maggie's very hard up and he can't get her to accept a loan; she'd like to stay here a bit longer and go on with her reading but thinks she'll have to return to London and take a job."

"What?" In Eleanor's astonishment and anger she spilt tomato juice on her glove.

"Magda's hard up? How do you know?"

"Tuesday told me."

"That girl seems to repose a lot of confidence in you," Eleanor commented acidly. "If Magda's worried about money why didn't she tell me? I could have—"

"As well as a rent-free cottage? She'd hardly want that."

"But she's one of my greatest friends!"

"Are you one of hers?" he asked.

"Charles! What's got into you? Probing and analysing and scrutinising like this—it's not like you—"

"I have more opportunity now, I suppose," he said vaguely.

Eleanor frowned, considering expedients against this new threat to her plans.

"I'll have to go and see Aunt Julia," she muttered, mainly to herself, "try and get her interested in the idea of a clinic. Heaven knows she's rich enough."

As so often happened now, Charles's mind had moved peacefully away among the brightnesses and summits, the absorbing intricacies of his new life.

"Clinic," he said, "what clinic?"

"Thyroid disorders; I've told you all about it before. But the council are so slow making up their minds and it needs capital. If Magda had an inducement like that to stay down here—"

"Would she ever?" Charles said dubiously. "She's hardly a country bird."

"She doesn't care where she is, if she can do her work." Eleanor picked up her bag. "How are you getting back to Watertown?"

"Meeting Claire; she'll bring me."

"Oh well, see you later then—"

"So," Charles went on, "I may as well come out to Aunt Julia's with you."

"Oh, very well." Eleanor was slightly put out.

"I won't interrupt while you are trying to wheedle money out of her," Charles said kindly.

XVI

UNEXPECTEDLY, MISS FOLEY approved of Claire's Jaguar; she went along for the ride when Claire drove Charles back to Watertown. Eleanor was greatly startled, and rather displeased, on making her way down to the cottage through a heavy rainstorm with a couple of library books for Magda, to find a sort of conversazione in progress: Charles was there, Kormendi was there, Claire and Aunt Julia were there, and Magda, and John Fitzroy, and the girl, all sitting on crates and Snowcem tins, very much at ease, wreathed in cigarette smoke and apparently talking about English fiction.

Kormendi, it seemed, had been asking what he should read to acquire an understanding of English *mores*.

"In Hungary I am reading Dornford Yates and zis P. G. Woadhouse for learning English, but when I am come here I am not finding life is lived like such books."

There was a roar of laughter and everyone began making suggestions. Eleanor shrugged with exasperation and looked for sympathy from Magda, who never read fiction, but Magda was earnestly recommending Kormendi to read a liberal magazine called *Witness Box* which would unveil the seamy side of British life to him, and remained unaware of Eleanor's efforts to catch her eye.

"Wine, Dr Foley?"

The girl Tuesday was solemnly offering a jam-jar full of an unhygienic-looking yellow fluid; everyone else had containers of the stuff in their hands.

"No thank you," Eleanor said with a tight-fitting smile.

"It's—really excellent—you ought to try it—Nell," Aunt Julia croaked. "Gorse-flower wine—tastes of peaches. It might soothe your disappointment—a trifle." Her face folded into its eldritch smile.

"Mrs Prothero at Santewan gave us a keg for helping with the chores while she had her bad finger," Tuesday explained. "She's going to show me how to make it."

"Oh? Will you have time?" Eleanor said inattentively, wondering how the girl had managed to get so thick with the Protheros; she began to have an angry, baffled feeling that undesirable connections and alliances were forming, weblike, all about her; conspiracy could be smelt; if it were not stamped out it would spread like a canker. Aunt Julia, now—there she was by that wretched drunken painter chatting away like an old friend. And Claire, tiresome creature, with her usual indiscriminate amiability, was promising to take Magda to some specialist library in Plymouth, and to drive John and Aunt Julia to St Ives to look at statues, while Charles, Kormendi, and the miserable girl, thick as thieves, were all talking about the pig, and making plans for more and more pigs.

Eleanor laid Magda's two books on a shelf and began moving towards the door.

"Don't go!" Magda exclaimed, abandoning a discussion about arrangements with Claire. "Stay while I tell you what I have been doing today."

"I'm afraid I really mustn't, I have all my notes to write up." Eleanor gave a tolerant glance at the idlers, and jerked open the front door which, since Kormendi had fixed it, fitted tighter than a bulkhead. In all but the worst weather, consequently, it was left open. A blast of rain and wind whooped in; during the few minutes she had spent at the cottage the weather had worsened.

"You can't go out in that!" several officious voices cried.

It was plain that Eleanor would be a fool if she did; the rain drove down with a fury that could hardly last; already the little stream outside the cottage was in spate, pouring over the stone-slab bridge and drowning part of the front garden.

"Will not last long," Kormendi said, moving up behind her to assess the storm.

Eleanor stood impatiently drumming her gloved fingers against the doorpost. Pink lightning flickered garishly against a black sky; in the foreground the viaduct shone as if carved from pale cheese; she heard a mutter of thunder.

Nin, whose attitude to bad weather was wholly irrational, would be having hysterics up at the house if someone did not arrive soon to keep her company.

Meanwhile Charles and the girl Tuesday had started to play silly games with a breadknife, spinning it on top of a box and telling fortunes.

"How many piglets your sow is going to have—eleven, twelve, thirteen. She'll have thirteen, Mat!" the girl called as the knife spun to a standstill.

"Is unlucky number; one will have to be roasted," Kormendi said cheerfully.

"Let's see how soon she's due." Tuesday spun the knife again. "This week, next week, sometime, never. This week, next week, Charles!"

"We used to play that game at my first school." Magda was suddenly invested by one of her moods of elephantine gaiety. Leaning past Tuesday she spun the knife. "We used to play, First to die, first to be married, cleverest, stupidest, prettiest, plainest."

The knife whirled, snatching pink gleams from the tiny window. Tuesday looked uneasy, Eleanor noticed; moving away from Charles she picked up the jug of wine and went round the room filling people's cups and jars.

As the knife dwindled to a rest, pointing at Maggie, there came a phenomenally loud crash of thunder, almost directly overhead. Everybody gasped and laughed; Charles said, "I thought they'd got us that time."

"Oh lord," Eleanor sighed, "Nin will be having conniptions. I ought to try and get to her."

"Don't be crazy," Charles said. "She wouldn't want you to turn up half drowned. Relax for five minutes, can't you? What was that spin supposed to prophesy, Maggie?"

His tone with Magda was teasing, brotherly; how on earth had they come to be on such affectionate terms, Eleanor wondered.

"Cleverest, of course," Tuesday said quickly. "Maggie's certainly that."

Eleanor smiled her little, stretched smile. Tuesday was spinning the knife again.

"Never mind the cleverest," she said, "let's find out who's the happiest."

Another peal of thunder rocked the cottage; as it died, Aunt Julia could be heard saying detachedly,

"In my young days—knife blades—were supposed—to draw down lightning."

"Do you think the cottage will be struck?" Claire sounded sceptical.

"Mass cremation would be a tidy finish," John muttered.

"Some of us, who have work to do, would prefer to stay alive," Eleanor said lightly.

The knife whirled to a stop, its blade aimed at Charles.

"Charles, you're the happiest."

"Of course I am," said Charles. Avoiding his sister's eye he smiled at Tuesday. "Why wouldn't I be? I have the loveliest house in Cornwall, and not a care in the world."

"Well, make the most of your lovely cosy cocoon then, you bloody Mishkin!" John Fitzroy exclaimed with the sudden violence of extreme exasperation. "Not a care in the world! Christ! Evolution must have taken a short step from the ostrich to you, or else you've a skin like foam rubber!"

Charles said, "What do you mean?" He spoke simply, unperturbed, unaware, it seemed, of the impatient hostility in John's voice and the sudden tension it had caused in everybody else.

John stood, staggering, drained the wine-jar in his hand, and placed it with care on the dresser. He said, "If you're really so thick that you don't see what's brewing, it's certainly not my business to wake the fatted dog. Pardon me, I mean the sleeping calf, of course." He began to make his way towards the door, adding with savage irony, "I daresay calf love is better than no bed, but it's the golden calf that lays the cockatrice's egg *isn't it*, Dr Foley?" Coming face to face with Eleanor by the door he gave her a mirthless grin.

"I'm afraid I haven't the faintest idea what you're talking about," she said, stepping back sharply so that he gave the appearance of pushing her out of the way. He lurched out into the rain, splashed heedlessly through the ford, and was soon out of sight.

"Oh, poor John," Tuesday said, distressed.

"Poor? Poor manners, I'd have said," Eleanor corrected coldly. "Why on earth you have such friends, Magda—however! It seems to be slacking a little and I really must go and do some work. How about you, Charles?"

But Charles said that he would stay at the cottage until it was safe for Aunt Julia to cross the bridge, and as Eleanor left she heard them all beginning to make up limericks.

Like a lot of children, she thought, frowning, as she hurried up the hill. Giggling, insubordinate children, ready to poke spiteful fun, no doubt, as soon as one's back was turned.

XVII

IF THERE WERE a Ship Cult in England I'd join it. I'm a born expecter—I seem to spend my life waiting for occasions, for arrivals, for news, for results, for reactions, for something to happen. In Cornwall, since there was nothing specific to wait for I found myself hoping for letters. It wasn't that I was discontented with my lot or bored; probably, I suppose, that tranquil cruising, idling period was or will be the happiest time of my life; it's just that I have this inbred craving for something to *come*; the sail over the horizon, the gift-bearing god.

So I used to wait for the postman, whose name was Fred; I can still remember every crag of his kind face, the way he rolled his trousers under the bicycle clips, and how he used to bring us lettuce and blackcurrants and great bunches of rhubarb, which we'd swap for watercress and parsley and green gooseberries. He was like a coastal trader, tacking along on his bike from one port to the next with these articles of barter. I'd see him come over our horizon at about half past eleven, then there'd be an interval as he went down a hidden hill along a bridle-path; then suddenly he'd spin round the high-banked corner of the lane, ringing his bell like mad to warn the unpredictable milk-lorry which turned at the bottom of our hill and then used it as a sort of launching-ramp to get up speed.

Sometimes Fred passed right by and those days were black and sunken like mute keys or decayed teeth; I felt a personal sense of grievance as if he'd slapped or slighted me; and I think, bless him, he came to realise how much store I set by his calls because he took to stopping for a chat even if he hadn't any mail for me or library books for Maggie. And then I felt at least he'd done his best for us.

On the morning that I'm thinking of he stopped and scuffled in his satchel while I waited breathlessly, and fished out a letter for me in my mother's usual thin grey foreign envelope and purple typing. I hear from her so rarely that her letters have scarcity value even though in general they consist of half a dozen lines asking why I haven't written for so long, sent from Naxos or Mozambique or Monomoy, seldom with complete address, therefore impossible to answer. I have a sheaf of them, almost identical, saved over ten years or so. Still, it's always agreeable to feel one has a relative, and I took this envelope with the usual joy, thanked Fred, and asked him about his dermatitis (it was better, that day) and gave him half a dozen paperbacks that I'd read and Maggie wouldn't. They went down well because he was a Chandler fan, so we had some literary talk and then he went stomping off up the hill to deliver medical journals to Eleanor and a lot of brochures to Charles, who had a passion for buying electric gadgets.

I took another look at my letter wondering what had seemed odd about it at first glance, and realised that contrary to custom the stamp on it was not black, foreign, or three-cornered with camel, but a common English one; the postmark was London. Mother was in England.

I started counting on my fingers, trying to remember when I had last seen her, gave up, and opened the envelope. Out fell a cheque for two hundred pounds. It nearly glided into the stream (I was standing on the little stone-slab bridge in front of the cottage) but I grabbed it and tucked it into my jeans pocket.

Darling Aulis, Mother said—she is about the only person who uses my real name—*here I am, as you see, only to find that you have left London for some damp (no doubt) and inaccessible corner of the country. Come back, come back! I shall be here only till the 13th and must of course see you. Vanessa. PS The Oppenheimer Award amounted to £10,000, so here is some pocket money.*

Mother, who is half French, has an immense vocabulary, and fluent Greek, and no imagination, so about twenty years ago she very sensibly turned her talents to translation, cornering the rights in a ponderous nineteenth-century Greek novelist called

Vassiliaides. He wrote about thirty books which she is slowly working through and as it turns out that his symbolism and mysticism and doomed view of life are just to the contemporary taste, she is on to a good thing and keeps winning tremendous literary prizes with her translations; some of them have been turned into plays (horrid dull watching they are too), others have been televised, and every year Vanessa scoops in more and more honorary degrees from far-flung universities like Athens, Ill., and Potakohua. If I haven't mentioned her much up to now it can easily be seen why: travelling round as she always has done even when married to my father (who was an archaeologist and died) she has hardly had any opportunity to come in contact with me or supply those things that they always expect in biographies and curricula vitae: background and influence Such background as I have lies too far back.

It was on the rebound from not seeing Vanessa at that publisher's party after a four-year gap that I took up with Maggie; all very explicable.

So naturally I was delighted to receive this maternal bombshell; a Happening indeed, no dug-out canoe but a full-rigged schooner. I went in to where Maggie was scribbling among toppling textbooks and boiling coffee in a cosy womb-corner.

"Look!" I said dropping the cheque in front of her. It took her a moment to detach herself from the thyroid gland but when she did her eyes lit up.

"Marvellous! But that's marvellous! Now we shall be able to stay down here at least till I've finished working on this paper. Two hundred! We can live on that for months."

"I shall need a little of it to get up to London," I said. "Mother's there now and wants to see me."

"Well of course you must have a little," said Maggie. She is not unreasonable. "It's very convenient that you are going; I'll give you a list of books to get for me at Foyles. Perhaps your mother will give you some more money when you meet."

"She might, at that; she seems to be very rich. It'll be fun seeing her."

I hadn't thought much about Mother till that moment, I'd been too occupied with the thought of Maggie's pleasure, but now I began to look forward to our reunion. I'd worked out that it was nearly six years since we'd met, time for me to have changed a lot, grown up really. Mother wouldn't have changed, I was sure, she was always the same: a little, brown, elegant monkey with wispy dark hair and huge mournful violet eyes (mournful, I hasten to add, only with a monkey's uncomprehending grief, actually Vanessa hasn't a mournful atom in her, the essential quality of her is that she is such fun to be with).

"This is a great relief, I must say," Maggie went on comfortably. "Eleanor keeps working on me to persuade me to start some thyroid clinic in Truro; I am sure it is just her kindness, trying to find me a paid occupation down here. I should hate to take that kind of money."

I had heard all about the projected clinic, and formed the opinion that this wasn't so much altruism on Aspic's part as a wish to keep Maggie near her for company. It was becoming more and more embarrassing, too, as she tried various possible sources of revenue; there had been a blazing row with her old aunt, I gathered, who wasn't prepared to part with any cash, and now Eleanor was going the rounds of wealthy connections, and the end of it, I could see, would be that after she had demeaned herself to such an unaccustomed degree she'd feel Maggie was in honour bound to come in on the project. I wasn't sure Maggie would feel it that way, though; old Maggie has a fine vein of tough realism where her work is concerned.

Anyway the two hundred pounds certainly eased our lot; we needn't accept charity and could even pay some rent. The thought of Aspic's annoyance at this stroke of luck gave me a warm tickle of malice and I began to make joyful plans for my trip to London. Charles's friend Claire wanted to drive up some time soon, I knew; she had sublet her flat and it was giving trouble. I thought I might hitch a lift with her.

"We must celebrate!" said Maggie, who was slowly notching herself up into top gear. "We must give a party!"

"Oh, no, really, Maggie! Besides, there isn't room in the cottage." I was daunted by the very idea. Maggie at parties is frightening; she hardly ever attends one but when she does it is funny and piteous and horrific and embarrassing, like a maniac child or a dancing bear; she throws herself into them with dread abandon, never seeing that she has outdistanced everybody else. I suppose only with-it or witty or decorative people should go to parties; for her age Maggie is more without-it than anybody I have ever known.

"Perhaps not," she said, brought back to reality. "Then we must go out and celebrate. Isn't there a circus in the neighbourhood? Let's take everybody tonight."

"Good heavens," I said weakly. "Do you think they'd enjoy it?"

"Certainly they will. Everybody enjoys a circus."

It was astonishing the force that Maggie could command when she was doing what she conceived to be her social duty; I was pretty sure that Charles and Eleanor and John all loathed the very smell of a circus, but she soon had them organised into this fearful excursion, not to mention Charles's friend Claire and the three protégés; she would have been pleased to include old Miss Foley too, but Miss Foley had strong views about cruelty to animals and roundly declared that nothing would persuade her. It was an unwieldy party enough : we all went off in two cars like a school outing. Eleanor drove Maggie and John and me; Maggie and Eleanor sat in front talking nonstop about the thyroid gland while John and I scowled silently at one another in the back. John had been in a black mood for days, he fell easily into these deep depressions when the merest risk of human contact rasped him to screaming point. I wasn't surprised when, as soon as we reached the floodlit circus field, he left us and rapidly made off into Lanrith.

"Where's John gone?" Maggie said, turning from her absorbed discussion, anxious as a mother partridge over an errant fledgling.

"Cigarettes," I improvised quickly. "He said not to wait, he wouldn't be long."

Luckily at that moment Claire's Jaguar arrived with the rest of the party, and we shuffled towards the entrance, weaving into the familiar embarrassment about paying—"Let me!" "No, please, let me, I *want* some change!" which Maggie quelled firmly by getting the most expensive tickets for the whole bunch. She would have made a beautiful eighteenth-century nabob, except that she was rather too intelligent.

In we went. There was the usual dismal smell of hot bodies and peppermints and animals and sawdust. Our seats were the best all right : bang on the ring. Most of the tiers behind us were empty—it seemed all too plain that this was a small and second-rate circus; the opposite ringside seats were taken by a group of people who, even to my unaccustomed eyes, appeared stranger than the average Cornish crowd. Most of them stared dully straight ahead without taking the smallest interest in their surroundings; a few were unnaturally excited.

"Who the devil can they be?" Charles said. Claire, who

always knew everything, told him they were favoured patients from the local mental hospital. This seemed a bad omen for our evening—not that I begrudged the poor dears their treat, but even in the most roseate circumstances it would have been difficult to let joy be unconfined with their vacant, uncaring faces looking past us to Nirvana.

I didn't try very hard. I was sitting between Charles and the boy called Chad, the fair one, and I had my own problems. In the last few days I had felt growing and growing in me a terrifying consciousness of Charles; like a magnet or a geiger counter I always knew his exact whereabouts, and if we were together I had the impression that I echoed all his physical feelings, breathed with him, vibrated with his dicey heart, shared his hungers and fatigues and enthusiasms. Coupled to this, bad enough in itself, was the nerve-racking fact that I hadn't the faintest notion what he was thinking about—if he thought at all; the whole situation was more than I could cope with, which was another reason why I was glad to be bound for London, a safe insulated distance away. I ought to have been immune to Charles and I couldn't understand why I wasn't; I couldn't understand anything.

So I turned my shoulder from him, feeling as if I were leaning casually against a sign that said "Danger, 120,000 volts" and instead talked to gentle, sensitive Chad, who had calloused ploughboy's hands and a compassionate mouth and the frightened eyes of a schizo. It turned out we knew people in common at a London art school but I soon saw that he loathed that sort of conversation, so instead we discussed cooking and stately homes. He was so well-informed on both topics that we were almost halfway through the circus before it occurred to either of us to look at the ring; the dead silence from the audience, and the whip-cracking and cursing finally caught our attention.

There was a man with a leopard. We gathered he wanted it to jump through a hoop held over a sort of trough from which blue flames spouted. The leopard didn't want to, however; it had had enough. I didn't blame it. The trainer was repulsive : fat and weaselly and jowly and pale with rage. Each time the leopard refused he poured out curses as if he really loathed it, and slashed at it with his whip. My sympathies were all on the side of the leopard, which was holding its own pretty well, snarling and spitting and hissing with flattened ears; it made several attempts to tear chunks off him, but unavailingly because his reach with the whip was far longer.

At last even from that apathetic audience there were some cries of "Shame!" I noticed that several of them came from Eleanor who seemed very angry over the leopard's treatment; I was interested to see that something could shake her loose from her prefectorial calm.

The ringmaster was standing not far from Eleanor; when a particularly vicious slash by the trainer drew a sort of yell from the leopard she jumped up, leaned over the rail, and said something quick and sharp in his ear. He demurred, shrugging, with a patronising smile, but it was soon wiped from his face; I think she pulled her medical authority and every other stop from the RSPCA to the House of Lords. She had in any case a fairly formidable presence; in that black-and-gold-spotted silk raincoat and orange scarf she might have been own cousin to the leopard itself.

So the ringmaster blew an admonishing whistle and the trainer furiously drove his unco-operative charge back between the barriers of steel netting to its cage. Just before he slammed the door it made a sideways darting rush, swiped with a clever paw, and drew a fistful of blood from the man's white-breeched leg; although satisfying, I could see this was not really good policy on the part of the leopard. Reprisals were bound to follow, specially after the fiasco of the act. The door clanged shut at last and the cage was wheeled out. Some comic monkeys came in, and some clowns.

"I'm not going to be able to stand this," said Chad. "I'll wait outside."

Patrick and Kuniang seemed to be enjoying the circus with uninhibited, extrovert enthusiasm. Feeling sorry for Chad, who looked more than commonly lost, I said,

"I'll come with you. I don't like it above half myself."

We slipped out, unobserved, I hoped.

Outside Chad began to cry. "It's the hate," he gasped. "The hate and disgust, like horrible blowholes piercing right down to what's underneath. If we stay, the whole surface may crack open."

"All right, my dear, take it easy," I said. "We won't stay, we'll wander quietly down the town and have a hot coffee and a hamburger."

114

I hadn't eaten for god knows how many hours and I daresay Chad hadn't; he was thin as a knitting needle.

"Try to stop crying," I suggested. "It only tires you out and doesn't do any good."

He gulped and shook a while longer but gradually drew himself together as we walked slowly along, and gave me a cautious, sideways, measuring look.

"I shouldn't have said what I did," he remarked coldly after a time.

"About the surface? Why?"

To this he made no answer, but hunched his shoulders forward till they nearly met under his chin, and walked on as if the furies were after him. I said almost without thinking, the words just came out,

"Oh, Chad. Poor Chad. Will you be punished for telling me?"

There was such desperation in the look he gave me that I was sorry I had spoken. I added quickly,

"Never mind. Don't say any more. Tell me about Nonesuch, you were just starting to when all the trouble began."

That helped, for the time, anyway; he pulled his surface together and gave me a very intelligent and perfectly normal lecture about sixteenth-century great houses which lasted until we found a coffee stall. I had a little money on me luckily.

"Would you like some soup?"

"Soup?" he said vaguely as if he had never heard the word. "Oh, soup, yes." After the soup we felt better—at least I did, it was impossible to guess what Chad felt—and turned back, in case the circus had finished. On the way up the hill we overtook an unsteady figure which turned out to be John.

"Weren't you at the circus?" he said, rather puzzled.

"We sneaked out. It was too painful."

"I could have told you it would be."

"Well," I said crossly, "I wish you had thrown in your influence at an earlier stage to dissuade Maggie from the idea."

He stopped in the road and said with careful articulation, "Look, Tuesday, don't argue with me, like a good girl, will you? I'm just not in the mood for it now."

"Okay, John."

We walked on in jagged non-communication, three abreast but as separate as the components of Orion's belt, and were presently picked up by the headlights of Eleanor's car as it nosed out of the circus field.

Nobody spoke on the ride home.

In Lanrith we stopped to exchange Chad for Charles and called goodnights to Claire's carload; as soon as we reached Watertown John leapt out of the car and strode away fast, out of the headlights down in the direction of the river.

I could feel that Eleanor was bursting with unspoken criticism, to be kept for a private inquest with Maggie next day, no doubt. She and Charles said polite thanks and disappeared into their warm and well-lit house where old Nin was almost certainly sitting up for them with sandwiches and Ovaltine.

Maggie and I walked to the cottage in silence.

"Well!" she said heavily, just when I was beginning to hope that the silence might last till I could escape to bed. "That was a pretty piece of behaviour I must say! Walking out in the middle of the circus with that beatnik boy, going to a pub with John—you might at least have the decency to help make my party a success. But no, as soon as there's a chance, off you go with the first male you can grab."

"Chad isn't a male," I said, but hopelessly, "he's a child, and a badly disturbed child at that. You of all people ought to recognise a schizo when you see one. I went out with him because the circus was more than he could bear; he was coming apart. And we didn't go to a pub."

"I suppose you just leaned against a wall in a dark alley," Maggie said furiously.

"Oh, for god's sake, Maggie!"

She started a tirade against my wanton ways and because this time it was undeserved I felt no particular resentment but just a dispirited wish that I could dam the flow. There I hung, like a pingpong ball on top of a jet of water, defenceless against her force; it did seem silly. By degrees I began to pity her because her party had been a failure (worse than I knew, I heard later; after the show Eleanor had gone round and upset everyone by making a scene about the disgraceful conditions in which the animals were kept).

"Look, Maggie," I said in a pause when she had run down and was re-charging, "honestly you're barking up the wrong tree. I'm just not *interested* in John or Chad. If you really—"

Then I stopped and started again.

"Hell, you're supposed to be John's friend. If you'd lifted your nose out of your books long enough to look at him in the last four or five days you'd know that he's in a very bad way just now, utterly depressed. That's why he went off to a pub. As for me, he doesn't give a damn if I live or die. And I can tell you," I went on, working myself up, "if I were you I'd be worried stiff about him; instead of ripping into me for things I haven't done, you'd be better occupied looking for John to make sure he hasn't chucked himself in the river."

"Oh, rubbish," Maggie said. I noticed—as I always do when I'm annoyed with her—that Maggie's English has the inflections of over fifty years ago, she must have learnt it from some teacher who migrated to Europe before World War I. She added after a pause, more doubtfully,

"Do you really think so?"

"Damn it, Maggie, you're the doctor round here. Can't you see what's under your nose?"

"Very well," she said, "in that case we must go and look for him."

To my amusement she put a kettle on the stove. "Like having a baby," I suggested, but she said sharply, "If this is serious, do not make a joke of it." We took torches and went out into the starlit, tree-smelling night. The lights of Watertown were out; godly repose reigned up there.

"Where do we go?" said Maggie. She had never yet been down to the river. I showed her the way in silence. Short-sighted at all times, she had practically no night vision and fumbled along, half a step behind me, grabbing at my arm for support when she tripped over roots or into ruts. She detested the country really because she hadn't the physical nimbleness to cope with its requirements and because there was such a lot of it; when we reached the stone-walled landing-stage where I had stood with Charles she stopped and said plaintively, "How much farther do we have to go?"

"It depends on where John has got to, doesn't it? We've the whole of Cornwall to look in."

Maggie was discouraged. "I shall sit on this wall and shout for him," she said. "And if he doesn't answer I shall go back to the cottage and do some work."

"Don't shout."

"Why not?"

I couldn't explain. The great rift of sky overhead, full of stars, hung silent between the black wooded valley-sides; the river slid past like oil, without a ripple. If we had the valley to ourselves I didn't want to spoil it with noise. If there were other people I didn't want to know.

Maggie, however, threw back her head and let out a yodel, which is one of her accomplishments that I can't bear. There is something embarrassingly unrestrained about yodelling.

"Yodelay-ay! John! Can you hear me?"

His voice came from somewhere quite close, almost under our feet.

"What do you want?"

I nearly shot out of my skin.

"John! Where the devil are you?"

"I'm here," he said. There was the hollow plock-splash of a boat rocking on water and his shape materialised in the dimness under the wall as he pulled himself towards us; he was sitting in Charles's dinghy.

"For heaven's sake! What are you doing there? Why didn't you call out when you heard us?"

"I hoped you'd go away again. What do you want?"

"We were worried about you," Maggie said. "You should have told us where you were going."

She sounded so like a mother scolding a small boy that John burst out laughing.

"Oh, Maggie!" he said affectionately. "You get on with your work of genius. Find a cure for whatever it is. Never mind about me."

"It's not a case of curing—" she began to correct him, when he said, "Hush—"

We listened. Somebody was coming our way, down the path from Lanrith—two people in fact, crunching over twigs, breaking through bushes, sometimes bursting into song. Bits of songs collided in discord and meandered apart again; one voice was young, male, and tenor, the other thin, eldritch, cracked, and in no register whatever; still, the effect was somehow rather endearing.

"What is it?" Maggie asked, peering. She isn't deaf, but her hearing is not a hundred per cent; sometimes I think nature deliberately stinted on Maggie's externals so as to make her concentrate more on her true function.

"Quiet!" John said.

Another little spate of singing floated our way, with bits of different songs in it; one of the voices was energetically waltzing Matilda while the cracked one contested with some unpolished piece about girls in calico drawers.

118

"Lay off it, you old cuckoo, you've got the wrong tune."

"Why should I lay off, it's you that's wrong, not me!"

"Peter Lannick!" I breathed in Maggie's ear. "Come along, he'd hate to know we'd heard them. That must be his mother."

Maggie ignored my tug on her arm. "Who's Peter Lannick?"

One of the two figures fell down and was hauled up by the other.

"Come on, get up on your old pins, you needn't think *I'm* going to carry you all the way back to Acacia Cottages. Time you were in your bed."

"Bugger my bed," the other voice said plaintively. "It beant comfortable. Full of crumbs, 'tis."

"Who's fault's that? Crumbs or not, it's time you were in it. Come along, I've got to be on the job tomorrow at seven. Stir your stumps, you old soak."

"That's no way to speak to your own mother! You'm cruel, that's what you be, cruel! I'll be telling your dad about you, when I see'm in heaven. Proper shocked, he'll be."

"Oh, for Christ's sake—!" Peter Lannick said, half laughing half exasperated. Then Maggie switched the torch on and he started violently.

"Who the hell's that?" His voice turned harsh with shock and suspicion; in the torchlight the frowning, angry, handsome lines of his face were grotesquely lengthened so that he looked like a fallen angel.

"Hullo, Peter," I said lamely. "It's us, from the cottage. We came for a walk.—*Maggie, will you please put the light out?*" I muttered, but its beam had already found Mrs Lannick in all her startling deshabille. She was dignified with it, though: an old, moulting camel.

Maggie, never one for social nuances, suddenly took it into her head to try and put the Lannicks at ease, adopting what she thought was the correct manner for the English countryside, a sort of huntin' and shootin' idiom.

"You live in a beautiful part of England, Mrs Lannick."

"Who's she and who's she think she's talking to?" Mrs Lannick grumbled, peering through her elflocks.

"It's the people from Watertown Cottage, Mum." I knew that would be no recommendation; a violent mutual dislike had grown between Peter and the Foleys because of Eleanor's view that Mrs Lannick should be in a home; Eleanor had also made her views on this matter known to Mr Rowse, whose patience was already tried pretty high by the amount of time Peter was absent.

Maggie's misplaced overtures were cut short by Peter snapping "Goodnight" over his shoulder as he steered his mother along the home track with a mixture of shove, drag, and carry; I saw that her legs were trailing backwards along the ground before I managed to locate the torch in Maggie's hand and switch it off.

John had vanished at the beginning of the encounter and when we got back to the cottage we found him in the kitchen reading the *New Statesman* as if his life depended on it, while the room filled with steam from the boiling kettle.

XVIII

CHARLES WAS IN the orchard with Tuesday when Claire waved from the road gate, opened it, and came climbing towards them up the steep slope.

"Hi!" she called. "Isn't it hot! I've brought you the staples you ordered from Whites."

"Thanks, Claire! Come and see our pig-fold."

They had enclosed an irregular bit of ground between the trees with the electric fence and Bland the pig was now ruminatively taking stock of her new territory.

"Very nice."

"I don't like that ticking noise it makes, though," Tuesday said. "It's like the sound track in a psycho film; puts me in mind of somebody creeping along with a knife."

"You have an overstimulated imagination," Charles told her.

"Can the pig really not get past that wire?"

"She could perfectly well if she tried but she's been conditioned to electric wire ever since she was a weanling and had a tender sensitive skin."

"Does it give much of a shock?"

"Very little. Try."

"No thank you," Claire said drily. "You mightn't believe it but I've still got a tender sensitive skin."

They were still laughing at her when Peter Lannick passed by, taking a shortcut across the orchard to where the rest of the builders' men were assembling for their lunch-break. He gave them a brief glance; Claire was vaguely surprised by the look of dislike, almost hate, in his black eyes; then she remembered that, acting on Eleanor's advice, Miss Foley had paid him off and no longer employed him in her garden. He had become too unreliable, she told him; but he would be more likely to put the blame on Eleanor, or on Claire for having supplanted him.

"Come and have some lunch," Charles invited. Claire refused, but was persuaded to stay for a glass of cider.

"Have you any commissions for me in London?" she asked. "That was really what I came to find out. And can you be ready at eight tomorrow morning, Tuesday?"

While they were making arrangements for the journey Charles strolled on to pick a handful of narcissus for Nin's kitchen. They grew in clumps everywhere through the orchard—profuse, starry, sharply fragrant. Those in the middle of the orchard were beginning to brown, but there were still fresh buds on the shaded bank below the row of cypresses. It's more like a Mediterranean landscape than an English one, Charles thought, moving slowly towards the gate, picking as he went, the flowers and the steep hill, the black trees and the white house.

He came to a sudden stop. He had heard Tuesday's name.

". . . Proper little bitch," the voice said. "Met that sort before; dead spit of a bint I had in Marseilles once. Easy as butter one minute, and slap your face for nothing the next."

Charles stood motionless by the gate. His face whitened with shock.

"Ah, come on now, Peter," someone said sceptically—the men were eating their lunch seated on a pile of planks and empty Snowcem tins at the side of the road, just beyond the gate, "how do you know she's so easy?"

"How do I know? I'm telling you. Because I do. Do you know what she did?"

Charles felt a presence at his back; without turning he knew that someone had come up and stood silently close behind him.

"I was fishing the other morning from the Town Quay," Peter Lannick went on, having paused for effect, "early it was, nobody about, and she come along, stops for a chat, and then, calm as you please, she up and kiss me. What d'you make of that, then?"

There was a roar of derisive, half-incredulous laughter from the other men.

"Fancies you, do she, Peter? Did she ask you home with her?

When's the knot going to be spliced? Whyn't you tell us a proper fishing story while you'm at it, boy?"

" 'Tis the gospel truth!" Peter Lannick repeated angrily. "Sure as I'm standing here she kissed me!"

"Do I gather you're talking about me?" said Tuesday. She walked past Charles, opened the gate, and faced the circle of men. There was an audible gasp from someone, and a voice muttered, "Blimey. Now for trouble."

"Are you telling them I kissed you?" Tuesday asked Peter. He was silent. He had turned a dusky red and was staring at the ground but as she confronted him he slowly lifted his black eyes and returned her straight gaze with a look of malignant intensity.

"That's what he *said*," someone murmured. Charles glanced at the other men, who seemed put out and embarrassed. It was plain that none of them had much sympathy for Peter.

"Well it was the truth!" Tuesday said suddenly. "I kissed him because he'd told me about his troubles and I felt sorry for him, because he looked miserable and I wanted to cheer him up. But fair's fair—since he's chosen to brag about it, I suppose I'd better kiss you all round. You're not the only apple on the tree, Peter Lannick!"

And taking them all by surprise she walked lightly from man to man round the group, giving them a kiss apiece with an exaggerated musical-comedy flourish. A shout of laughter went up and the men looked slyly at Peter, whose knuckles were clenched white with suppressed feelings. "Now," Tuesday said to him—she was breathless and rather flushed—"have you got it into your thick head that so far as I am concerned a kiss means friendliness and nothing more? Have you?"

"Yes," he muttered, hating her.

"That's all right, then. Goodbye!" she called to the others, and swung off quickly down the hill towards the cottage.

"Well, by damn!" some of the men said.

"Back to work!" Kormendi called sharply. "Is five minutes past time already."

The group scattered in selfconscious haste. Only Peter Lannick was left, kicking angrily at a clod of earth on the bank. Kormendi said something to him in an undertone, took his arm, and hurried him off up the hill. Charles then realised for the first time that Eleanor and Maggie had been spectators of the scene; they must have come through a little lych-gate from the walled kitchen garden and were standing on the other side of the road—like a pair of Erinnyes, Charles thought angrily; why did they always have to be on the spot when anything went wrong, flapping their black wings? Then he was vaguely puzzled at his own feelings.

"Well! What a little baggage!" Eleanor remarked distastefully. "Really, Magda, I wonder why you put up with her."

Maggie said heavily, "I feel responsible for her. But perhaps it is as well she is going back to London for a few days."

"I should advise her to stay there and not come back."

"Oh no! She is better with me. On her own I think she would run into trouble."

"She'll be in trouble soon wherever she is if she continues to behave like this."

Tired of their gloomy chorus Charles, who was still inside the orchard gate, turned and went back the way he had come. There was another gate beyond the cypresses which led down to a cascading little stream, and here he found Claire, thoughtfully picking watercress.

"Your Aunt Julia has told me about putting this stuff into pasties," she greeted him cheerfully. "Twice the flavour, it's supposed to give them."

She looked up with a shrewd eye at Charles and added, "Is poor Tuesday going to get a spanking?"

He burst out laughing. "I shouldn't wonder! Maggie looked ready to murder her."

"Really in the circumstances I thought Tuesday managed pretty well."

"Yes, didn't she?" he said, warming to Claire.

"Of course she was a fool to have anything to do with Peter Lannick in the first place. He's a no-good, that boy; like an animal with a bad disposition, ready to lash out at anything. But she's too young to have good judgment; she just felt sorry for him."

"I'm surprised you think so poorly of Peter; you generally seem to find some good in the blackest sheep."

"He's weak," Claire said impatiently. "And he's a malingerer; he pretends to have migraines so as to get off work."

"He really does get them," Charles objected. "I don't like the boy, but I've seen him when he was obviously in torture; white as my shirt and could hardly keep his eyes focused."

"But old Rowse told me he often pretends a migraine because

he wants to get home and see what his mother's up to. Rowse turns a blind eye, three times out of four, because he's sorry for them, but I feel that's untidy behaviour, not a proper solution."

"Now you sound like Eleanor," Charles said gently. "You haven't quite adjusted to Cornish life yet, I'm afraid. Solutions down here are mostly a bit *comme çi, comme ça*."

"That's very sharp of you, my dear Charles," Claire said, smiling at him affectionately. "Also out of character! You and Eleanor certainly are the most dissimilar brother and sister I've ever met. It's surprising you get on at all."

"Oh, we've always got on all right," Charles said vaguely. But then, thinking of Eleanor and Maggie, still absorbed in their duet of denunciation higher up the hill, he did, for a moment, participate in Claire's surprise.

XIX

AFTER I'D LEFT the group of men I ran off down the hill to the cottage. But when I reached the stone-slab bridge among the mimulus and watercress I suddenly thought: no. Maggie will be after me, wanting to have it all out—as if you *could* have out any bygone action, like a tooth—and what can I say to her? I'm not ready for another commination scene.

So I went on past the cottage and took the river path; instead of turning left towards Lanrith I turned right through woods and followed the west bank of the river down towards the sea. These woods were neglected and the path wasn't much used, evidently; it was undrained and boggy, cluttered with fallen branches; my passage was accompanied all the way by the satisfying snap and scrunch of dead twigs as I trod them into the oozy ground. Some birds got up off the river shallows and flapped away protesting with long mournful cries. Soon I had to slow down because there were so many obstacles; you can't keep up a furious pace when you have to creep under damp black entanglements of leaning, half-dead trees, or skirt gingerly round patches of treacherous ground. The mud had that sinister yeasty, foamy crust on it which generally means it is at least three feet deep. And a blue, phosphorescent shine. There were pale, liverish fungi sprouting from the sodden black bark on fallen branches. John had pointed out these things to me before and I noticed them now, but with less than half my mind. The other half was still racing, moving twice as fast as I could walk, but not getting anywhere.

Here I was, in another predicament, and I had no doubt Maggie would say it was all due to my licentious, libidinous, man-chasing habits, but in fact I felt that my trigger-action had been innocent enough; hell, what are you to do when you behave one way, in all good faith, and the person on the receiving end takes it in the wrong spirit and volleys back something quite different? Why blame me?

Suddenly I felt disgusted with *females*—with their devious, manipulating, undercover approach to life, the way they read nonexistent meanings into actions, and take advantage, and put pressure, and endlessly confer and report and distort. No doubt they were at it now—I had seen Maggie and Eleanor on the far side of the road as I left. Peter Lannick's handsome miserable face swam into my mind and I thought, for the purpose of this argument he's an honorary female, he's certainly indirect enough in his approach, a sidewinder if ever there was one. Yes, like a snake, with a snake's inexpressive eyes.

I was pleased with this discovered resemblance between Peter Lannick and a snake, so I went on round the circle of my acquaintance, looking for more parallels. Charles was a deer, with his thin face and soft brown hair and honest, puzzled eyes; Aspic, cold and self-assured and scheming and sleek—what was she like? Some elegant, deadly fish, perhaps, a pike or a sword-fish. John had a gorilla's shambling, sorrowful, intelligent strength; and Maggie—where could I put Maggie? The more I thought about Maggie, the more she eluded this sort of simple definition; uncouth she might be, maddening, selfish, demand-ing, unreasonable, but she was a human being through and through, the world must benefit from her presence in it. Per-haps she is a saint, I thought gloomily, jumping over a small tributary stream that crossed the path, and landing ankle-deep in squelch; saints are proverbially hard to live with. Saints and females; the world would be an easier place without them.

I found myself longing for the company of Wal. He was so straightforward and direct in his wants : sex, food, a gay time, in that order. As soon as one need was satisfied, he went on to the next, then back to the beginning again. There was nothing complicated about my relationship with him, it was comfortable, seemed to have a natural virtue like being in the sun; we were at ease together, knowing that each could supply what the other wanted. I had been out with him, unknown to Maggie, half a dozen times before I came to Cornwall, and felt hardly any guilt about deceiving her because the pattern each time was so innocently identical : bed, first, in his colonel's flat in Curzon Street (a most extraordinary place; the bed was circular and the floor covered in fur three inches deep; I assumed the colonel had a private income, from oil perhaps). After bed we went out for a meal, Lyons' Corner House was Wal's preference, not that he begrudged the money for more expensive places, but he said snooty eating-joints gave him a pain in the gut. Then a cheerful play, none of your morbid problem stuff; then back to the flat for more bed. As with food, so with sex, Wal's tastes were simple; he liked it plain but good. No fancy trimmings, no fancy postures, just one dish and plenty of it. He was delighted with me and told me often that I was a grade-A pitcher, a real bit of crackling, as most as a mocking-bird. I adored Wal's use of the word most; it made me grin, now, walking along in the bog, to think of it. You really are most, he would mutter, taking a mouthful of hair and ear, getting a purchase round my neck with one arm and my knees with the other.

More most still, Wal? More most than anyone else you've met?

Don't distract me, honey.

He was delighted with my rapidly acquired proficiency in bed and I was delighted too; always diffident about my ability to learn anything new, I had been relieved to find that here, if nowhere else, I seemed to have a natural talent. Or so Wal told me and I believed him; he seemed to know what he was talking about. That was what I liked about our association; it was all here and now; cards on the table. He had even asked me to marry him, and promised to fix me up a little nest, so as to get me out of Maggie's orbit. I felt tender now at the thought of that little nest, but I had been evasive at the time, because I didn't feel capable of dealing Maggie such a blow. Also at bottom I knew that presently I would find sharing a little nest with Wal extremely monotonous. Oh, what is one to do? I suppose I am impossible to please because although I prefer simple characters I soon become terribly bored by them.

I wondered if I should ever become bored by Charles, but this was a dangerous line to pursue; the very thought of ever being on such terms with Charles as I had with Wal gave me a terrible pang, and I quickly pushed it away, down, down, to the very bottom of my mind, and concentrated on abstracts. The thing is, I thought, females travel parallel to one another and that is why they never understand one another, because they don't meet; but dealings between males and females are simple because they are travelling at right angles and sooner or later are bound to meet, no matter how briefly. I had travelled towards Wal, collided with him, and now we were travelling apart. Literally, too, it seemed; I'd had a sad letter from him that morning in answer to mine about my forthcoming trip to London, in which he told me he'd been posted back to Florida and would already be on his way by the time I arrived. He sounded truly sorry to miss me, but I guessed he'd already wiped me off his slate; practical Wal would waste no time without a bedmate. And I, what would I do? I was certainly sad at the thought of no more gambols in the big circular bed; having become accustomed to its benefits, would I ever be able to settle down without them again? It would be like going back to starch after discovering a high-protein diet. I was depressed at the thought of London without Wal. But maybe his absence was as well, really, since Mother would be there and I was looking forward with excitement and curiosity to our reunion; concentrating on more than one person at a time is something I find difficult and I'd hate not to make the most of Vanessa during what might be our only encounter for years. I had so many things to ask her; so many to tell; I thought of her as a sort of Delphic sibyl.

It was a good thing, too, I thought, that Maggie would be out of town while Mother was there; I couldn't imagine them coming to terms at all. They seemed hardly to be members of the same species and I had a notion that Mother, who considers life so inessential that its accessories *must* be highly important, would fail to realise that Maggie, who never thinks about life at all, must be considered as important in her own right. Vanessa might easily find Maggie a shattering bore; she has a low threshold to ennui. I suspect she was bored by my poor father and that is why he died of dysentery.

By now I'd thought myself clear of Peter Lannick and his troubles; I felt better. At the same time I'd come out of the woods at the foot of the estuary and was climbing up a bare sheeptracked field; the side of the cliff really but I couldn't see anything of the sea because a fine summer fog had settled, greying the grass and spangling the thistles with dewdrops and thoroughly soaking me. It wasn't cold, though; I swished my feet enjoyably through wet tussocks, cleaning off the bog-mud, and then turned homewards above the woods, planning what cooked food I'd leave for Maggie to eat while I was in London; I'd laid in two pounds of shin of beef which could be made into a stew; she'd eat it cold, I knew, Maggie could never be bothered to heat anything up, but at least it would nourish her; Matyas had brought us a hare, which I could roast, and there were plenty of eggs which she ate raw; also Eleanor would be sure to invite her for several meals. I reckoned she would be all right for a few days. Eased in my mind about her I hurried on to get home and make a start with the cookery; now I was beginning to look forward to my trip and felt better all round.

Unseen in the fog, seagulls laughed their Demon King laughter; often their cry seems a doleful noise but to me just then it sounded cheerful and heartening.

Dusk had fallen by the time I reached the cottage and a lamp shone in the window. Maggie, who never learns what she calls unnecessary tricks (a term which embraces cookery, typing, horticulture, anything to do with literature or the arts, machinery, or sewing) had reluctantly let me teach her how to light the simple oil lamps with which the cottage was furnished because otherwise she'd have been stuck in the dark, unable to work. Of course John might be there too but lately he had taken to hitching a lift into Lanrith when the builders' truck went home, and spending his evenings at the Ferry Inn. I suspected—though I'd never discussed her with him—that like myself he'd taken a violent dislike to Eleanor, who often strolled down after supper for a chat with Maggie. I generally sneaked off to read in bed on these occasions.

So it was a surprise to find Maggie and Eleanor and John, all sitting in the cottage parlour together. The first thing I looked at was the fire because such a glum atmosphere hung in the room that I felt it must surely have a concrete cause; true enough, the fire was almost out; none of them had the sense to look after it.

"Hullo," I said, "you are a set of knotheads, aren't you?" I fetched some dry kindling from the shed and balanced it over the warm ashes with a bit of coal on top; deciding against asking Aspic for the loan of her Diabolino I went through into the kitchen, lit the oilstove, and started chopping up shin of beef.

"Come in here," Maggie called.

It was pretty cold in the leanto in my damp jeans, so I gathered up the meat and onions on my chopping-plank and took them through. By now the fire was burning up quite well but nevertheless the social atmosphere of the room remained glacial. John was morosely reading the *Western Morning News* but I could see his mind wasn't on it. He had the appearance of an umpire waiting to score an unpromising game. Maggie looked sick to her heart, like Lord Rendel; Aspic was her sleek, righteous self with a "This is going to hurt me more than it does you" expression; she wore her usual good tweeds and that bloody leopard-spotted raincoat and even gloves, as for a funeral call.

"Somebody won the pools?" I suggested as I went on with my chopping.

"Where have you been?" Maggie said, sombre.

"Where does it look like? Down through the woods to the sea. Why?" Bits of Lord Rendel were still wandering in my head. "Where did you think I was? Been to my sweetheart?"

"Stop it!" said Maggie violently, and at the same moment Aspic's smooth cold voice cut in,

"Really, in the circumstances nothing seems more probable. Don't you think you owe us an apology for that disgraceful piece of behaviour this morning?"

"Owe you an apology?" I practically gaped at her. "My dear Dr Foley, my actions are my own and I'm answerable to nobody else for them. I really can't see that it's any business of yours how I behave."

I was rather pleased by this speech but Aspic's nostrils went white with temper. John buried himself even deeper in the *Western Morning News*; Maggie looked gaunt and racked and harrowed.

"It most certainly is my business," Aspic said coldly. "You're down here as my guest. You can hardly expect me to tolerate having my professional reputation associated by the locals with your dubious goings-on."

"Tenant, not guest," I pointed out, tickled to death at the thought that we had paid her some rent.

"Tenants can be given notice to quit."

"Okay, give us notice," I said. "Maggie will be better off back in town where there are some decent libraries."

"Please," Eleanor said with patience, "don't wilfully misunderstand me. Magda is resting down here and doing useful work. But you—now let's be honest my dear—" she smiled at me, her little half-rictus bedside smile and I grinned back, thinking, God pity her poor patients—"let's be honest, you don't really fit in with us down here, do you? So why don't you just go back to London where you are much happier, and stay there?"

"Civilly spoken," I said. "But if I don't choose to? After all, it was my money that paid the rent—"

"Tuesday, really!" Maggie burst out and in the same breath Eleanor said, "You can have it back. Every penny of it."

"—though I suppose mentioning that is just another example of my nasty unfitting-in ways."

I was getting a bit cross, which is never good, so I took my chopped meat into the kitchen and put it in a pressure-cooker (I never go far without one, it's about the only habit I learned from Vanessa) and, returning with the hare, began to skin and gut it.

"You'll excuse my getting on with this, I'm sure," I said, "but Maggie and John will be needing something to eat while I'm away."

John looked up from the *W.M.N.* and said, "I'm leaving too."

"Why, John?" I asked, diverted. "Maggie will miss you."

"I've a show coming on in town. Have to fix it."

"Oh—I'm glad. I thought perhaps Dr Foley was giving you the push too; it's a thing she'd like to do with all Maggie's friends."

"Tuesday, *will* you be quiet."

Maggie was suddenly blazing angry. I'd hit on a sensitive spot, I suppose; deep down she knew, but wouldn't accept, the reason why Aspic wanted to get rid of us; and rather than acknowledge the truth Maggie as usual let fly at the wrong target. I heard all over again how ruttish I was, how untrustworthy, mentally dishonest, morally turpid, utterly without a sense of right and wrong. I began to get sore, tugging at the hare's guts and dumping them on the fire. To me, right and wrong are so much more elastic than Maggie seemed to find them; surely keeping people fed and warm is right, as blackguarding them for their inescapable instincts is wrong?

I said, "Maggie, you take an exaggerated view. I am not a

sort of female Don Juan. It isn't like that. Maybe if you entered into the subject rather more yourself—"

"Don't be vile," Eleanor snapped. She was smoothing the fingers of her elegant grey gloves; I noticed that even her calm was less than total; her hands were shaking a little and she pressed the left one against her ribs.

"Not like that? It certainly is!"

Maggie took some deep breaths. Aspic's keyed-upness had communicated itself to her. She stood, massive, hands on the table, staring at me like an Assyrian lion, with all her concentrated power. She said, "I'm beginning to think Eleanor's right. You're nothing but a little slut. If I didn't stop you, you'd probably take up with any man who looked at you. For all I know, as soon as you reach London, you'll start trying to get into bed with John here!"

That really hit me. I was brought up short, mouth open like a fool, taking in the implications of what she said, of what she thought.

I did something I hadn't done for ages, I began to blush; I could feel the blush swamping me from head to foot. The thought of *John*—we'd known him for so long that I took him wholly for granted, like a brother, up to this moment. With difficulty I lifted my eyes from the hare, trying dumbly to think of words in which to frame a protest.

None came. Instead, I met John's eyes. We exchanged a long, queer, unguarded look. It was the first time our boundaries had, so to speak, touched; I felt the recoil of it as if someone had held a knife against an area of scar tissue on my skin.

John said, "Here, leave me out of this, please. It's none of my affair. And, Maggie, stop railing at the girl like a fishwife. Can't you see she's wet, she ought to change. Besides, she didn't do anything so terrible as all that."

He sounded bored and disgusted by all this female carry-on and I didn't blame him. But his eyes avoided mine.

Maggie never did anything by halves. She had long since given up worrying about my physical health; solicitude was not something she could maintain for very long at her pitch; anyway I had recovered.

But now she leapt at me, full of concern.

"Of course you're wet, you're sopping, why didn't you change when you came in, stupid child? You must get out of those wet clothes right away."

"Keep your hair on," I said crossly. "I shan't die before I've finished this job."

"Well—I must be getting back. Have a pleasant journey." Aspic gave me an acid smile, smoothing her gloves. Something had restored her composure. "Think about what I said. After all, we're both interested in Magda's welfare, aren't we—in seeing she is enabled to do her best work undisturbed."

"Oh, sure, sure," I snarled. I do hate hypocrisy. Maggie could work on the edge of a clothesline.

John said, "I'm going to bed."

While we were all standing about waiting for someone to make the first move the front door opened. A damp draught blew in and a voice called, "Anybody at home?" and Charles stepped into the room.

He was carrying his mother's guitar in its brown canvas case; he said simply, "So this is where everyone has got to," and then to me, "I was wondering if, as you're off to London tomorrow, you'd give us a tune or two this evening?"

I could have laughed—or cried. Charles certainly did pick his moments for jumping in with both feet. This was perhaps his worst yet.

"Oh really, Charles," Eleanor said, "Don't you think it's rather late? I was just coming home. You mustn't trespass on people's goodnature, you know."

"It's only eight," he pointed out.

"I was just going to change out of my wet things, actually," I said. The hare was done and I'd put it in a baking pan.

"That won't take you long," Charles said.

"I—I suppose not." Rather astonished, I went up to my tiny room at the back and lit a candle. Charles wasn't usually so persistent; had he guessed what had been going on? Was this a show of partisanship? If so I felt it was ill-timed for both of us, like Aspic's with the leopard. But I couldn't refuse. He was too innocent and vulnerable.

I peeled off my damp jeans and wandered naked round the shadowy uneven little room hunting for a clean pair and some dry socks; as usual everything was piled on the bed because there was no chair and nowhere to hang clothes. Out of the corner of my eye, suddenly, I noticed something white behind me and turned sharply in time to see a pale face pressed against the window. It vanished like lightning.

I'm not easily rattled as a rule but I daresay I was a bit

strung-up from the scene that had just taken place—I screamed.

Feet pounded up the stairs—Maggie's; she said, "What's the matter?"

I'd swallowed and taken breath by this time. "It was a man's face looking in," I said, hurriedly pulling on trousers and sweater, shuffling my feet into espadrilles. "Sorry I screamed—stupid thing to do. It just took me by surprise for a moment."

But Maggie was perturbed. She said as we went down,

"A man's face? At your window? Are you sure? What was he doing?" questions which were echoed by the others in the parlour. Eleanor had changed her mind about going and was all set to enjoy this new scandal.

"Someone at the window?" Charles said angrily. "Who? What a damn nerve! Let's get out and look for the beggar." He picked up his torch.

"Of course the garden slopes up very steeply behind the cottage, doesn't it?" Aspic said in her smooth tones. "It would be very easy to climb into those bedroom windows. Who was it?"

"Are you sure you didn't imagine the whole thing?" John gave me an irritable glance; I could see him wondering if this was just more exhibitionism on my part. I met his eyes firmly.

"No."

"Then who was it, could you see?"

I couldn't help it—I started to giggle in a hysterical, hiccuping, weak way.

"Oh, lord, can't you guess? Who else could it be? It was Peter Lannick."

XX

"ELEANOR," KARL'S VOICE said softly, mockingly "Eleanor dear, I'm afraid you're going to have to take off that costume. Blue doesn't suit you today, you know?"

Eleanor stood staring into the mirror; she had been giving her hair its intensive morning treatment. At the sound of Karl's ironic voice, his sweet, sybillant German accent, her whole body hunched forward rigidly, heron-angled, into the posture of old age. She flung down the brush on the marble table.

"You must take the clothes off, Eleanor dear. That's right. Hang them up, then. I regret to see that you are putting on weight a little; yes, I'm afraid you have lost your figure, my girl. Now—I should advise the green tweed, I think—green will perhaps do for today."

Angrily she struggled into it, and put up her hair, hurrying, without her usual dexterity, in case the voice should suddenly countermand its last order and bid her change yet again. Sometimes, almost weeping, she was obliged to change two, three, even four times before the autocratic voice was satisfied.

"Don't forget the gloves, sweetie."

She snatched them from a drawer and practically ran from the room.

It was in her bedroom and bathroom that the voice came loudest. Elsewhere it was generally no more than a murmur, drowned by the presence of real people.

"You're late," Nin said in the kitchen, pouring a cup of coffee. "That's every day this week you've been late down to breakfast. I'd better start calling you. You look tired, too; need a tonic, I daresay."

"There's no such thing as a 'tonic'," Eleanor said irritably. "Besides, I'm perfectly all right. No thanks, I don't want any coffee this morning."

"No *coffee*!" The old woman was outraged. "After I've made you a pot special? Come on, sit down, don't be silly. You've got time for that, and a bit of toast."

"I don't want it. I'm not hungry. And I'm giving up coffee."

"Giving it up?" Nin was so thunderstruck that she put the glass carafe down in a wet patch on the draining board; it promptly slid, fell, and smashed. "Drat, now look what you've made me do. Give up coffee? Well that's news I *must* say. You just about live on the stuff and all those pills you swallow. Mind, I've never thought it was good."

"Then you ought to be glad I'm giving it up. Goodbye, I'm off. See you tonight." She pulled on her gloves.

"You come home for your one o'clock dinner. I've got a lovely drop of broth," Nin called after her. But Eleanor was already in her car. She swung it neatly in a circle outside the cottage, paused to swallow a couple of capsules, and shot off up the hill, having observed with satisfaction that Claire's Jaguar was parked there with Tuesday and John sleepily packing rucksacks into the boot. When those three were back in London (and please heaven let them stay there) the Watertown valley would be inhabited only by Foleys, for Nin counted as family. And by

Magda, of course. The thought soothed Eleanor, and she dealt more leniently than usual with the follies and obstinacies of her surgery patients. Later she had another stroke of fortune. Looking out of her little office window she saw Aunt Julia, in an ankle-length dress of rusty black silk, silver-fox stole, and black toque, her brilliantly striped carpet-bag on her arm, hobble across Fore Street on the arm of an aged man. This must be the day for her monthly visit to old Canon Pollard, who had been up at Cambridge with her in the nineties.

Eleanor glanced at her watch. Claire's Jaguar, with its freight, would be well away by now; Aunt Julia never returned home until after tea on the Canon's days; the coast was clear. After a rapid check through her list of calls, Eleanor went briskly out to her car again, crossed the ferry, and took the steep winding road to Khartoum Cottage. Her arrival could not have been better timed. Those two disreputable young men and the extraordinary girl were out in front and what were they doing? They had stripped down a motor mower to its smallest components on the rough patch of lawn which was now liberally smeared with black grease; they seemed to be amusing themselves with the bits. At least the boys were; the girl Kuniang, as usual, sat watching them with a remote, contented, faraway expression, like a baby. She was even sucking her finger.

As Eleanor left her car and approached they watched her warily.

"I'm afraid Miss Foley's out," Patrick said politely.

"Is the house locked up?"

"Yes it is, I'm afraid."

"Well that's something," Eleanor said with a short laugh. She added curtly, looking at the display on the grass, "What an absolutely disgusting mess. I'm sure my aunt never gave you permission to do that here—did she?"

Nobody answered.

"You're just playing, aren't you. It would be too much to expect you to do anything useful in return for the hospitality you have been receiving."

The three pairs of eyes studied her in silence.

Eleanor went on irritably, "Anyway, clear it up now. You'd better put it all in a box, in the boot of my car, you can't just leave it lying there. Go on, hurry up! I daresay Mr Pearce at the garage will dispose of it. And get your clothes packed, I'm taking you to the station. —Well, don't just stand there, get moving."

They seemed more dazed than surprised, too dazed to protest. The boys carefully piled all the components of the mower into a crate, while Kuniang took some jeans and sweaters off a clothes-line—also in Aunt Julia's front garden, Eleanor noted angrily, the place would soon have degenerated into a slum—and wrapped them in a piece of newspaper. This seemed to be all their luggage.

"We haven't any money," Patrick pointed out as Eleanor drove them, not towards Lanrith Station, but to Pollank Road, the next stop up the London line.

"I'll buy you three singles to Paddington," Eleanor said. "And please stay in London; we don't want your kind down here."

"Have you a pencil and paper?" Kuniang suddenly asked in her self-possessed little voice. "I'd like to write a goodbye note to Miss Foley. She has been extremely kind to us. She'll wonder where we've gone."

"For heaven's sake," Eleanor said sharply, "why do you think I'm taking this trouble? Miss Foley wants me to put you on this train; she couldn't think of any other way to get rid of you."

That silenced them satisfactorily. They stood mute on the crumbling little station platform with its tall rampart of rhodo-dendrons, from which the hot sun of midday produced a resinous smell. Presently Eleanor had the pleasure of seeing the three of them climb into the long empty train and be drawn away in the direction of London.

Then she took the mangled mower to Mr Pearce's garage.

"Heh, that don't lose no time in comin' back," Mr Pearce said. "Patrick find it too much for him? Well I *am* surprised. Born mechanic, that boy is."

"Indeed?"

"Bought the mower off'n me last week. Leastways he done two half days' work for me last weekend and when I went to pay him he say he'll have the old mower instead. Been standing in the corner for dunnowlong. What you want a mower for, boy, I sez, and come out 'tisn't for him, 'tis for old Miss Foley as only 'as 'and scythe. Take 'er and welcome, boy, I sez; rare old job she be but you got the time and patience I reckon you'm able to make 'er go again. Pleased as punch he was; wanted to give the old lady a surprise, see."

"I see," Eleanor said. "Well, if you can't make it work, Mr Pearce, better throw it out. Patrick and his friends have gone back to London."

"Ar, I'm sorry to hear that. Proper good helper that boy was. Kind of a farewell present, then, would it be been?"

Eleanor left the garage feeling somehow affronted, but was soothed a little by Karl's soft laughter in her ear as she drove homewards.

"That was very neatly done, my pretty. You see how easy it is, once you make up your mind to act."

Having returned home unexpectedly for lunch, Eleanor annoyed Nin by eating nothing but an apple and a glass of milk. In the midst of the meal the doorbell rang: a young soldier stood there with a tracker dog.

Nin conferred with him in a lugubrious and lengthy mutter which at length roused Eleanor's annoyance.

"What's all the moaning about?" she said, coming briskly into the hall, pulling on her gloves. Nin turned a shocked face.

"Oh, Miss Nell, what do you suppose has happened?"

"I can't guess," Eleanor said lightly. "What has?"

"We shall all be eaten in our beds! There's a ravening leopard escaped from that circus at Lanrith, and they think it might be heading this way!"

"No," the soldier corrected politely, "we're just warning all the outlying farms to keep a lookout. It may have gone up on the moor; in fact it's more likely. And they don't reckon it's ravening at present; it's had a dozen fowls and a lamb at Trenna Down. But you'd better shut up your stock at night."

Eleanor, interested, questioned the man and heard the story of the escape. The trainer, his judgment impaired by a good many drinks, had gone into the leopard's cage late at night swearing to "teach that damn brute a trick or two." There were no witnesses to what happened then but it was plain that the leopard had outsmarted him and escaped; he was generally considered lucky to be alive with forty stitches and the loss of an eye.

"Oh well, tell Charles, will you, Nin," Eleanor said carelessly when she had heard the tale. "I'm sure he'd hate to lose his cherished pig, or any of those gilt-edged chickens. Thanks for warning us," she said to the soldier.

But in her heart she felt a strange satisfaction that the leopard had triumphed over its loutish trainer and escaped. Probably its freedom would be shortlived; but she hoped that it would make the best possible use of its time.

XXI

THE FIRST PART of the drive up to London was silent. I sat in front with Claire and addressed a few remarks to her, but then she said, "Don't be offended, but on a long trip I really prefer to concentrate on my driving. You and John talk as much as you like of course."

Naturally this permission totally spiked our ability to converse for about an hour. I was, anyway, riding a crescendo of excitement at the thought of seeing Vanessa. I'd received a long, characteristically extravagant telegram from her that morning asking for a pound of Cornish cream, several family heirlooms that weren't in my possession, and some of the works of Barbara Hepworth. Impossible as most of these requests were to fulfil, they did at least give me a powerful foretaste of Vanessa's personality, and I was all impatience to see her.

We stopped at Crewkerne for sandwiches and beer, and I moved to the back intending to get some sleep (last night had been pretty distracted, with an unavailing search for Peter Lannick and a lot of recriminations). After a while, though, I found myself not asleep but holding a conversation with John.

"Shall you be coming back?" he asked.

"Oh yes. In a week or so. I don't suppose Mother will be staying in London long; she never does. And I promised to bring back some books for Maggie."

"In spite of that scene? You don't bear a grudge for the names she called you?"

"Maggie? Good heavens no. Anyway, perhaps some of them are deserved. Well," I said, blushing a little, "not all of them. But it's like a thunderstorm with Maggie, the air's clearer when it's over. And my memory's too sievelike to bear grudges." The dislike I have for Aspic isn't a grudge, I thought; it's because of what she is, not what she does.

"That's a good thing, then," he said.

"Why, John?"

"I'm not happy about Maggie down there. And she's your responsibility."

"So you told me before," I said crossly. "But I haven't saved her life. We aren't living in China. Why don't you do a stint?"

"Because you're the one she needs. You're all the family she hasn't got. Anyway, I may not be about much for a while. When my show's organised I'm probably sailing in the Gull Race."

"In a dinghy? Across the Atlantic? You must be crazy."

"No, why? Anyway, you work on getting Maggie back from Cornwall."

I hardly noticed what he said, I was so surprised at this new manifestation of him; John was not the sort of person to take part in sporting events. Then it struck me that sailing a small boat across an ocean must be one of the very best forms of escape.

"I want to paint some skies," he said. "You see them very well from a small boat."

We went on talking about skies, in a peaceful scrappy way. There was something oasis-like about this journey; we had left the tensions and complexities of Watertown behind and by unspoken agreement didn't refer to them again; London was still far away. And Claire's silence as she drove was not severe but rather sympathetic. I had come to like and respect Claire, little as I knew her; she seemed one of the personalities that are complete in themselves, not demanding or competing but perfectly at ease in the world. I could understand why she and Charles were friends. Furthermore she was a solvent, one of those elements that clear a situation without adding any further complication. Even her silence seemed to help straighten my thoughts, and during that drive it was really borne in on me for the first time what an extremely odd atmosphere existed at Watertown.

Analytical thinking is not my strong suit, but trying vaguely to sort out the cause of the tension I thought that its eye seemed centred on Eleanor. Not that I could find anything too odd about Aspic herself except that passion for gloves; indeed she was overnormal, if such a state is possible, but she certainly did contrive to bring out the old Hades in other people : John's melancholy, Maggie's puritanical streak, Charles's doomed condition, and perhaps my divergencies from accepted behaviour. In fact the idyllic retreat that was supposed to refresh and restore us had worked in reverse, and I felt in an undefined way that this was Eleanor's fault, that she was almost encouraging such a state of affairs in order to bring about—what? A crisis? But what sort of crisis? And how could it benefit her?

In spite of, perhaps because of this pressure of emotional tension I began to feel longingly that Watertown was the most beautiful, desirable place in the whole world, with its woods and fields angled up the steep sides of the valley and its sculptured dark trees and the ubiquitous murmur of the three streams. This acute sudden feeling of deprivation crystallised in resentment against Eleanor who had wanted to drive me out. Not entirely logical I will admit, since I'd been going anyway.

As we neared London the contrast with Watertown became sharper and sharper until I ached all over with homesickness. I always loathe returning to London at any time, though it's not a bad place once you are living there and involved. But this evening the outskirts looked their greyest, drabbest worst, whereas Watertown when we left had been hushed and dewy, lit by the heavenly morning light of early summer. Although this was supposedly a pleasure trip I began to feel drained of exhilaration, and set my hopes quite desperately on Vanessa the way one sometimes craves a drink, not with physical relish, but in the knowledge that it will presently have good results. If it weren't for seeing Vanessa, I thought, I'd rush to Foyles, get Maggie's books, and go back on the night train. To add to my gloom I realised that I was starting a cold; my throat was sore and gritty, my feet were like ice, always a bad sign with me. I hoped Vanessa wouldn't catch it.

Claire dropped us in Guilford Square which she said was only a stone's throw from where she lived, and mentioned that she hoped to drive back in about three days' time. John said he wouldn't be returning to Cornwall but I fixed to ring her next evening about my plans, not knowing how long Vanessa proposed staying in London. This arrangement was a small comfort, like clutching the key that would let me back into paradise.

My hopes were fixed on Vanessa like a homing signal. I thought: in an hour's time I'll be sitting in some expensive place with soft lights and soft cushions, drinking an expensive drink and listening to some of the most amusing and informed conversation I'm ever likely to hear.

Claire waved goodbye and the Jaguar moved off; with a pang I noticed a frond of fern, the last of Cornwall, tangled round the rear fender.

John and I climbed the stairs in silence, already separated by our different plans.

From a dozen steps below I saw something white on the door of Maggie's and my flat: a sheet of paper dangling from the letterbox with a note in Vanessa's elegant, flying script:

> *Terribly sorry, precious child, I waited as long as I could but a man has just offered me a seat on his plane going to Mustang where polyandry is practised; too good a chance to miss you will agree. Do use tickets. See you another time. Love Ma.*

Underneath was an envelope with pairs of tickets for three different plays.

"Bad news?" John asked, pausing on his way to the flat above.

"*Blast* her!" I burst out. "She didn't wait as long as she could. She didn't wait at all!"

"Who? Oh, your mother."

"She's gone off with a man to Mustang." This sounded like a piece of limerick and I started to laugh and then found to my annoyance that I was nearly crying; my emotional reactions just at present seemed dangerously out of control. "Where is Mustang?"

"On the Tibetan border, I believe. What will you do?" John said, sounding unwillingly concerned.

"Go back to Cornwall, I suppose," I said drearily. Such is the perversity of my nature that the beckoning image of Watertown had now ceased to beckon; I imagined it hostile, withdrawn in darkness; the thought of my unexpected arrival there filled me with a vague discomfort as if I were trying to thrust myself in where I wasn't wanted.

A tear splashed on the tickets I held. "Here, would you like these?" I said. "They're no use to me."

"Certainly not. You must use them. And I tell you what, you need some food. It's hours since we ate. Have you anything in the flat?"

I shook my head. Before we left for Cornwall I'd made a clean sweep.

"Well, hang on just a minute while I dump this pack and we'll go down to Chez Annette. I could do with a bite myself."

"Okay," I said without enthusiasm. The thought of food did

not appeal, but I could not bear the prospect of being alone. It was nice of John to bother. I wandered despondently into our flat which, with its unnatural tidiness and five weeks' dust all over, looked thoroughly inhospitable. A pile of mail had accumulated in spite of our forwarding arrangements—mostly bills and medical advertising. In a minute John came clattering down from his flat upstairs. By this time I'd remembered that he probably had jobs he wanted to get on with, so I began to protest and ask him not to bother about me. He told me to stop arguing and come along, he wanted a meal, so we went down to Chez Annette which was a tiny little place where Maggie and I sometimes ate if I didn't feel like cooking. The food wasn't good and the service was slow, but it was cheap and convenient. I sat crumbling a roll, not feeling very grateful to John because I was so low-spirited that the additional burden of gratitude would have been too much to bear. It didn't occur to me that John could have his own reasons for wanting to avoid solitude; I had too much respect for him to think that he might be glad of my company.

"Do have these theatre tickets," I said again as we ate our brackish soup—which was at least hot; I had to keep blowing my nose. My cold was coming on vigorously.

"Certainly not. Surely you can find someone to go with?"

"I don't want to go with anybody; I'm too disappointed."

"Poor Tuesday," said John, but added, "I didn't know you had this mother fixation."

"I have not got a mother fixation. I've only *met* my mother half a dozen times."

"Who brought you up, then?"

"Oh, various extremely capable people. It's not an interesting subject."

I had the uneasy feeling that he was studying me, which I hate, and it was particularly unnerving from John, whom I had known for so long, who had seemed securely fixed in my surroundings as Maggie's friend, half hostile towards me, half tolerant, not really interested. I drank some wine; it was Portuguese red, violently acid. I didn't like it but hoped it would do my cold good though it would probably give rise to hell's own hangover. For reasons best known to himself John had ordered a huge carafe of the stuff.

"Why did your parents give you that damn silly name?" he asked irrelevantly.

"Aulis? Because I was born there."

"Where is it?"

"On the Boetian coast. My father wanted to call me Iphigeneia, but Vanessa felt the name had unfortunate associations."

"I agree with her," John said solemnly, drinking a third glass of the fierce red wine. "You would have had a hideous time at school. Not that what you've got is much better." Then he surprised me by saying, "I read your book once."

"Did you, John? I didn't know you ever read fiction."

"I never do. I wanted to see what sort of a witch had got her hooks into Maggie."

"I'm not a witch."

"Yes you are. Broomstick and all."

I met his eyes—he was scowling—and for a second time felt that queer shock, of two live organisms touching, that I'd experienced in the cottage parlour. But with a remote quality this time, as if it were happening to a couple of other people, not me, not John. He had an unfamiliar look about him this evening, disjointed, reckless, his focus set at long range, as if he'd sloughed off his usual skin. I felt uneasy because he didn't seem to be looking at me but at some image of me that he'd thrown up in his own mind.

"Well, thanks very much for the meal, John," I said. "It was a work of rescue. And do please have these tickets, I really don't want them. I'm going to bed, and coddle my cold." As if they were a sort of talisman that would wipe out obligation I handed him the tickets again.

He took them and carefully shredded them into little slips which blew about the table.

"Hey! What a waste," I protested.

"Don't you want your wine?"

"No, I've really had enough, thank you."

He drank it and stood up.

"Come on. I know what you need for that cold—you need a double whisky and lemon. We'll go to the Museum Tavern."

He put a heavy hand on my shoulder and steered me to the door.

I suppose my superego had been issuing warnings for the last hour but it was at this moment that these really began to penetrate. By now, though, the red wine was taking effect. Alcohol doesn't dull my awareness or my conscience, it just wipes out my willpower.

Outside, rain was flogging down in a regular cloudburst; the empty street was half an inch deep in water and little droves of splashes went scudding along it like tenpins. We ran a few yards, John still guiding me by my slippery bare arm, and then he said, "This isn't going to do your cold any good."

Neither of us had coats on.

"No," I said, relieved. "I'm going home."

"That's a much better idea."

"No, no," I objected, realising that he meant to come too. "You go to the Mus. Tavern. There'll be people you know there."

He didn't answer, but steered me purposefully back to the front door in Guilford Square. We climbed the stone stairs, dripping.

By now the screams of my superego were so loud that I felt it was unfair they weren't reaching John. I pulled out my key when we reached my front door saying ineffectually, "Well, thanks again for the meal, John, it was nice of you to bother, see you tomorrow, perhaps—" but he took no notice. With a blind, set look on his face he propelled me on, up the stairs to his door. I felt the heat of his wet hand trembling on my wet arm, and I thought: What we are doing is wrong. I shall regret this bitterly.

I suppose that was my first true conviction of sin.

John took out a key, unlocked the door, and shoehorned me inside, all in one neat movement; although he'd drunk by far the larger part of the wine it had had much less effect on him than on me.

He lit the gasfire and said, "Take your wet things off."

I said, "No, John, really, I—"

"Come on. Take your wet things off." He found a bottle of White Horse and splashed out two glasses full.

The trouble was that even while I was protesting and trying to hold back, my body had already ratted and gone over to the other side.

My clothes were sodden; John peeled them off me, seriously and efficiently, and then, standing very straight, with a strange, fixed, almost dedicated look, he strained me against him in a long, tense, mute, trembling kiss.

"This is all wrong," I said; my final protest.

144

"Shut up." He gave me my drink and took his.

I was glad of the fire's warmth on my bare skin, and knelt on my strewn clothes in front of it. John pulled a chair up and sat with his arms round me, his eyes shut, the lines of his face tight with anguish. Then he began to stroke my skin, ritually, still with that drawn look of pain and desperation. Finally his head fell forward against my breasts as if he had completely given up some interior struggle, and we stayed still like that for a long time. I thought again, we are two strangers. This is not John, not the John I know. This body that he holds is not my body.

At last he stood up and moved me over to his bed, which had blankets folded on it, no sheets; John was very tidy and methodical; he had probably sent the sheets to the laundry before leaving for Cornwall. He looked at the blankets in a baffled way, then gave up the problem, shook one out, and gestured me on to the bed. And I lay down, thinking, this is all wrong, the worst kind of wrong, wrong from beginning to end.

By now rain was beating against the windows in great shuddering gusts. There wasn't a sound of traffic outside; we were as isolated as if we'd been on Mars.

Isolated from ourselves, too; when he stripped and lay beside me and our bodies began tremblingly, intricately communicating, I thought again, this is two other people making love, this is not us.

The voice of guilt, the voice of denial.

And neither of us spoke; in anonymous silence the two strangers on the bed conducted their blind ceremony of attack and surrender among the rumpled blankets.

At some silent zero hour (the rain had stopped by then and the last tube-train had gone home) John gave a deep, groaning sigh, that seemed to come in its despair from the blackest depths of his being.

"Oh god. Oh god."

What was there for me to do? I didn't dare try to comfort him. I thought he would hate me. I lay still as death in his arms and then gently started to slide away. But he held me tighter than ever and surprised me by suddenly kissing me and saying,

"I've wanted to do this for the last three weeks."

"Oh no." I was appalled. "Oh no, that can't be true."

"Perhaps not. But I thought of it, when you used to come

silently like a cat and look at the picture on my easel and then go away again. Didn't you guess?"

"No never. How could I? You rather disliked me, I thought."

"So I did. That didn't affect the issue. I thought women always guessed."

I kept silent, while guilt burned in me like a poisoned arrow. Because the reason why I had been so oblivious of John was rooted in a double treachery; not only had Maggie been betrayed by her two friends, but I had been unfaithful to my first, unpromised, unspoken love.

"Of course it was that scene with Maggie that sparked it off."

"Yes. . ."

I remembered the dislocated, fatalistic look on John's face as she said, "You'll start trying to get into bed with John, here." Intention, simple and naked. Don't poke beans up your noses. You might say Maggie had no one to blame but herself for putting the idea into our heads. Herself and Eleanor who had come down and prodded her into making the scene. Except that my action in kissing Peter Lannick had started the whole course of events. But it was Maggie—activated again by Eleanor—who had dragged me down to Cornwall.

Which she did to get me away from Wal.

At this point I felt my face set in a vicelike mask, and the tears begin to trickle out of the corners of my eyes, back through my hair, freezing cold.

"What's the matter?" John's voice said in the dark, unsympathetically. "It's men, not women, who suffer from post-coital depression."

I could hardly explain that I was crying for Wal's colonel's big bouncy bed, that I was crying for nice, simple Wal, no sort of menace at all to Maggie if she'd only had the sense to realise.

"This is going to crucify Maggie," I said.

"Shall you tell her?"

"I don't think I'll have to. She'll know. But I shall, anyway."

"Oh," said John, and nothing more. We lay side by side in silence for some time. Then, angrily, I thought, he began making love to me again.

At one point he said,

"We could go off to Portugal or Peru."

"And dump Maggie? What about my responsibility? And anyway I don't love you, John," I said.

"No, I suppose not. No, there is that."

"You don't, do you? Love me, I mean?"

"Love?" he said. "No. No, Tuesday, I don't."

"Well, then."

Luckily sleep and this final conclusion hit us at about the same moment.

I had dreaded waking next morning, to hangover and mutual horror; but luckily I had such a cold by then that all other considerations were drowned. John was rather nice about it, he made me stay in bed while he went out and bought lemons and oranges and a squeezer. He was much kinder and more thoughtful than Wal would have been in such circumstances. He also went to Foyles and found the books that Maggie wanted.

In the evening I telephoned Claire to say that I'd go back to Cornwall with her.

All day long, when he was at home, John had manifested a curious need to touch me. While I was frying chops for his lunch or sneezingly sweeping his flat he would seldom be more than an arm's length away; whenever I was unoccupied he would come and huddle against me like an animal craving warmth. While I made the telephone call he had his arms tightly wrapped round me, his fingers tucked under my arm close against my breast.

But when Claire and I had talked and I'd rung off, he said,

"That's that, then," and, getting up, walked away to the other side of the room where he stood with his back turned, looking out and down at the lighted street.

"Well—" I said. "Perhaps I'd better go down to my own flat tonight."

"Perhaps you had."

"Goodnight, then. Goodbye, in case I don't see you in the morning."

"Goodbye," he said.

So I slept alone in my own narrow bed. And half wished that John would come down in the middle of the night to share it with me. But he didn't; and as I tossed and turned and sneezed it occurred to me to wonder whether I'd ever share a bed with any man again.

XXII

Eleanor braked at the top of Watertown Hill and, before engaging low gear, paused a moment to give the scene before her a reflective, satisfied scrutiny. Afternoon rounds and evening surgery were behind her, she had encountered Mr Rowse in Lanrith and told him firmly that he would be well-advised to pay off Peter Lannick, now she was returning home with a virtuous sense of dull duty done. She felt that at last her Cornish existence was becoming orderly and purposeful. The disparate elements were being sorted out, the rest marshalled into a tidy pattern.

Ahead of her the deep little valley lay tranquil, its woods and fields sunk in evening peace. Late golden sunshine bathed one slope, the other was already shadowed. Soon, thought Eleanor, the alterations to the house will be finished, the builders gone, and we shall have the whole kingdom to ourselves.

Below her the chimneys of Watertown House were crowned with a drift of woodsmoke. The railway viaduct marched with classic formality across the southern end of the valley, fencing it in. She thought, it is like a holy place, there should be an oracle here, and a priestess, and sacrificial mysteries. No doubt there had been once; she remembered the arched-over well in the garden under the great yew tree, with its crumbling statue, supposedly of the Virgin, but so battered and weatherworn that it could have been Demeter, or some earlier, more primitive divinity.

Letting in the clutch she allowed the car to move slowly down the steep, twisting hill. At one point the orchard gateway gave a glimpse of the cottage below and Eleanor caught sight of a tall, black-clad figure standing on the bridge. With total certainty, like a message from on high, the realisation came to her: there is a priestess, a sibyl, here in the valley. I have installed her myself.

Leaving the car outside Watertown House, with its nose jammed against the bank, Eleanor walked down to meet her friend: Magda, the goddess-queen, tall and massive in her shabby clothes, with her coronet of black braided hair. The calm valley's elegiacally dark, upward-pointing trees made an appropriate background for her. Its quality of expectant hush was matched by her abstraction and slow unerring logic and long, ruminant silences; its primitive graces of earth, water, and rock were mirrored by her archaic tranquillity.

I have installed her in a fit setting, Eleanor thought. I found this place for her; Claire and Charles were no more than my instruments. I can manipulate people as I wish, fire them off like rockets or crumple them like paper. Soon Charles will be gone too, we shall rule our kingdom undisturbed.

Blackbrowed Magda, queen of the evening valley, peered myopically and, seeing Eleanor, waved and came strolling uphill towards her.

"Did you remember my cigarettes?" she called. "Isn't it quiet here without Tuesday and John! I thought I should be able to work better on my own, but I miss them. It is quite difficult to concentrate. I wonder if they've reached London yet."

"If you can't put them out of your head it is certainly time they went," Eleanor said. A little black-purple pustule of anger swelled in her mind; it was intolerable that, even when absent, her enemies should still have power. "Don't think about them," she said harshly. "As you said yourself, they are a worthless pair. Forget them. Tell me what you have been doing today. What point have you reached?"

The two tall women swung into step along the peaceful dusty road, which already smelt sharply of dew on bracken and damp moss. Karl's ghost, half mocking, half acquiescent, shuffled a little way in the rear, as if subdued by Magda's presence.

But then Maggie said again, "Did you remember my cigarettes?"

"No." Eleanor was irritated. "Don't you think you smoke too much?"

"You *forgot* them?" Sincere astonishment widened Maggie's eyes and creased her massive, intelligent brow. "But how am I going to get through the night? Tuesday *never* forgets them. This is terrible! I have only five left. And now the shops will be closed—you will have to get some at a pub in Lanrith."

"You're not seriously suggesting I should go back for them?"

They had turned and were facing one another. Karl laughed a little, behind Eleanor's shoulder. Then she said, "Charles may have some, I suppose..." and moved uphill. Charles had just emerged from the henyard, wheeling a barrowload of straw. She called to him coldly, "Charles, have you any cigarettes you can lend Magda?"

"Only a couple, I'm afraid. I've been trying to cut down, letting stocks run low."

"Seven won't last me through the night," said Maggie.

Into the resulting silence came Nin, from the front door, beckoning vigorously.

"Oh lord, *now* what?" Eleanor said.

She moved towards the house, Magda following; Nin met them, portentous with news.

"It's that leopard, Miss Nell! You're to go at once. Police call. It's savaged a person now, what did I tell you! If it isn't caught soon we shall all be devoured in our beds. Fine state of affairs! We'd have done better to stay in London."

"What nonsense," Eleanor said shortly. "After all, leopards don't regularly roam loose in Cornwall. Well, where have I got to go?"

"Lanrith police station. One of the soldiers found her in the woods, they don't want to move her till you get there. The sergeant's waiting to take you."

"They haven't caught the leopard?" Eleanor said, checking.

"No, that's still stravaiging loose, worrying sheep! Hoskinses have lost two, now, the postman said, though whether you can believe him ... No, but think of that poor woman, that boy's mother; not that she'll be much loss if she does die," Nin said with gloomy relish.

"Which boy?"

"Peter Lannick. Daresay she was wandering about tipsy as usual."

"Oh," Eleanor said impatiently, getting into the car. "That's the end of her, then. Don't keep supper for me or wait up."

She accelerated down the hill, turned the car, and came up again. Magda was calling something; she slowed and opened the window.

"... my cigarettes. You won't forget them this time, will you?'

From behind, on the back seat, Karl's laughter pealed out, shrill as the maniac chatter of a hyena.

Eleanor loathed pubs. To her they seemed purely evil, and not even attractive: dark, dismal places where people idled away their time, spending money on wasteful objects that were neither nutritious, instructive, or in any way beneficial. The people in them seemed Hogarthian, maliciously unpredictable; she imagined them pointing fingers and leering behind her back, whispering lewd comments. The first two she tried, the Ferry

Inn and the Godolphin, did not have the brand of cigarettes that Magda smoked. Gritting her teeth in exasperation, she imagined the reception of any other kind—"But, Eleanor, you know I can't smoke those! You'll just be in time to change them before the pubs close."

At last she found Magda's brand in a third pub, a tiny, smoky hovel where the customers, regulars obviously, fell silent and stared at her with frank hostility all the time she was in the bar.

"What ever kept you, Doctor?" the sergeant said when at last she reached the police station.

"I was held up," she said coldly.

After a bucketing ride through woods in a borrowed jeep they reached the spot where Mrs Lannick lay, but one of the men who had stayed with her shook his head.

"I doubt she's gone," he said.

Eleanor examined the untidy, mangled wreckage of Mrs Lannick and concurred; there was nothing to be done. "It wouldn't have made any difference if I'd got here earlier," she added. "I see she was in her usual state. Strong smell of spirits even now. Too drunk to get away, I suppose. You think it was the leopard?"

"Tracks round about same as those in the cage," the police inspector said. "And some bits of fluff, see, on a bramble."

"Where's the woman's son?"

"They haven't found him yet," the sergeant said. "He come home from work, the neighbours said, found she was missing, and went out looking for her. Not long after, one of the army chaps found the body, but no one seems to know which way Peter went."

"It's to be hoped he didn't meet the leopard too. It's not been caught yet?"

"No, Doctor. One chap thought he saw it and fired a shot at it, but evidently he missed."

"What a fool," Eleanor said. "It will be twice as dangerous if he wounded it."

She escorted Mrs Lannick's body back to the police station, made out a report, and then went to the Lannick cottage in case Peter had turned up. But he was not there.

By now dusk had turned to dark. She started towards home, driving less carefully than usual because she was tired; her bones ached with tiredness.

About halfway along the Watertown road there was a sharp

151

double bend at the top of a steep hill, and it was here that she met the leopard; she was in low gear for the bend, not doing much over twenty m.p.h. She saw the eyes first, blazing red, automatically dipped her lights, and braked to a stop, switching off the engine.

The leopard, crouching in the narrow, high-banked lane, seemed undecided which way to escape. Its tail swung, it flashed black and gold, its blunt cat-face stared straight at her, snarling distrust of the lights, and she stared back spellbound, her identity, surroundings, governing impulse, all equally lost and forgotten.

After an immeasurable length of time the leopard yawned, turned profile-on, and sprang upwards in a figure-three curve, lightly striking the bank halfway, rebounding, and disappearing over the top into darkness. Not without some effort, however, Eleanor noticed, her professional habit of observation surmounting even the intensity of this encounter; the beast had, it was plain, fed recently and heavily; its belly hung low. Hoskins had probably spoken the truth about his sheep. Its killing of the drunken Mrs Lannick might have been an act of panic; perhaps she had mistaken it for a dog.

Much more time slid by, unmarked. At last Eleanor started up again, mechanically, and, without noticing what she did, drove the remaining distance to Watertown. She put her car away, gave the cigarettes to Magda, who was absorbed in work once more, said goodnight to Nin and Charles, wrote some reports, and went to bed, all without the least awareness of her actions.

She did not mention what she had seen, then or later.

XXIII

N THE END I went back to Cornwall by train. Claire rang me and said she might have to stay in town a fortnight; something about her lodgers getting involved in a court case and she was likely to be called as a witness; I didn't exactly take in what it was all about. After that, because my cold was still streaming and I felt the inertia of depression, over a week went by before I could stir myself to go. I just stayed in the flat and ate oranges and indulged in an orgy of gramophone playing, since Maggie wasn't there to disapprove.

John never came near till the last day when, rather to my surprise, answering the bell, I found him outside. He wouldn't come in but stood there as remote, unsmiling, formal, as if we were strangers and had never spoken in our lives.

"When are you off?" he said. "I thought you'd have gone by now."

I explained about Claire, and that I was leaving later that morning. He nodded absently, and said, "Get Maggie out of there, won't you."

"Out of Cornwall, you mean?"

"Yes, Cornwall, Watertown, that whole crazy setup," he said impatiently. "It's high time she came back and settled down to proper work. She can't do much more down there. And you're the only person who can persuade her to budge."

"What about you, John?"

"I'm not going back. The Gull Race starts in five days; I'm up to my eyes getting all my gear together."

"I see."

Of course I had known that it would be like this, but just the same I felt a sad, dragging ache; loss, regret, isolation.

John frowned as if the effort of communicating were almost more than he could bear, and said,

"There's something quite abnormal about that whole arrangement. You must feel it."

"I certainly feel there's something abnormal about Eleanor Foley."

"Of course there is!" He gave me a quick, irritable look; it was the first time our eyes met. "She's paranoid—on the way to being a complete nut-case I imagine."

"I'm relieved you think so too." Here at least was common ground.

"The thing is to do something before it's too late. The Foley woman will turn dangerous, mark my words, as soon as she stops getting her own way. She's possessive and jealous to an absolutely terminal extent; she might easily go to the lengths of destroying something rather than have it taken from her. So go carefully."

"You make it sound as if a moonlight flit was our only hope. You don't think you're exaggerating?"

"You know I'm not. Foley wants Maggie all to herself—this

precious notion of a thyroid clinic is only a means to that end. She's as calculating and devious as a cat," said John, who hated cats. "I bet the only reason she moved to Cornwall was so as to get her hooks on rich old aunt thingummy and isolate Maggie. God knows, too, what she intends for that wretched brother of hers; she certainly hates his guts. However that's not your worry."

"No."

"So make an effort, will you."

With these final words he turned to go upstairs again and had reached the corner before I said,

"John."

"Well?"

He didn't look round.

"You—you might—it might help if you wrote to Maggie."

He stood still for a moment in the same position, without turning, then said, "All right," and went quickly on out of my view.

I didn't see him again.

So there I was, sitting in the train, sick with dread at what lay before me. Nobody had seen me off, nobody would meet me, as nobody knew I was coming; I felt like a space-craft making an unscheduled voyage to a doubtful landing.

The train reached Lanrith at four. I walked down to the town, expecting that I'd have to walk on to Watertown, a prospect I contemplated without enthusiasm, but in Fore Street I had the luck to be hailed by plump little Mr Rowse who said that if I liked to wait ten minutes I could go with him; he was taking the truck out to inspect progress and pick up his men.

"Save you an hour's walk that will."

My rucksack, full of Maggie's books, weighed like lead, so I dumped it in his cab with relief and went off to buy bread and groceries as the larder would no doubt be empty.

On our way out I asked how the work was going and heard a long diatribe against Peter Lannick. Mr Rowse apologised for the incident on the night before I left, so I said, think nothing of it, the boy had enough troubles without getting landed in Peeping Tom actions.

"I know the boy's got troubles," Mr Rowse said, "but I've made allowances for him, lookso, till I've none left to make. Say what you like, 'twas a merciful release when his mother got took, and if he'd any honesty he'd admit it."

"She died?" I was startled. "That was very sudden, surely?"

"Leopard got her," Mr Rowse said, and told me about it.

"Good heavens—what a frightful thing for Peter," I said inadequately. "Still, at least now I suppose he can go back into the navy?"

Mr Rowse shook his head doubtfully as he negotiated the steep, crevice-like lane with practised skill. "Boy's not too peart since it happened. I reckon it shook him up bad and he can't seem to pull himself together. Full of bloody ridickerlous notions he is now—saying he's going to get his own back for his mum's death."

"On the circus people? I suppose they might be held responsible? Has the leopard been caught?"

"No, not yet. No, it ben't the circus Peter's after—'tis Dr Foley he blames for not getting to his mum quicker."

"Surely that's a bit unreasonable?"

"There ben't an atom of reason in Peter just now," Mr Rowse said. "I offered him a week's leave, he said no. But he's hardly done a hand's turn of work since it happened—and quarrelsome! Bite your head off as soon as look at you. Kormendi's proper fed up with him, and as for Dr Foley! Blazing row they had 'count he'd been wandering round the cottage at night, then another when he was chucking broken tiles off the roof and one hit her mudguard; she said he'd done it a purpose and she'd see he got his cards if he didn't mend his ways. Which is awkward for me."

"It certainly is," I said, trying to be sympathetic. "Naturally you wouldn't want to sack a man who'd just been bereaved." But I was so strung-up that I could hardly follow what he was saying. A terrible current of emotion had control of me; I felt dry with anguish and terror at the thought of Maggie, yet paradoxically as we neared the head of our own valley and the hillsides drew into familiar contours with the viaduct striding from wood to wood and the Watertown chimneys silhouetted below, my dread was almost matched by an uprush of simple, homecoming happiness; and what was the use of that when my present task was to get Maggie out of here the quickest way I knew how?

Mr Rowse drove down to the bottom and turned his truck on the gravel patch by the cottage. I went through the open door to find three days' dirty dishes, a dead fire, and no Maggie, so after piling some sticks hopefully on the ashes I walked up to the house. Maggie might have gone out with Eleanor—whose car was absent—but, more probably she had gone up to the house to use Eleanor's reference books. In fact, taking a short-cut through the garden I saw her by the back door in a group that consisted of Kormendi, Mr Rowse, old Nin, and Peter Lannick, who was standing a little apart. Peter's appearance shocked me; he seemed to have lost a couple of stone since I'd been away; his face was white and drawn and the expression on it, compound of derision and despair, was not a pleasant one.

"Ah, come on, sack me and get it over," he jeered. "British justice that is; always sack a man when he has a headache."

"Headache—!" said Kormendi with a Hungarian oath. "Today, headache; yesterday, stomach-ache; tomorrow I suppose it will be leg-ache! I tell you he gives *me* the ache, that one; he gives me the ache in the neck."

Friend, you keep your mouth shut, I adjured myself; this is one place where you don't go clumping in with your hobnailed feet.

Just the same, Peter did look to me as if his head ached; he had that tight look round the eyes. But Maggie seemed to be in charge of the situation and I knew she could be relied on in a straightforward crisis such as this.

Marching up to Peter—she was quite as tall as he—she laid a palm on his forehead. He made as if to twitch away angrily, but then suffered it. After peering at his eyeballs and feeling his pulse, Maggie announced,

"This man is not well. *You* should have seen that," she said sternly to Kormendi. "He should have aspirin and lie down for half an hour and then go home."

"I'll get the aspirins," proposed Nin, fussy with self-importance, "there's some in Mr Charles's bathroom cupboard—"

"Come along," Maggie said to Peter, ignoring Nin. Too dazed, apparently, with the pain of his head to put up any resistance, he followed her obediently. Mr Rowse, promising to take Peter home in half an hour, disappeared with Kormendi to inspect the work. Old Nin, muttering to herself, went down the garden to fetch some washing from the line; I strolled after Peter and Maggie with a feeling of respite. She had seen me, registered my arrival, but no more; it was not her way to make personal contact until she had dealt with the matter in hand.

I waited, flipping through a copy of the *Lancet* that lay on Eleanor's scrupulously tidy kneehole desk in her office, which was opposite the downstairs bathroom. The *Lancet* was full of nice juicy reading; but my heart wasn't in it.

Clinks of bottles being moved came from the bathroom; then a tap running.

"Ergotamine would be better but aspirin will do," I heard Maggie say. "Do you take aspirins for your headaches?"

"Yeah."

"Then I will give you four; here you are. Now you had better lie on Mr Foley's bed till Mr Rowse is ready to drive you home."

She steered him into Charles's room, next the bathroom; he went docilely. Nin had returned and was chuntering to herself in the kitchen, thumping the iron about. "That's right, make yourself at home; use the place as if it belonged to you," I heard her mutter. She had never taken to Maggie, whom she mistrusted as a foreigner, though oddly enough she quite liked me.

"Where are Charles and Eleanor, Nin?" I asked, going through to her.

"Over to Camelot. She was taking a clinic at the hospital, he went with her to get some more pig-wire. Then they was going on to dinner with friends on Bodmin Moor. Back about eleven, they said. Want a cup of tea? I just made some."

"I'd love one, Nin." For days I'd been unable to eat but parched with thirst; probably the effect of my cold. And tea with Nin, I thought, would postpone a little the long evening's tête-à-tête that lay ahead.

Nin poured me a cup and then called ungraciously, "There's tea, Dr Tassák, if you want."

Maggie came in, preoccupied over Peter Lannick and his migraines. "If he were my patient he should have a thorough physical check-up and also see a psychiatrist. Thank you." She accepted the cup with absent-mindedness that looked like condescension; I could see Nin taking it as such.

"Maybe he'll be all right when he's back in the navy?" I suggested. "Change of scene and more congenial occupation—aren't migraines caused by strain?"

"Not *caused*; the causes are more complex than that," Maggie said seriously, and began discussing them in detail. It was soothingly impersonal and I kept her going with questions. Midway through, I thought I heard footsteps; then suddenly there was a heavy thud from Charles's room and a crash of breaking china.

"What goes on?" I said. Maggie spun round and hurried

back to where she had left Peter; I followed with Nin at my heels.

Charles's room, originally a pantry, was small and simply furnished; a divan with a dark blue cover; a pine chair, dressing-chest, and wardrobe; a bedside table with a lamp and some books; a dark blue carpet. On this Peter Lannick now lay, having rolled off the bed, apparently, and taken the lamp with him in his fall. He was deeply unconscious.

Nin made the next few minutes chaotic with exclamations but Maggie, taking no notice, carefully examined Peter all over again.

"I do not understand it," she said then, sounding disturbed. "While we were talking just now I thought I heard him go to the bathroom and back; do you think he could have taken anything else?"

"I will look," she said, and came back, frowning, with an empty aspirin bottle in her hand. "He has taken the rest but there were not many—" She bit her lip, then said to Nin, "There would not be anything but aspirins in this bottle?"

"I don't know, I'm sure, miss," Nin said, dissociating herself completely from the matter. "I never touch them myself."

"I had better empty his stomach," Maggie decided.

"Can you? Have you the tubes and things?"

"Eleanor will be sure to. Help me get him back on the bed."

He was dreadfully thin; it took no great effort to lift him. Nin, with compressed lips, produced a spare key for the large locked cupboard in Eleanor's office; Maggie hunted methodically through it, found a hypodermic and gave Peter an injection to stimulate his heart, which was slower than it should be, she said. Then she emptied his stomach, while I helped, and Nin stood tut-tutting by, and then crossly removed the resulting pail of fluid.

"He doesn't seem to have eaten anything for the last twenty-four hours," Maggie said. "That may partly explain his reaction." But I could see she was still puzzled and worried.

Presently Peter's eyelids fluttered; the whites showed, then the pupils rolled down into view and focused on me. For a few minutes he lay gazing at me with a strange simplicity and trust. "Ah, then, so it's you, is it," he muttered, half to himself, and something that might have been a smile twitched his mouth.

"You're all right now, Peter," I said.

But soon his forehead furrowed and he began staring about him in a baffled way.

"Here, what—" he said gropingly. "What am I doing here? What the hell d'you think you're all playing at?"

He put a hand up to his forehead. The lamp or the table had cut it quite badly and there was a sizeable lump.

"You fell off the bed?" said Maggie. "Don't you remember?"

"Off the bed?" he said suspiciously. "You kidding?"

Nin was now fussily occupied with a brush and pan, clearing up the broken lamp.

"Stupid boy," she scolded. "How ever did you come to do a thing like that? Look at the mess you made."

"You fainted," I said.

"Fainted?" Peter suddenly became violently angry. "Here, what the hell's going on? I never fainted in me life. You trying to put something over on me? Make out I'm going barmy or something?" He tried to sit up, swayed with weakness, and had to lie back. "What were them pills you gave me?" he said to Maggie. "That wasn't aspirin. Aspirin never made me faint before, and I took hundreds of 'em. It was that stuff made me faint. You done it on purpose."

"Nonsense," Maggie said. "You had perfectly harmless aspirins which, as you say, you have had hundreds of times before. But you went back and helped yourself to some more. That was a stupid thing to do, wasn't it? How many did you take?"

"Wasn't working fast enough," he muttered, and his eyelids drifted shut. Maggie checked his breathing and pulse, which were better now, and we left him with the door open. She took the aspirin bottle into Eleanor's room and tested the powder that was left in it by licking her finger.

"But no, this is aspirin; it is most odd. Can he have taken anything else?" I heard her mutter, and she checked through the little medicine cabinet in the bathroom, but apparently the rest of its contents were innocuous.

"I am going to put a dressing on his head," she told me. "I think you had better call Camelot hospital and ask them if they can take him in for observation. See if Eleanor is there; if she is I should like to speak to her."

Peter was indignant when he heard this. "You just bloody leave me alone, see? You don't get me into no hospital."

"Come, come," Maggie said firmly. "I am only acting for

your good. Be sensible, please! Before, you were angry because you thought we did not believe that you were ill. Now you are angry because we do believe it. There seems to be no pleasing you."

She managed to quell him by her mixture of calm and authority; meanwhile I got through to the hospital who promised to send an ambulance, but said Eleanor had finished her clinic and left.

"See if you can get hold of her at her friends," Maggie said when I told her this. "Their name is Trubshawe and they live on the moor."

I looked through the directory for Trubshawes but the area seemed to be studded with them and Maggie didn't know the address or initial.

On the bottom shelf of Eleanor's drug cupboard I had noticed a small gilt-embossed leather address-book lying with a pile of notebooks and folders; it seemed worth trying this before phoning every Trubshawe in turn. Its pages were interleaved with loose memoranda and the whole thing was secured by an elastic band to prevent the contents falling out. I took off the elastic and hunted through the T section; no Trubshawes. But the loose bits of paper also carried addresses, in no sort of order, and I began going through them. An envelope near the front contained small squares of paper, leaves torn off a little telephone memo-pad. I recognised Charles's writing on the top one and—I suppose inexcusably—pulled it out. It said,

Dear Nell,
I am sorry to take what you probably think is a coward's way out but I cannot stand the prospect of what you told me last night so I am getting my death over quickly for both our sakes.
Goodbye. Love, Charles.

It was dated London, Christmas.

I stared at it for a few moments, in shock.

Christmas, I thought. Last Christmas. At the time when Maggie and I were having our first touch of crisis, Charles was going through one a good deal more drastic. But he had changed his mind. Why, I wondered, and then remembered something he had once told me. Claire had talked him out of the notion of suicide. But how very odd of Eleanor to keep this note; how odd of him, too, not to have made certain that such an embarrassing reminder was destroyed. With guilty haste I started to put it back in the envelope, glancing automatically at the slip beneath.

It had exactly the same words on it.

No, not exactly; the heading was Watertown and instead of "I cannot stand the prospect of what you told me last night," it said, "I find I cannot stand the prospect of the painful months ahead."

Suddenly I couldn't bear the sight of the notes—they gave me the horrors. I slid them back into the envelope and put it in my jeans pocket. In the middle of the address-book was a bit of paper with the name I wanted: Trubshawe, Little Moor Farm, Bray Down, Levernick. I rang Inquiries, who told me they weren't on the phone.

Snapping the elastic band back over the book, I put it away, locked the cupboard, and gave the key to Nin, who hid it inside a small pink teapot. While she did this I opened the lid of the Aga stove and dropped the envelope well down into the heart of the fire.

Then I went to inform Maggie that we were out of luck as regards Trubshawes.

By now the men were beginning to pack up for the day so Maggie went out to tell Mr Rowse that she was sending Peter in to hospital and not to worry about taking him home. I wandered back to the kitchen with my mind in a high state of upheaval; too many things were happening that seemed, in a murky way, connected and if they were connected I didn't like it.

Nin was at her ironing again, agog to discuss Peter's peculiar condition, so I pushed the door to, leaned against the dresser, and provided an audience. For the second time I heard all about Mrs Lannick's death, and about Peter's unreasonable dislike of Miss Nell, only trying to do her best by him, and how the leopard was still at large.

"I wouldn't go out after dark not for a fortune," Nin said. "I carry a big heavy stick with me everywhere now, even down the garden to pick a bunch of parsley, and you'd better do the same when you go down to the cottage, Miss Tuesday."

"Oh I daresay the leopard's miles off by now."

"Well, I made Mr Charles get a bigger gun, that little rook rifle he has would be no good; he borrowed one of Colonel Pascoe's guns that he had for his big-game hunting; it never hurts to have a gun in the house," Nin said with satisfaction, "not when you live isolated like this. Loaded ready in the feed store it is, case that nasty beast should come prowling after the animals. I will say, Mr Charles quite saw the sense in what I said, once the little pigs was born. So proud of them he is, you'd think he'd had 'em himself."

She chuckled drily.

"Oh, she's had them at last, has she? How many?"

"Twelve, and one that died. Charles and that Kormendi was like two children the day they come—quite tried Miss Nell's patience. Though as I see it, anything that takes his mind off his health is all for the best."

"How—how do you think he is, in general?" I understood that Nin had been told about Charles's heart condition, but not how serious it was.

"Charles?" She gave me a shrewd look. "Never better. Country air has put him right on his feet again."

"Does he have to take anything for his illness?" I asked and hoped it sounded casual.

"Little red tablets night and morning," Nin said, demolishing my vague speculations. "I don't say they don't do good, but good cooking and good air's better still, in my opinion."

"I'm sure you're right." My mind was wandering again, back to Maggie; Mr Rowse's truck, with the workmen, passed the window and departed; somehow the next few hours had to be undergone. But then the ambulance arrived, postponing my confession once more.

Two uniformed attendants poked inquiring heads round the door and Maggie came out of Eleanor's office where she had been making notes, and led them to where Peter was resting.

But Peter wasn't resting. Peter had gone. He must have slipped out through the window, which stood open.

We felt proper fools, of course. At least I did. Maggie scolded me roundly for not having heard anything, though it seemed to me that she bore an equal share of blame. However there he wasn't, no use crying over spilt milk when the horse is gone. The ambulance men helped us hunt round the house and outbuildings, but I could see them thinking that anybody able to scarper so fast couldn't be in dire need of hospitalisation. Nin, of course, kept up a Cassandra chorus in the background to the effect that the leopard, having despatched Peter's mother, was now probably close at hand, raring to do him in too, and us to follow; this didn't make the ambulance men any keener. It was growing dark by now and as one of them suggested Peter could easily be in Lanrith by this time. In the end they left and we walked down to our cold empty cottage, Maggie promising Nin that she'd come back later when Charles and Eleanor returned, to report to Eleanor on all these goings-on.

Nin wasn't grateful.

I've mentioned before that entering the cottage felt like climbing into a coffin. It was too damp, too dark, too narrow, set in under the steep hillside. This evening the half-open door looked like the entrance to a trap, the windows were eye-sockets in a skull. Menacing. I suppose it was the pathetic fallacy getting its hooks in me.

"Maggie, there's something I've got to tell you . . ."

XXIV

"I HOPE MAGDA'S HAD the sense to stay up at the house." Eleanor said, changing down for Watertown hill. The vertical banks flung back a blast of engine sound; wet rock and harts' tongue ferns gleamed in the headlights.

"Worrying about the leopard?" Charles said. "It's not likely to go into the cottage, surely?" The slight mockery in his tone nettled Eleanor, who retorted,

"Why not? It's used to being in a cage. And you know how hopeless Magda is about leaving the front door open."

As they came round into the wider stretch of road by Watertown House their lights showed two figures walking uphill.

"Why!" Charles said, "Tuesday's back!" At the unguarded pleasure in his voice Eleanor's foot jerked on the pedal and the brakes squealed. "Anyway your anxieties about the leopard seem to have been unjustified this time at least," he added as he got out of the car, "though I suppose I'd better go and check on the pigs."

He did not do so immediately, though; while Eleanor ran the car into the lay-by and sat for a moment, gripping her gloved hands on the wheel, he went forward and greeted the other two; there was something in the warm, laughing tone of his voice, in the eager set of his shoulders and head as he met them, that brought a choking wormwood bitterness into Eleanor's mouth and sent heat coursing along her veins until even her fingertips tingled.

Careful, though. Careful. We can easily put a stop to this.

With satisfaction she switched off the headlights, plunging them into dark.

"Hey!" There was a cheerful protest from Charles. "Have a heart, Nell, wait till we're in!"

Nin, however, had heard them. The light over the front door came on, showing Charles holding Magda's hand, and with his other arm round the girl.

Eleanor noticed, though, that the cheerfulness was all on Charles's part; Magda looked as if she were under severe strain; the girl, even more skinny and scrawny after her week in London, had the air of someone who has been put through a wringer. With a leap of the heart Eleanor thought: Magda has been telling her to go back where she belongs. Patience; you are sure to win.

She walked into the house, listening with half her attention to Magda's story of Peter Lannick—"Oh, another of his so-called migraines? They have about as much relation to a real migraine as what most people call flu has to the real thing," she said impatiently, dropping her handbag on the desk, scanning the telephone pad for messages. The aspirin bottle still stood there; she frowned at it absently.

"I think Peter should see a psychiatrist," Magda was insisting. "This could have been attempted suicide."

"Did you keep the contents of the stomach?" Eleanor said sharply.

"Unfortunately Nin threw them away without telling me," Maggie was obliged to admit. "But if the whole thing was hysterical, or if he has a cardiac neurosis, that makes him even more of a case for psychiatric treatment. He seems to have strong delusions of persecution."

"Don't we all?" Eleanor said lightly. She heard Karl chuckle behind her. "But most of us struggle along without resorting to psychiatrists. Oh, all right—" as Maggie, serious and concerned, opened her mouth to argue—"I'll try and get hold of Peter tomorrow, see what I think. Where is he now?"

"That's what nobody knows."

"Do we have to go out with ropes and lanterns?" Charles, who had been visiting the pigs, armed, on Nin's adjuration, with his

.350 double-barrel, came into the hall followed by the girl. She doesn't lose a minute, Eleanor thought.

"Oh, hardly that. But perhaps we should ring and ask the Lanrith police if he has reached home?"

Humouring Magda, Eleanor did so; the sergeant promised to check and ring her back.

Nin, once she saw they were safe, had gone to bed; the others had moved into the kitchen and were making coffee; Eleanor joined them, noticing again the sense of strain, which seemed to have extended to Charles. He was, Eleanor observed, with the acutely heightened perception which visited her where those three were concerned, showing a curious gentle solicitude towards Magda, as if aware that she had suffered some painful blow. And all the time, though they never touched, spoke, or met each other's eyes, electric currents of communication were vibrating between him and the girl Tuesday. What had passed while they were outside? Eleanor wondered, absently pouring coffee and then pushing it away. Why was Magda looking so stricken? And yet she seemed to be responding with a sort of bewildered gratitude to Charles's overtures, smiling faintly at his little jokes, accepting coffee and a cigarette from him ... What was going on?

"Are you all right?" Eleanor said in a low voice to Magda.

"Yes, why?" Magda's tone was brusque, almost curt; she bent her head sideways to Charles's lighter.

"I thought you looked rather tired."

"I'm all right," Magda said impatiently, without meeting her friend's eyes.

Eleanor stood motionless for a moment, then shrugged, and went into the office to answer the telephone which began ringing at that moment.

"Peter's not home yet," she reported briefly when she came back into the silence that seemed to have lasted since she had left the room. "The police are going to keep a lookout for him. —Well, if the leopard gets him, that will really give his delusions of persecution something to feed on."

Nobody smiled. Magda said heavily, "It is time we were in bed," rose without a glance at anybody, and made for the front door at her usual rapid, blundering pace—Eleanor heard her trip over a mat in the hall. The girl followed her.

"I'll see you both home," Charles said quickly, and picked up a torch.

Left alone, Eleanor stood for a moment, smoothing the fingers of her gloves. Unacknowledged rage had risen to such a magnitude inside her that she would gladly have dashed a coffeecup on to the granite floor. "But that would be stupid, wouldn't it?" Karl's voice said gently. "We don't want to waste energy, do we?"

Eleanor turned sharply on her heel, took another torch from the dresser, and went out the back door, through the feed store, and the farmyard, meticulously shutting and relatching doors and gates behind her.

She made her way up through the orchard towards Charles's pig-pen. A barn-owl called; in the mild night, scents of bluebell and late narcissus mingled, not unpleasantly, with that of pig. Glancing back, Eleanor saw a light come on in the cottage.

If the place were to burn down, she thought; if the viaduct were to fall on it, if there were a landslide—But not on Magda. On those two. If a runaway truck could hit them, a boat sink under them—Why won't she go sailing with Charles? Some absurd excuse that sailing bores her—

A slight noise to Eleanor's left made her turn; the light from her torch travelled up the bank to the scrappy hazel hedge that topped it.

This time the leopard had the advantage of height. Perched like some golden heraldic beast among the leaves, it glared down but seemed disinclined to risk a leap into the dark behind the torch-beam. Its pupils narrowed, it crouched lower, spitting, wrinkling its face at the light. The blunt, elegant head turned from side to side, she saw the flash of whiskers and the lighter-coloured fur in its ears.

"Oh, you beauty," Eleanor said softly. "You beautiful thing."

She felt no fear; the leopard seemed neither stranger nor more hostile than people; people with their schemes, their lies, their malicious betrayals. She would have gone forward to it without hesitation, but that was not her plan; instead, after a last look at the dazzling eyes—why did they seem so familiar?—she walked calmly on uphill to the farrowing pen where the mother pig and piglets were incarcerated. There were two doors, large and small; she pulled up the small door to open it, and shot the bolt so that it would not slide down again.

Then, still with the same deliberation, she made her way to the top of the orchard, where a second gate led out into the lane. She did not see the leopard again but addressed it silently in thought as she went back down the road towards the house.

Just wait, she told it, just wait patiently a little time. I am doing my best for you. We are friends. Friends, of course; now she knew why the topaz eyes seemed so familiar. They were Karl's eyes, shining at her with Karl's bright, passionless scrutiny out of the leopard's face.

She paused by the car and locked it, then cocked her head, thinking she heard a footstep on the hill above. Could Charles—? But the sound was not repeated; she must have been mistaken; when she went indoors she found Charles there already, stoking the stove. His movements were slow and imprecise; dejection or fatigue had made him absent-minded.

"Oh, hullo, have you been out?" he said in surprise.

"Locking the car."

"You think our furry friend might make off with it?" he suggested in an attempt at lightness.

"No," Eleanor said patiently, "but if Peter Lannick is really wandering round in the dangerously unstable state that Maggie would have us believe, it's just on the cards that he might do something foolish to the Ford."

"Oh yes, maybe.—Poor Maggie," Charles said irrelevantly. "Goodnight, Nell."

"Goodnight," she said, and directed an expressionless look after his retreating back.

XXV

Next morning was Saturday, which I hate, and to make matters worse it rained. I got up quietly—Maggie would sleep for hours, yet, thank god, if undisturbed—and went out into the shining, dripping world. Why did the bloody place have to be so beautiful when I was trying to leave it? Brunel's viaduct soared up into the cloud like the Pillars of Hercules and the cedars behind Watertown House were solemn as a sacred grove.

I was just about as wretched as I could be. Or so I thought.

Even Aspic's manifest rage at my return didn't amuse me as much as it would have done a few weeks before. She was beginning to frighten me a little; once or twice on the previous evening I'd caught a rabid gleam in her eye, as it skimmed me, that fairly gave me the grue; if she could have dumped me in an acid bath she'd have done it without a second's hesitation. I began to think that John's warnings, which I'd taken as at least in part the product of alcohol and remorse, were not exaggerated in the least. Maggie must be rescued, and it would be real Sleeping Beauty stuff because unless I pointed out that her dear friend was going as daffy as a coot she'd fight every step of the way; and if I told her, she'd say that Eleanor needed her even more. So there was a problem right off.

And Charles. Oh, Charles. Thinking about him was like taking a dive through a liquidiser but I couldn't help doing it. There he was, two hundred yards away, asleep in his square white house, and if I had any sense I'd see that the distance between us never grew any less.

Breaking my news to Maggie last night had been just as bad as I'd expected; she'd been really crushed by it, she just sat staring at me, numbly repeating, "But why do you *do* these things? Why do you do it?"

"Oh god, I don't know, Maggie; deprived childhood, I daresay. Or like putting beans up your nose."

"*Beans* up your nose?" She rubbed her noble brow, smearing it with cigarette ash, looking utterly at sea.

"Surely you know—if you tell someone not to do a thing often enough, they're hypnotised into doing it."

"You aren't as spineless as that, are you?"

So it was a considerable relief, really, when we heard Aspic's car returning and could limp out, licking our scars, to tell her about Peter Lannick. I hadn't really intended to go along, but then I thought, if I was there Maggie wouldn't be able to unroll the latest instalment of my vice to Aspic, at least till she'd slept on it; and as well I could see that she didn't get eaten by the leopard; oh, really I just wanted to see Charles again, I suppose, I was that sore and miserable. Maggie had it in one: spineless was the word.

And then the simpleton had to go and look so goddam *pleased* at the sight of me, and, when Aspic turned the headlights off so that we were all groping about in the dark, he found me with the precision of a magnet scooping up iron filings and gave me a tremendous homecoming hug, as if we'd been doing it all our lives. And kissed me. I shall remember that kiss to my dying day and it's probably all of Charles I shall have to remember so I might as well make the most of it: one quick gentle kiss lasting approximately 4.005 seconds if anyone had been timing us. I worked it out afterwards.

For the rest of the evening I felt as if I'd been taking mescalin; things went on happening, and I could perceive that they did, but I was in another dimension and quite separate; just a meter, registering reactions to Charles.

I'd had the presence of mind to whisper to him, when he came in from looking at his pigs:

"Charles, I've done something perfectly dreadful to Maggie. Please, can you be extra kind to her?"

He gave me one naked look, taking in everything I hadn't told him; and then he was extra kind to Maggie. Poor Maggie.

A great jossop of rain pelted down my neck and I sneezed, reminding myself that no one was going to be pleased if I got pneumonia again. So I took the path which circled the Watertown fields, sunk well out of sight, and joined the Lanrith road up above at Santewan, the Protheros' farm. They always had a roaring kitchen fire and I could stay for a cup of tea and a gossip till the morning was a bit further under way. And I even had a good excuse; I'd brought Mrs Prothero an ovenware funnel and a bundle of filter-papers for her wine-making.

Fred the postman was there, fortifying himself for the next long wet reach of lane.

"Ow be, me 'andsome?" he greeted me.

I sat down and got the cream of the gossip at once: Peter Lannick hadn't been home all night but he was still alive and uneaten by leopard because he had turned up at Santewan earlier that morning and been given breakfast.

"Ate like a madman he did, poor soul; been roaming about the woods all night a-looking for the old leopard and not finding 'er, seemingly, and a mercy 'tis! And not a decent meal in him since last Tuesday week, proper skin and bone he was. Never've I seen the like."

Mrs Prothero gazed at us round-eyed and I felt guiltier than ever; why hadn't we given Peter something yesterday, at least a hot drink?

"And what do you think he did tell us? 'Tis a dreadful thing if it be true."

"What did he tell you, then, missus?" Fred said, finishing his mug of tea and swinging the satchel round his shoulders.

"Why, that last night, when 'e was a-searching Watertown orchards—"

"Where 'e'd no manner o' right to be, midear, an' up to no good I'll be bound—"

" 'E did see Dr Foley, 'er own self, come up orchard, pussyfoot soft all in the dark, and what do you suppose 'er did?"

"Changed into the leopard-puss?" Fred suggested cheerfully. "When I was in the Dardanelles, last war but one, before your time my lover, I heerd tales of chaps as could change into a wolf of a night-time and run about on four legs, seeking whom they could devour. Proper handy that'd be for some of us, eh?"

"Now, Fred!" cried Mrs Prothero, scandalised. "Don't-ee be frittening us with such unchristian nonsense! No, 'tweren't that, but nigh as bad; Dr Foley went up to farrowing-pen and opened the door for to let out Mr Charles's little pigs. What do-ee think of that, then? 'S own sister to serve him such a trick?"

"You mean," I said blankly, "let the little pigs out so they'd die of cold?"

"Ess! Or for the old leopard to get en! 'S own sister!"

But Fred looked sceptical.

"How do-ee know it ben't all a tale, like? Maybe her never let out the farrows at all? Maybe 'twas Peter as let en out? Niver credit all ee do hear, Missus!"

"Now, Fred! Peter Lannick's my own sister's husband's nevvy, an' a decent chap afore 's mum turned so poorly-like and no-account. But that Dr Foley! Tis just the like of thing her might do. 'Twas wicked cruel what her did to our poor old Tibbie and I've heerd a-plenty other tales tew! Some do say 'twas she let the beast loose from the circus."

"I'm sure that's nonsense, Mrs Prothero," I said.

Fred, still sceptical, left to go on with his round, but paused in the doorway.

"Nearly forgot this, midear, for your friend, t'other lady."

It was a postcard for Maggie, from John. "Dear Maggie, don't blame Tuesday too much. It was my fault really. And come back to London. *This is important.* John."

My eye skimmed it before I thought. When I did think, I thought, sourly, just as well I'd already made my confession.

Mrs Prothero was still dying to discuss Peter's story.

"Do-ee think it *could* be true, midear? Dr Foley's a proper queer 'un."

I thought it *could* be true, all right; but I also thought a lot of harm could be done by spreading it.

"Don't you suppose he imagined it? If he was ill and starving?"

"Ess, maybe," she agreed regretfully. " 'Tis true 'e did seem feverish. I was fair frit by the look of 'en; like as not 'tis all a pack of moonshine."

On this I left her; it had struck me that part of the story, at least, could easily be checked.

In fact, when I walked down the hill to Watertown there was no need to make tactful inquiries; I could see at once that all hell had broken loose.

Mr Rowse, with a small party of workmen, stood outside the house in the rain, listening respectfully to Charles, who raged up and down the road like judge, jury, and a chorus from Euripides, all in one. He had no jacket on, raindrops spangled his sweater and his brown hair. I had never seen him so angry; indeed, thinking it over, I had never seen him angry at all, and I began to worry; what would such a state of emotion do to his heart? Poor Nin evidently worried about this too; she pattered up and down behind him, wailing, "Master Charles! Master Charles! Don't upset yourself so, dearie, *don't*! There's a plenty more pigs in Cornwall. And you've still got the sow!"

But to Charles these were his pigs, ones that he himself had successfully engineered into the world, and he would not be comforted. He took no notice of Nin.

"Savaged, every one of them. Nothing left but bloody gristle. When I find out who opened the pen I'll—I'll—"

Eleanor came out of the house, neat and immaculate in her silk leopard-pattern raincoat; she said calmly,

"You really must not excite yourself so, Charles; it is very bad for you. Here, take these." And she handed him a couple of red tablets.

"Oh, for god's sake, Nell! Don't fuss!" Impatiently disregarding her he shoved the tablets in his pocket and strode indoors. "I'm going to ring the police and then I'm going out with my gun; that leopard's going to be sorry it ever tasted pig! If we meet I'll give it such a pantsful of lead that it'll have to be fetched home in a colander."

"Eh dear now!" said Mr Rowse, and dispersed his fascinated men with wavings of his fat little arms. Peter was not there, I noticed.

Eleanor, very pale and with compressed lips, got into her car and drove off, ignoring me as if I had been a notifiable disease in somebody else's patient.

I went down and made a pot of coffee for Maggie and woke her; she instantly began reading one of the books I'd brought her, a massive tome called *Harvey's Analysis of One Hundred and Sixty Five Cases of Thyroid Deficiency*, as if it were a prophylactic against me; I suppose in a way it was.

"Here," I said, and gave her John's postcard. She stared at it blankly; several minutes went by before she seemed to register that it was in a language she understood.

"He says it was his fault?" she said at last. And after another pause, "Does he love you?"

"Good god, Maggie—" Of course not, I was going on to say, but a black police MG spun past our windows, turning neatly and pulling up with a scrunch of gravel. There was a knock and a sergeant put his head in the open door.

"Morning, miss. Just want to make a check on the whereabouts of this leopard as has savaged Mr Foley's pigs. Mind if I take a look round the back?"

"Do," I said. "We'd hate to think we might meet it face to face in the coal shed. It definitely was the leopard that got them, was it?"

"Inspector's up there now, looking at the remains, miss. You didn't catch a glimpse of it, or hear anything suspicious in the night? Squeals, or yowling, or anything like that?"

"Not a thing, I'm afraid."

Maggie had been slowly hingeing on to the purport of his questions.

"Do you mean," she said, horrified, "that the leopard has killed Charles's pigs?"

"Looks like it, miss."

"But this is dreadful! Charles must be terribly upset."

"That's putting it mildly," I said.

"I must go and tell him how sorry I am."

"I should leave it just now—" I began, but she was out already, ignoring the rain on her black sweater and trousers, making a beeline for the house. With a strong effort I stayed where I was. The cottage parlour looked up towards the orchard; presently I could see Maggie's black figure arrive up there, joining the navy-blue dots of police who were weaving about among the trees, and the particoloured blob which represented Charles's white sweater and brown corduroys.

172

I shunted my mind away from them and coupled it on to the idea for a plot, which had suddenly sprung out of nowhere in the unaccountable way they do, just when I'd begun to give up hope.

After some time—four hours and twenty pages as it turned out—I came to the end of that burst of impetus and began to wonder where Maggie had got to. So I left a pot of soup warming on the hob, put on my anorak, and went out into the wet, which had thickened and become a nice solid, west-country, Saturday-afternoon brume. Mr Rowse and men had departed; glad to leave the leopard's latest stamping-ground I daresay, though one might assume that at this time of day it would be dossed down somewhere and sleeping off last night's orgy of pork.

I went up to the house first but nobody was about except Nin who told me disapprovingly that Charles was out on a leopard hunt and Maggie with him. Down through the Watertown woods they'd gone, she said, towards the river. I was startled to hear of this activity on Maggie's part, but also pleased; it seemed Charles was taking me at my word, really putting himself out to be nice to her. Only one thing made me uneasy; were the pair of them competent to deal with the leopard if by bad luck they should encounter it? Maggie would be useless in such a contingency, I thought, remembering the time we'd found a rat in the flat kitchen and how she'd panicked; and suppose Charles had a heart-attack? I could see why Nin disapproved of their going off; certainly if Eleanor had been at home there would have been twenty-carat trouble, but she was out delivering a baby.

Probably there was not much real risk; Nin said the police had gone the other way, up towards the moor, on a hot tip from a tracker dog which presumably knew what it was about.

I started off to look for Charles and Maggie; urged by Nin I carried our firewood chopper though I sincerely trusted I wasn't going to get within chopping range of the leopard. And I hoped, too, squelching down through the wild, wet, overgrown woods, that Charles didn't suffer from an itchy trigger-finger; not that my red anorak could be thought to resemble a leopard's spots but the visibility was bad.

As I ploughed along I brooded unconstructively about Eleanor and Peter Lannick, wondering which of them would be more predisposed to an act of wanton, malicious destruction; in present circumstances the odds were about even, I thought; I wouldn't care to meet either of them alone in a dark lane.

Was it going to be possible to tell Maggie what I had heard at the Protheros'?

Finding it a bit spooky in the mist under the trees I kept myself cheerful by singing, and presently had the relief of seeing Charles and Maggie in the distance. They didn't look like big-game hunters; they were walking slowly, engrossed in talk; Charles carried his gun but the leopard could have ridden past them in a troika and neither would have noticed.

"Boo!" I shouted.

They looked up and I received the daunting impression first that I'd been the subject of their talk, second that neither was pleased to see me. It was the first time for weeks that I'd met Charles without his face lighting up and I felt it like the first twinge of a mortal disease.

No need to waste time asking if they'd seen the leopard; obviously they hadn't; instead I said to Charles,

"Will you help me persuade Maggie that she ought to come back to London?"

"Why?" Maggie said bitterly. "Because John is there?"

I didn't look at Charles. He didn't look at me.

"No," I answered tiredly. "In case you'd forgotten, John takes off in the Gull Race on Tuesday. Simply because you need to be within reach of hospitals and libraries if you're to do decent research. And you know that too."

Charles said tentatively, "It does sound like sense, Maggie. You mustn't let Nell persuade you against your better judgment. She's apt to let her enthusiasms run away with her, I'm afraid."

"I'm glad to stay here and help her get settled," Maggie said gruffly.

I kept my mouth shut. There were things that couldn't be said in front of Charles.

When we reached the road and could see as far as the entrance of Watertown House, it was plain that yet another dramatic scene was in progress there. I wondered idly, as we quickened our pace, whether people become more inclined to behave like characters out of grand opera if they live in roman-tic surroundings. A camera shot of the gathering on the hill would have looked exactly like some fearful climax from a last act, with skeletons tumbling out of cupboards—mist-dripping

174

cypresses up above, two square white buildings asymmetrically arranged on either side of the steep road, chorus of constables, etc., on either side, Inspector Pollard, upstage, centre, between Peter Lannick, pale and dishevelled, and Eleanor, trim as a pin in her leopardskin raincoat. Two police cars parked, U.R.

Oh, oh, I thought. Now we shall see some fireworks. But perhaps a few things will get straightened out.

"That's a downright lie," Peter was saying with passion as we came within earshot. "I tell you I saw her with my own eyes lift up the hatch so's they could run out."

Eleanor gave a shrug and glanced at Pollard expressively.

"Honestly, Inspector. I ask you! I'm afraid it's a simple case of delusions—at least that's the most charitable construction to put on his story."

"Delusions! I'll give you delusions!" Peter said with an ugly oath. He started all over again giving an account of how he had seen Eleanor in the orchard. It sounded circumstantial enough but his feverish appearance and state of disarray weren't helping the audience to believe him, I could see.

"He's in a very disturbed state at present," Eleanor went on with perfect calm, addressing the inspector and ignoring Peter. "My friend there, Dr Tassák, will confirm that. Yesterday evening she had to treat him for a hysterical faint; in fact he knocked his head and may be slightly concussed. We meant to send him to hospital for observation, as you probably know, but he ran off before the ambulance arrived."

"You mean," said the inspector, "it may be a case of—?" He tapped his forehead.

"Bloody hell it may!" burst in Peter furiously. "Don't you go a-pinning it on me that I'm mental, Jake Pollard! I'm as sane as you or anybody else. Though by god it's enough to drive a man barmy, what she's been a-doing to me! First-all she deliberately terrified my mum, always going on about having her put away in a home; oh yes, and one of the neighbours saw you there that last afternoon," he said savagely to Eleanor. "It was most likely your narking and nagging at her that made the poor old sod so miserable she went wandering out in the woods half-cut. You *wanted* the bloody leopard to get her, didn't you? Kind of a pet for you, isn't it? Like to make sure it gets plenty of tit-bits, don't you? And then when the cops found her and called you, you took so long coming, a-purpose, that the poor old girl was a goner before you got there, so's you wouldn't have the bother of looking after her." He thrust his face forward at Eleanor; a muscle in his cheek kept jerking uncontrollably and his eyes were full of tears. "Poor old soak, you just don't think people like us oughta be *alive*, do you? You think they're just a mess that oughta be swept up and tidied away. And now, thanks to you, old Rowse has paid me off with two weeks' sick leave. Sick leave! When I come back it'll be, Oh, I'm afraid we've filled your place now. You told him I was going barmy, didn't you? By god, do I wish you'd never come here, you and your fancy London friends. *She* did her best to poison me yesterday," he said, nodding towards Maggie, "and 'tother one's no better than a little tart, ask any o' Rowse's men they'll tell you the same—"

"Here, here, that's enough of that sort o' talk!" the inspector exclaimed, scandalised. "I'm going to take you into custody, my lad, for behaviour liable to cause a breach of the peace, and you'll be lucky if Dr Foley doesn't bring a civil action against you for slander. I never heard such stuff in all my life, never!"

He nodded to two of his men; they stepped forward and took hold of Peter's arms.

"Come on, boy," one of them said, not unkindly. "What you want is a cup of tea and a lay-down."

"What I want is justice!" Peter shouted furiously as he was hurried away to the police-car.

"I'm sorry about that, Doctor," the inspector told Eleanor.

"Oh, good heavens, I'm quite used to such scenes," she said coolly. "I assure you he's merely suffering from minor mental disturbance and the best thing you can do for him is get him to a doctor, preferably a male one. Obviously it's no use my trying to examine him in his present frame of mind."

"I'll do that, miss," Pollard said. "I'll call Dr Trevelyan."

"Excuse me, sir." The driver had got out of one of the cars. "Message just come through on the radio from Camelot division —there's been a serious multiple car-crash upalong the A.30 at Gweer Downs and can you spare four or five men? Coach overturned in the fog."

The inspector looked put out. "As if we hadn't enough tribulation already with this blowstering leopard," he said, slipping into more of an accent than I had yet heard from him. "Here, let me have a word." He went and argued on the radio, but unsuccessfully, it appeared; presently he came back to say to Charles,

"I'll have to take my men off for the time, I'm afraid, sir. I was meaning to leave a couple out this way, case the leopard comes back; they lost his trail up on the moor but seemed like he might be circling down here again. So I must ask you to use extra precautions tonight. I'll warn Kormendi and the Protheros as I go up."

The two police cars drove off, in close formation.

Eleanor, Charles, Maggie, and I were left standing about on the road in a silence that nobody seemed keen to break. But presently Maggie said,

"Where did they find Peter?"

"Not far from here," Eleanor said. She turned and walked indoors. We followed. "They were coming back, apparently, to warn us that the leopard's trail had been lost, and caught sight of Peter in the woods between here and Lanrith, dodging about; it took four of them to collar him."

"Poor chap," Charles said, "he does seem to be in a state."

No one made any comment about Peter's accusation against Eleanor. Nin appeared just then and said that Claire was on the phone, ringing from Exeter to say could she do any shopping there for anybody? She was pausing for a meal on her way back to Cornwall.

"Good old Claire!" Charles was delighted. "She can get some cartridges for the .350, I haven't all that many."

He went off to give specifications. Glancing at Eleanor I surprised a look of straight, uncontrolled rage on her face before she pulled herself together and began talking to Maggie about Peter Lannick. Why does she dislike Claire so much, I wondered. Simply because she is Charles's friend? Or because she is living with old Aunt Julia and may be an undesirable influence on her?

"I daresay he'll be remanded for a medical report and then just shunted quietly off somewhere," Eleanor said. "It would really be kinder. But if it should come to evidence in court you could confirm that he was in an odd mental condition. After all, you were the one who was urging that he should see a psychiatrist."

"Certainly I could confirm it," said Maggie. She turned to me. "That is another reason why we cannot leave Cornwall at present."

"Leave Cornwall? Who suggested you should?" Eleanor's voice had risen half an octave; her eyes flew from Maggie to me.

Charles came back. He said, "Right, Claire will be here in a couple of hours. I asked her to stay to a meal before she goes back to Aunt Julia. Now I'm going out to have another try at shooting the hide off that bloody leopard. I hope the inspector was right and that it *does* come back this way."

XXVI

ELEANOR TOOK OFF her raincoat and went upstairs. She stood for a moment breathing deep breaths, then let down her hair, brushed it smooth, and recoiled it. This was usually a tranquillising process. But her hands were shaking so much that she had to do it three times before she was satisfied, and the effort of holding her arms above her head made her breathless all over again.

"You *are* in a rage, aren't you, liebchen?" Karl's voice teased her. "Won't they leave you alone? But you got rid of Peter Lannick very creditably; old Trevelyan, who's an utter moron, will pronounce that he has St Vitus' Dance or diminished responsibility, with a little guidance from you, and that will be the end of the matter."

What's the use of that? she retorted furiously in her mind. He's not nearly such a threat to me as the other two.

"You can deal with them, dear, you know you can. All in good time."

And then there's Charles and the leopard. Suppose he shoots it?

"Perhaps the leopard will get Charles, dear."

At this thought she put down her brush and walked over to the window. As afternoon turned to twilight the fog had thickened and filled Watertown hollow with sodden greyness, through which the cottage and viaduct looked like ghostly shapes in an over-exposed photograph. Trees dripped audibly; then their sound was drowned by the slow clank of a goods-train crossing the viaduct, exploding a fog signal every few hundred yards. When it had gone the hush settled down once more.

Yes, she thought. Yes I can deal with them. All in good time. She went downstairs and was immediately angry again.

"Where's Dr Tassák?"

"Went back to the cottage," Nin said placidly. "Work to do, she said."

"But I asked her to have a drink and spend the evening here."

Nin shrugged. "All I can tell you's what she told me. Anyway, not very cheerful, here, is it? Sittingroom fire's all but out and I've no time to tend to it, not if Miss Dean's coming to supper."

The sittingroom fire was completely out. Tight-lipped, Eleanor fetched wood, coal, and the Diabolino firelighter, piled up the fuel, and began blowing it into a blaze. There was at least considerable satisfaction in wielding the powerful, efficient tool, directing a blast of invisible, searing heat until the heap of stuff began to smoke and smoulder, and suddenly crackled into flame. She was about to put the firelighter away when she heard an outbreak of frantic screeching and cackling from the hens up in the yard, followed by two shots. The fog made them sound shatteringly close.

There was a wail from Nin, and a crash of crockery.

"Mercy on us! What was that?"

"How should I know?" snapped Eleanor, but she made her way quickly up to the henyard.

Owl-light had given way to true dark now, and she paused at the henyard gate looking out into the shadows of the orchard. Then, up towards the top of the hill, she saw a circle of torchlight wavering over grass as it came nearer; it was Charles, but he seemed to be limping or halting—was he hurt? At his approach the hens shrieked and cackled again, flying crazily against the walls of their roosting-house.

"Are you all right?" Eleanor called.

He said, "I've shot the leopard."

"*What?*"

He turned the torch backward and she saw that it was true; he was dragging the black-and-gold body by its hind legs. The face, fixed in a last grinning snarl, bumped sideways through clumps of narcissus.

"He came back for some more pickings, the brute! Well he won't try *that* again. And if the circus people want to sue, you can bear witness, Nell, that he was sneaking round our henyard..."

Eleanor made no answer. She turned on her heel and strode back to the house, leaving the yard gate wide behind her and the back door swinging.

"Hey, what's up?" Charles called, bewildered. "Hey, Nell! Where the devil are you off to?"

"Where's my spotted raincoat?" Eleanor demanded of Nin. "I left it hanging up here."

"That Dr Tassák borrowed it to go down to the cottage," Nin said, primming her lips. "I don't know why she bothered, I'm sure—she was wet enough already. Some folks treat other people's property as if it was their own—"

"Oh, good heavens, it doesn't matter!"

"Where are you off to, this time of the evening?" said Nin, full of disapproval, as Eleanor pulled out a white PVC slicker and shrugged into it. "Don't forget Miss Dean will be here any minute."

"Out on a call. Anyway Miss Dean's Charles's friend—he'll entertain her."

"*I* never heard the phone."

"Getting deaf, then, aren't you? Don't keep supper for me, I'm not hungry."

A moment later her car roared up the hill in bottom gear.

XXVII

W H E N   W E   G O T   back to the cottage—Maggie, it seemed, was dying to return to Harvey on Thyroid Deficiency and I'd no wish to stay on at Watertown, which felt particularly inhospitable just then, I wanted to reread my twenty pages—Maggie plumped down in the Windsor chair, raincoat and all. Then her real reason for leaving came out. She said,

"Sit down. I want to talk to you."

"What about?" I said nervously.

"Your future."

"Oh, Maggie. What is there to say?"

"There's a lot. I've been talking to Charles—"

My innards did an appalling lurch. It was exactly like going down too fast in a lift; I almost expected my ears to pop. I swallowed, hoped my voice wouldn't shake, and said,

"I really fail to see why poor Charles should be dragged into it."

Maggie gave me her professorial look; she had put on black-rimmed glasses and stared over them. She said,

"Charles is a very good, very kind, very disinterested person."

You're telling me, I felt like shouting. As if I didn't know that, with every hair of my head.

Maggie's large, luminous grey eyes were shining, her cheeks were almost pink. I suddenly thought, she doesn't look like Maggie, she looks like a woman. Keeping a grip of my eyes, she went on,

"Charles made me see that in a way I've been selfish, trying to hold you back, cramping your development because I'm so fond of you; he says you're maturing faster than I realise."

Maggie in this rare concessive mood always reduced me to inarticulacy; I muttered gruffly,

"You haven't been selfish, you were trying to improve me—"

"Well, Charles has showed me that there's a point beyond which you have to make your own decisions." Every time she said *Charles* her voice deepened in tone. It was like reading old texts where the name Jesus is printed differently in Gothic type; and just about as revealing. Myself, I always avoided talking about Charles when I could. I said, stammering slightly,

"You mean I ought to go off on my own? But how would you manage?"

"Oh, I'd be all right," she said with the certainty of the knights who had seen the Holy Grail.

"You'd have to come back to London, though, Maggie. You must come back."

"No," she said. "I need to stay here."

"But why? *Why?*"

This time Maggie didn't mention Charles. Perhaps she didn't even consciously think of him. She said, "Eleanor's not at all well. It isn't simple for her, this adjustment to a country practice. She needs me down here."

My having expected something like this made it no easier to tackle. I began cautiously, "It seems to me that she's a bit shaken off balance at present—maybe she's the one who could really do with psychiatric help," thinking, a strait-waistcoat would be nearer the mark.

"No, you have it quite wrong. You know nothing about it," Maggie said shortly. "In any case that's not the point. I can't go back to London yet but you must. Charles made me see that

181

it would be thoroughly selfish of me to stand in the way of you and John marrying."

I was so completely thrown by this that I just stared at her with my mouth open, feeling as if I were headed in the wrong direction up a dual carriageway. She looked back at me, a clear, gentle serious look, with goodwill and sincerity shining out like a lighthouse beam. Only it had missed its mark. For some reason at that moment I was reminded of the little crystal bird and wondered in a distracted way what she would do when I declined the offer of her greatest friend—toss him out of the window as well? But he had already tossed himself, and for this and various other reasons my throat constricted and tears began swarming out of my eyes.

"But it isn't—you don't—I can't—oh, blast it. Where's a handkerchief?" I mumbled, and found the towel we used to dry the dishes.

"It's all right," Maggie said earnestly.

"It's not all right, Maggie." Somehow I had to explain the whole situation to her, but as I nerved myself for this north face we heard a knock at the open door and Charles came in.

His appearance was odd—pale, bright-eyed, with his brown hair all ruffled up.

"Why Charles," Maggie said, "what's happened?"

She's observing, I thought marginally, she's actually reached the stage where she notices other people even when they're not ill.

Charles said, "I did it! I shot the leopard!"

He looked with triumph at our blank faces. After a pause Maggie said faintly,

"You mean you killed it?"

"Yes."

"Well, congratulations," I said, trying out my voice cautiously. "That ought to be a little compensation for all your pretty piglets."

"Not really," he said honestly. "I felt like a murderer when I saw it close to—it was such a beautiful beast. Nell was pretty upset, I think—I got it in the neck at fairly close range. She took one look and rushed off somewhere."

Sweet mayhem, what'll she do, I thought, remembering how she'd taken the leopard's part at the circus and her obvious sympathy for it. She's had enough to swallow today, this may blow her sky-high.

"Where—where did she go?" I said.

Charles looked at me in slight surprise.

"Oh, just off on some case. She'll be all right by the time she gets back."

Old one-track Maggie wasn't greatly interested in the leopard once it had been dealt with. She had set her hand to the plough and wanted to push on along her furrow.

"Charles," she said, "we've just been talking about what you and I discussed this afternoon on our walk—"

Oh no, I thought. This I am not going to bear.

One quick glance at Charles's face showed me he wasn't going to bear it easily either.

I said rapidly, "Maggie, Charles has had a pretty hectic day, he doesn't want to be bothered with our problems now—"

The defenceless face he turned to me was like a stab in the guts.

Maggie, of course, was all contrition at once.

"Yes, yes, I am sorry, you are right. Charles, you should be in bed."

"Actually," he said, "I'm expecting Claire any minute. I must go back. That's probably her car now."

I went to the door, relieved to escape from the submerged emotions drifting like mines about the room. Sure enough, Claire's Jaguar was just pulling up outside Watertown House. She didn't hear my shout, but walked round to the front door.

Charles had come after me but stopped abruptly when he found I was still standing on the little bridge; which made me shoot away into the dark as if I'd rebounded off him.

"Well—goodnight," he said, hesitating, dividing it between Maggie indoors and me by the stream. "Just thought I'd let you know there was no more danger."

"Thank you, Charles," I said. Then we heard Claire's lusty shout as she came striding down the hill.

"Hi—hi Charles? Are you down there?"

"Here," he called, starting towards her. "Nice to have you back, Claire."

Claire wasn't wasting time on civilities. She said to Charles,

"Nin was on the phone when I went in—it's bad news, I'm afraid. Khartoum Cottage is on fire—in fact I saw the engine start out as I came through Lanrith but of course it never occurred to me that it would be Miss Foley's place. Want me to take you out there?"

"Oh good lord, yes, thanks, Claire," said Charles, horrified. "What a frightful thing—I know we've always said she'd set fire to herself but you don't really expect—I'll just leave a message with Nin in case Nell comes back—"

He went quickly up the hill. "Shall I come along too?" I said to Claire. "An extra hand might be some use with the buckets and I know first aid."

"No harm," Claire said.

I went back to tell Maggie. She was already at grips with Harvey on Thyroid like a woman in labour gulping at her gas-and-air.

"Aunt Julia's house is on fire," I told her. "We're going to see if we can help—do you want to come? A doctor might be useful."

Slowly and reluctantly she surfaced out of Harvey. "Come? No, why should I? Eleanor's sure to be there and they won't want too many outsiders in the way."

She was probably right but a powerful instinct was prodding me to go along as a witness. What of? I didn't know. I simply felt that too many eccentric things had been happening too fast—Peter Lannick, the leopard, now this—it couldn't be pure coincidence that the Foley household were attracting such a lot of catastrophes. People drop their guard and behave spontaneously at scenes of crisis; I wanted to be there to observe. Besides, I liked old Aunt Julia.

Maggie was disapproving. "You had much better not go," she said. I forebore to remind her we had agreed Tuesday was to make her own decisions from now on and merely said, "You never know, I might be some use. See you later."

She grunted, already withdrawn into Harvey, and I ran out to Claire, who was turning the Jaguar on our gravel-patch. Just before I got into the car I glanced back and caught a glimpse of Maggie through our open front door—hunched over her book, wreathed in cigarette smoke, reaching out a blind hand for the dregs of the coffee.

As I had seen her so many times before.

XXVIII

CHARLES ASKED CLAIRE, "Did you hear if Aunt Julia was all right?"

"No," she said. "No, I didn't hear."

They were lucky with the ferry at Lanrith; an attendant was just casting off as they came down the ramp, but waited for them since there were few cars at that time of the evening.

"Ten minutes later," Claire said, "and we'd have had to go round by Tregonnoc Bridge, like the fire-engine. It's too big for the ferry."

During the rest of the drive, which took about eight minutes, nobody spoke. Claire drove with her usual concentration and skill, weaving the car like a shuttle through narrow foggy lanes. Before they reached Khartoum Cottage, when they were still half a mile away, they could see a reddish glow, diffused and wavering in the misty sky ahead. Claire pulled up before they got there, in a turning downhill, to avoid blocking the approach.

As they walked up Charles muttered, "At least there's no wind, that's one mercy."

The fog, even denser up on this hilltop, had been dispersed to some extent round the burning cottage itself by the sheer heat of the blaze, giving them a fairly clear view of what was happening. At present the fire seemed to be mostly at the back, but it was gaining a footing on the roof in front as lighted wisps of straw, borne on the updraught, sailed over and fell in new spots.

Like red-hot lizards, Charles thought, seeing a claw-shaped fan of sparks dart wriggling across the thatch. No wonder the Chinese used to call fire a dragon-god.

He made for the fire-engine, which was drawn up on the grass verge in front, with its hoses snaking through the garden, found a man making an adjustment to the water-pressure, and said urgently,

"Miss Foley? Where is she? Is she all right? I'm her nephew."

"We'm afraid she may still be in there, sir—nobody's had a glimpse of her yet. The stairs has gone, you see—they was at the back. We'm rigging a ladder now. Could be the lady was stupefied by the smoke—'twasn't she gave the alarm, 'twas neighbours, Jagoes down to Lannivet, called up to say they could see fire a-glowing on hilltop and thought it must be here."

Charles ran through the trampled garden to where the men

were working with the hoses, throwing long silvery broken plumes into the heart of the fire. Plainly this was where it must have started; the whole rear side of the house was ablaze up to the roof-ridge. Great tassels of flame detached themselves and floated upward into the fog; the thatch burned fiercely with a crackle like breaking eggshells.

They had set the ladder against the end wall; as Charles came round a black-faced fireman emerged from one of the windows and climbed down, making a no-go sign.

"That's not her bedroom!" Charles shouted. "It's at the other end. *Other end!*"

His voice was drowned by the roar of flames and hoses; he grabbed the arm of a thickset curly-haired man who seemed to be directing operations and pointed, urgently, until at last the man nodded his comprehension and had the ladder shifted to the other end of the cottage. This part was at an angle from the burning area; by some freak of convection although it was only a few feet away from the flames, the end section of roof, with its protruding dormer window, was still almost untouched.

But now the men hesitated, looking doubtfully at the rear roof, shaking their heads. Here the thatch had burned so savagely that part of it, which had been all flames only a short time before, was already reduced to a soft, incandescent red mass, evidently liable to fall in at any moment. It seemed unreasonable to expect anyone to risk his life under such a hazard.

Charles, without wasting time, ran to the ladder.

"I'll go," he said to the man at the foot. "Give me an axe and something to put over my face."

Somebody handed him a wet cloth; somebody else tossed a bucket of water over him. He heard Claire call,

"Charles, do be careful—"

"It's all right," he called back quite cheerfully, from halfway up the ladder. "Don't you see it doesn't matter what happens to me?"

With a feeling almost of satisfaction he reached the sill of the dormer, flung a leg over it, and disappeared into the darkness.

Nobody could possibly have heard what he said for at that moment the entire slate roof of the leanto wash-house fell in with a great crumpling crash.

XXIX

THERE WASN'T THE usual ring of spectators at the scene of the blaze. Just us, and the neighbours from a farm below who had given the alarm, and the firemen. Khartoum was too isolated for the fire to attract casual sightseers.

I'd already assured myself that Eleanor wasn't there. While I was wondering if this were of significance, one of the men came out with his hand badly cut by broken glass, so I offered to tie it up for him.

"How did the fire start, do you know?" I asked, winding the bandage.

"Hard to tell, miss—it had got such a hold, time we come along. But we could see *where* it had started all right—'twas out in that wash'us at the back where Miss Foley kept all her coals and kindling and the paraffin drum for her lamps. So o' course once it got started, it would spread easy. Plenty to feed on."

Under his layer of grime and soot I now recognised Sam Bonallack, a part-time fireman who in the daytime drove a delivery van for the Co-op.

"Thank you, midear," he said. "Proper job you made o' that." Then, looking up, he exclaimed, "By gor, who let *him* go up, then?"

I turned round in time to see Charles climb the ladder.

You couldn't say that silence fell—the steady roar of the fire went on, with an occasional whoomph! as a new section of thatch caught—but the men paused momentarily in their operations, and everyone watched the window. A piece of roof caved in not far away, leaving a black hole like a tooth-gap. I dug my nails into my palms and willed frenziedly for Charles to be all right, for him to find Aunt Julia. At least he knew the layout of the house. Nothing happened. Unable to bear the wait, I went over to Claire, and heard her cursing to herself:

"Why the hell did it have to happen when I wasn't here? Ten to one the poor old girl was asleep; once she's off she wouldn't wake if the rock of Gibraltar fell through the roof. I suppose she'd been at her old tricks, dosing the fire with paraffin to make it burn up, and spilt some on the floor—how she managed to survive for so long I really do not know. I don't think, till I came along, she knew the difference between paraffin and petrol

—she used to keep a handy can of one or t'other, irrespective, in the ingle-nook—"

She was talking mainly to ease the tension as we waited and I didn't pay much attention, but one sentence pierced through and lodged in my mind :

"Another couple of hours and I'd have been back and it wouldn't have happened—I'd have stopped her doing whatever she did, or at least smelt the fire before it got a hold—"

Which was to say that, for anybody intending to set fire to Miss Foley's house, this would be the last opportunity. If they chanced, that is, to know that Claire was away, and was expected back.

But how can you prove that somebody started a fire?

"By gor!" shouted Mr Bonallack, stepping back heavily on my foot in his excitement. "He's got her! 'Tis lucky the old girl's a featherweight!"

He thumped me on the back, nearly dislocating my cervical vertebrae; I hardly noticed it, I was watching Charles as he manoeuvred a black, blanket-wrapped bundle through the window; one of the other men darted up to help him down the ladder, others clustered at the bottom to receive her. Someone pointed to a sofa which stood nearby among a jumbled mass of household gear, but I saw Charles shake his head, looking round for Claire, who hurried forward.

"We'll have to get her to hospital right away," he said, ignoring the fire-chief who exclaimed, "Well done, sir! Is she all right then? We feared as you'd both had it when that bit of thatch fell—"

Claire nodded and ran for her car. By the time they had carried Miss Foley across the garden the Jaguar was parked in front of the fire engine.

"Lay her in the back," Claire said, and opened the rear door. Then I heard her exclaim, "Good god, Charles—your hands!"

"Oh, they'll be all right," he said. "The curtains and bedding had caught; her bed was right under the back window—"

"You must come to hospital too, Charles; you ought to have those hands dressed properly. I'm afraid there won't be room for you," Claire said to me, "I'll come back for you—"

"Oh, good heavens, don't bother, Claire, I can easily get a lift back with the men. And I'll go and ring Watertown now, to tell Nin, and Eleanor if she's back; there's a callbox down at the corner."

"That's a good plan," Claire said. "Maybe Eleanor can take you back. I'll ring Watertown from the hospital later to find out where you are."

Somebody had just produced the gaudy carpet-bag which Miss Foley carried everywhere; Claire took it and got into the driver's seat; Charles slipped in beside her, holding his arms awkwardly. I shut the door for him and he gave me a quick, doubtful look as if he would have liked to speak but didn't know what to say.

Claire drove off and I ran down to the telephone box, which stood at the junction of five cross roads.

It took ages to get through; the exchange was not very well manned after eight at night.

"Hello, hello, is that you, Nin?"

"Hullo, hullo, who is that? This is Watertown House. Who is that speaking?"

She sounded frail and elderly and suspicious.

I explained myself and told her about Charles's rescue of Miss Foley. She didn't seem as impressed as I'd expected, appeared to take it as a matter of course.

"Is Miss Eleanor back yet, Nin?"

"No, she isn't, Miss Tuesday, and I'm worried half to death here on my own."

"You'll be all right, Nin—after all, Charles has shot the leopard."

" 'Tisn't the *leopard*," she said, "it's that Peter Lannick. Inspector Pollard rang to say he'd got away again. Give them all the slip when they got to the station in Lanrith."

Food for thought, as I walked back to the scene of the fire.

Khartoum Cottage was still burning fiercely, and the men, satisfied that nobody was now left inside, were simply bent on saving what they could.

" 'Tis pretty hopeless," Mr Bonallack confided to me. "We're running out of water, see? Not much to spare up this way."

I remembered hearing that Miss Foley's well had a dismal tendency to run dry.

"Can you save her books?" I said. "She sets store by them."

"Mostly went at the first, I'm afeered, midear. Her study backed on the wash'us."

There were a few books strewn about with the other stuff. I collected them together, piling up loose pages, and began to stack them in a box. Then it occurred to me that the loose pages were very numerous and had a faintly familiar look; I peered at one closely and found that it was an old-fashioned white five-pound note, much crumpled. The book it had fallen from, Browning's *Dramatic Idylls,* had been interleaved with about a dozen more.

I was still staring, rather blankly, at this trove, when Eleanor's voice close behind my shoulder made me start.

"What's happened?" she demanded. "Where's Charles? Where's Aunt Julia?"

She was as pale as her white PVC coat; understandably, no doubt; and her eyes looked black in the lurid light, with minia-ture flames reflected in the pupils.

"Claire took them off to hospital," I said. "Miss Foley was unconscious and Charles had burned his hands very badly getting her out."

Eleanor made no comment on this, but said.

"Do you want a lift back to Watertown?"

I said, "Thanks," warily. At that moment the chief fireman, recognising her, came to ask if she'd look at a man with a sus-pected broken collarbone. While she went with him I stacked the rest of the books in the box, carried it to a shed, and put a groundsheet on top, weighed down with bricks. I reckoned that box contained about £400 in old five-pound notes, tucked among the books. They were probably as safe there as any-where else, provided nobody took a fancy to burn down the shed.

Eleanor was busy fixing up the hurt man with a sling, so I went along to her car. It struck me that a heart-to-heart with her at this juncture might be very instructive. But what I saw in her car changed my mind about accepting the lift; it was a long, lumpy shape on the back seat, covered with a sack, and it looked uncommonly like the Diabolino firelighter. It was either that or a gun.

I decided to walk home.

XXX

"Aunt Julia?" Charles said.

The bandaged face turned a little on the pillow, showing closed lids behind the eyeholes in the mask.

"Don't try to make her talk," warned the sister. "And you mustn't stay long, Mr Foley; you really ought to be in bed yourself."

"Is that—Charles?" It was the scantiest thread of sound.

Charles started to move one of his swaddled arms, remembered, and dropped it impatiently. Claire leaned forward and laid a hand over Aunt Julia's frail claw, which protruded from more bandages. The eyelids fluttered and a speck of pupil showed underneath.

"You're all right, Aunt Julia. Bit of a fire, but nobody hurt. We've taken you to hospital. Claire's here too."

"Very—kind." There was a long silence during which she appeared to be trying to summon strength for another question.

"What is it, Aunt Julia?"

"Khartoum—Cottage?"

"Mostly burnt, I'm afraid. Never mind. You can come and live with us, like a queen, and blue the proceeds from the insurance."

Her teeth showed, rather horrifyingly, in what seemed intended for a smile.

"Never trust—insurance companies—too many—go bankrupt."

"Hush. Lie quiet and take it easy."

But she was struggling to speak again.

"Books—for Charles—all books—"

"Yes, we know. Don't try to talk."

"Bag—"

"Your stripey bag?" Claire took it from the locker. "Here, see?"

"Book—"

There was a volume of Browning in the bag: *Red Cotton Nightcap Country*. Claire showed it.

"Charles—"

He said, "Thank you, Aunt Julia," and cleared his throat.

Aunt Julia said in a full and carrying voice,

"Browning is a greatly underrated poet. His works contain some of the—"

The words petered out. Presently her eyes moved upward until only a line of white was visible under the lids. There was nothing on the bed now but a bandaged, empty shell.

Claire looked down at her hand, which still lay over the

wrinkled, freckled one on the sheet. After a pause she slowly withdrew it.

Charles stood up. He said,

"I think I—" looked about him in a puzzled way as if he had suddenly lost track of what was happening, and crashed full-length on the floor.

Nurses came running and carefully rolled him on to a stretcher. One of them picked up *Red Cotton Nightcap Country* which had skidded across the highly polished ward floor, disgorging an untidy shower of white five-pound notes.

XXXI

TWELVE MINUTES IN a Jaguar adds up to a good long way on foot. I'd hoped to get in to Lanrith and across the foot-ferry before Eleanor caught me up; then I could have slipped away along the shortcut. But I took a wrong turning in the maze of little unposted lanes below Lannivet, and that delayed me. I was on the long winding descent called Coultersmill Hill when I heard a car change gear at the top.

The loom of its lights flung out above me, magnified by the fog, and I stepped to the side of the road, flattening myself against the bank—here it was just a ten-foot wall of rock, prettily hung with fern and pennywort. Standing still, I turned my face to the oncoming car. It couldn't be the fire-engine because that would be obliged to go round by the bridge.

There had been a fall of stones close by where I stood, loosened by wet weather from the bank. One or two quite large boulders lay piled in the angle of road and cliff. It was this that saved me. Eleanor's white Ford roared past, cutting in so close that the wing-mirror snatched at my sleeve and nearly pulled me over—I staggered and threw myself backward against the rock, trying in vain to find a handhold, grabbing with bruised knuckles at flimsy roots and slippery wedges of stone. But the pile of rocks had prevented the car from coming to the extreme edge of the road; she accelerated on, down the hill.

It had all taken place so fast that even the moment after I could hardly credit what had happened; I pushed myself upright on to shaky knees, and stared at the twin red rear-lamps as they receded downwards and round the bend at the foot, still in a state of dazed disbelief. Could she really have intended to come so close? Had she deliberately set out to crush me against the bank? And if so, had it been a momentary impulse, intended as a threat? Or a planned, coldblooded attempt at murder?

I wasn't left for long in doubt. At the bottom of the hill a bridle path led off towards the Lan river; I heard the Ford reverse into this, turn, and begin coming up again fast, snarling in low gear. Unless I moved at once from where I stood she would get me this time, and paste me over a stretch of the rock wall like a pat of butter on a biscuit.

Looking back, as she approached me the first time, I had noticed a great beech tree, silhouetted in the headlights, two or three hundred yards uphill. I remembered that its massive roots thrust out from the rock face in loops and whorls, like a huge frozen digestive tract, forming a sort of ladder. If I could get to the tree before she returned, if I could reach the bottom root and pull myself up, it might be possible to climb out of danger. If not I was trapped like a rat in a drainpipe.

I ran uphill with bursting lungs, hearing the roar of the engine come closer, knowing that I wasn't going to make the tree in time.

But the Ford shot past without stopping. I had an instant's hope, and hesitated. Had I been mistaken? Were her intentions not what I feared?

No. The engine sound faded, died, then began to swell again. She had turned at the top, where four roads met. She had chosen a downhill run for my elimination, so as to have gravity on her side.

My beech tree was only ten yards away now—only five—the headlights blazing into my eyes made it hard to judge. Now the network of roots hung over me, black, outlined in silver. I launched myself at them diagonally, like a goalkeeper swooping at a wide-angled ball—caught hold with my right hand—felt my left slip on wet moss and drag away. I was dangling by one hand, high, but not high enough, feeling desperately with my feet for a hold on the rock and not finding one—I realised what the bait must feel on the angler's hook, waiting for the fish to snap it up.

Something struck me a violent blow on the leg. I distinctly felt the bone snap. At the same time the force of the blow, nearly wrenching my arm out of its socket, made me lose my grip. I must have swung right round as I fell, or Eleanor must have swerved at the moment of impact, because I landed alongside the car, not in front of it; my last conscious impression was of the sudden reversal from light to dark as the car passed; then my head hit the road and I blacked out.

XXXII

NIN ANSWERED THE telephone. By now she was nearly weeping with the anxieties of her lonely vigil.

"Oh, Miss Nell, I'm so glad to hear your voice! Wherever have you been? Did you know about Miss Julia's house getting burnt down?"

"Yes they told me at the police station when I made my regular check call. I'll be going to the hospital to see how Aunt Julia's getting on, so don't wait up for me. But make up a bed for Miss Dean, will you—it seems we're to have her for the night."

"Oh, Miss Nell—"

"What's the matter now?"

"I'm so worried about that Peter Lannick! Did you know he'd got loose again? It's not right he should be roaming round!"

"He's out, is he?" Eleanor said reflectively. "How very—what did you say?"

"And it's my belief he's gone off with Mr Charles's gun."

"Why?" Eleanor's voice sharpened. "How do you know?"

"I found the outer door of the store-room unlocked and the gun's missing. Not the rook rifle, the big one he used to shoot the leopard."

"I daresay he took it back to Colonel Pascoe on the way in to Lanrith."

"And I'm almost sure I heard a shot not long ago!"

"Rubbish, Nin. You're letting your imagination run away with you. Why don't you get Dr Tassák to come up and keep you company?"

"Go out in the dark? Not for anything you could offer me!"

"Well then go to bed and put your head under the clothes,"

Eleanor said unsympathetically. She heard a squawk from Nin as she replaced the callbox receiver, but whether from outraged feelings at this callousness or from some other cause she did not wait to discover.

XXXIII

MY WORST NIGHTMARE, which I get every two or three years, originated, I believe, in an early fright when some wellmeaning adult took me at the age of three for a ride in a fairground bumper-car. The nightmare consists of an endless, helpless ride, uphill and down dale, culminating in a crash, from which, of course, I wake.

Eleanor wasn't to know of this particular bugbear—luckily for me. If she had, she would hardly have given me the injection; it would have been more satisfaction for her to know that I was afraid to the extent of my capacity, that my sufferings weren't blunted by anaesthesia. As it was, when I came to, I thought at first that I was asleep and dreaming.

The circumstances were all too familiar—helplessness, inertia, pain, and the dark, rushing landscape ahead, which constantly swooped and flickered, always seeming about to engulf me, always parting to flow by at the moment of collision. But in due course I began to realise that there was a difference, and after another long period of slow, muddled analysis the reason for this difference became plain to me—I was not afraid. Far from it, indeed; never mind the helplessness, the pain in my leg, the fact that, as usual in dreams, my utterance was choked by some sort of gag and my hands fastened together; never mind all these unimportant factors. I lolled back in my seat and watched the landscape hurtle towards me with tranquil pleasure, in a state of dreamy euphoria. The fog had lifted, a beautiful moon-lit night displayed the rolling contours of south Cornwall to full advantage. I was positively enjoying my nightmare, quite sorry to think that in the end I'd have to wake.

The awakening came rather sooner than I expected. Eleanor turned her head from the wheel to look at me and said,

"Coming round, are you?"

Her voice was a shock because she had never previously figured in any dream of mine. Her reality forced my confused impressions to assemble themselves; also the vague pain in my leg suddenly crystallised into an appalling jab of agony.

"Good," Eleanor said. "I had to give you a small shot of chloral hydrate just to keep you under while I strapped you up and made a phone call, but I didn't want you out for long. Are you frightened?"

"Umhm," I croaked through the wide piece of surgical plaster which bound my jaws together. She evidently took this for an affirmative and said,

"I'm so glad to hear it. Do you know, my father—who was a complete megalomaniac—used to make my mother go out with him on his rounds. He was always slightly drunk, and a reckless driver at best. She was sick with terror every time... I used to promise myself that once, just once, I'd take him out and scare him sick. But of course I never got the chance. He did it once too often and killed them both. Still, it's some compensation to do it now to you."

She took a left-hand bend at seventy-five, judging it beautifully, swinging wide and then tapering her course in towards the left-hand verge.

Peaceful and serene from chloral hydrate I leaned back in my seat and watched the needle creep up towards ninety. We shot over a hump-backed bridge, leaving the ground I'll swear, all four wheels together, and landed like a bird twenty yards farther on. I felt like singing. It was a marvellously exhilarating ride, the best I'll ever have. Only one thing faintly marred my enjoyment: Maggie. Poor Maggie, I thought, she won't much like it when we are both killed. But it will probably be better for her in the long run, she'll be able to pursue her work without complications. Goodbye, Maggie, I thought, whoops, here we go.

This time it was a right-hand bend with a railway arch, a steep rise beyond, and a Z-bend-type crossroads. Eleanor flickered through at a nonchalant eighty, and then turned to see how I was reacting. Evidently not enough of my expression was visible behind the plaster; she leaned sideways and ripped it off with one deft tug. I let out a squawk.

"Be quiet you wretched little coward," she said, but I could tell she was pleased.

"Where are you taking me?" I asked, to encourage conversation. It seemed a golden opportunity, really, to discover what went on in Aspic's mind.

"Taking you?" she sounded vague, negotiating, at high speed, a long winding village. DOBHOUSES, on the nameboard, flashed towards us and then sped back into dark. I hoped, for their sakes, that the good people of Dobhouses were all in bed.

"Oh I'm just driving around," Eleanor said when we had left the village and were hurtling down into the valley beyond. "I'm waiting till the firemen leave Khartoum Cottage; the fire's dying down now, they won't stay much longer. Then I shall take you back there and kill you; your body will be found in the ashes and it will be assumed that you died in the fire."

"Oh," I said, and thought about this. Then I asked,

"Why do you want to kill me?"

"Because I'm sick to death of you hanging round Magda's neck like a dead weight, coming between us and holding her back. Because now you've even started interfering with my plans for Charles."

"Plans for Charles? What plans?"

"Charles is soft," she said, viciously zipping over a narrow bridge. "He's been soft all his life. I've always been able to make him do what I wanted."

"Perhaps he was humouring you."

"Hah!" she scoffed. We whizzed past a 30-mile restriction sign. "Charles wanted to be a vet. *I* persuaded him to go into the City."

"Why?"

"Why? Because I despise City businessmen, that's why! I thought he'd hate it, but he's such a fool he even found it interesting! Then I finished off his engagement."

"How did you do that, Eleanor?"

"Persuaded the little ass he'd fallen in love with to go and drown herself. I told her she had inoperable cancer."

Up to this moment I'd listened to these amazing confidences with drug-induced calm. But this was too much to swallow, even on top of a dose of chloral hydrate. I could feel the hairs prickle at the back of my neck. A girl had actually been *killed*, cold-bloodedly put out of the world, for no other reason than because Charles loved her.

"And now," she went on, irritably twirling the wheel between her gloved hands—we were on the coast, bouncing along the convolutions of a cliff road—"now he has to come down here, get all enthusiastic about a bloody pig, and you encourage him to fancy he's fallen in love with *you*."

"I certainly do not!" But my hairs were prickling again. I said with less certainty, "Besides, he's ill, dying. What difference does it make to you?"

"Dying! He's not dying!" she said contemptuously. "Can you imagine such a fool? He trusts me absolutely. He didn't even ask for a second opinion."

I opened my mouth but no sound came out—the shock of this information was so great that for a moment or two I really thought I was going to faint again. Eleanor took time off from her driving for another glance at me and smiled her little, cold bedside smile.

"That surprises you, doesn't it?"

"He's not really dying?" I said slowly. "Then why the move down here? Why all the elaborate build-up? I don't understand."

The road suddenly fell away before us in a series of steep gradients down to a small harbour village. Eleanor fairly poured the car over the edge, with the accelerator flat to the floorboards. I wasn't so resigned now; the effects of the dope was wearing off, I suppose, what with one thing and another. If my hands hadn't been bound with more sticky tape I'd have clenched them together as a lot of improbably white cottages, jazzed to the eyebrows with hydrangeas and carriage-lamps, came bursting up the hill towards us. But Eleanor fiddled through them somehow, dived up a pisky-lined, cream-lined main street, and took the clifflike gradient on the other side.

Charles isn't going to die; for all I know, isn't even ill.

Then I remembered the suicide notes. "Did you write them?" I asked.

"Write what?" There was a hairpin left bend halfway up the hill; it seemed impossible that we could get round at the speed we were going, but she took it with miraculous precision, doing a smooth double declutch.

"Charles's suicide notes."

Her face didn't alter but for the first time she misrevved a gear change and the engine howled. "I knew," she muttered, recovering, "I knew I should have got rid of you sooner, you scheming, spying little bitch."

"Well," I said comfortably, "you are getting rid of me now, so you might just as well explain the whole affair. You were going to play the same trick on Charles, was that it? Reduce him to such a low state of mind that he'd kill himself too? And you had the notes all ready, bits of paper with his fingerprints on, maybe? Only it misfired, because he was too keen on life, even a short-term life, to pack it in. But why did you want to get rid of Charles? For his life-insurance?"

"That wasn't the most important reason," she said.

"What was, then?"

"Because I hate his bloody guts." She didn't shout the words, she brought them out with a cold, clipped fury that carried frightful conviction. "I hate him and I always have! *No* man is ever any use. They're stupid, selfish, unprincipled—Why, Charles is so weak, he hadn't even the courage to kill himself."

"So then you thought you'd hurry it along by putting something in his aspirin bottle?"

Really, I decided, it's as well we are neither of us likely to survive the night, for what in god's name would I do with all this knowledge, if ever I returned to the real world? Go to the police and tell them that cold, elegant, efficient Dr Foley is the most ruthless psychopath they are ever likely to encounter?

She had run off into a stream of invective against Charles which made me shiver. Hadn't he ever guessed that this terrible avalanche was hanging over him? But then, had any of us? Had Maggie? Had John?

"Pulpy, commonplace, complacent, *stupid*—and, what really made me sick, people used to say he was like Mother. As if there could have been the slightest resemblance! *I* was the one who took after her!"

"You?" I was so fascinated that I forgot caution. "But, my dear Aspic, isn't it obvious that you are the living image of your father?"

She turned on me a face so distorted with rage that I thought, Now she really will put us both over the cliff.

Maybe it would have been for the best if she had done so. But she recovered her self-control at the last millisecond and said through her teeth,

"Do you know how I intend to kill you?"

"No, and to tell the truth, I don't greatly care to hear."

She took no notice of that.

"I'm going to burn you to death. I don't suppose it will take more than ten minutes but they will probably be extremely painful. I've got the firelighter in the back of the car. Then your suitably charred body will be found in the ashes."

I didn't fancy the prospect of that much. Nor did I like the notion of leaving Aspic behind me to go on her destructive way. After all Charles, once she was removed, would have the opportunity of a long and possibly happy life ahead. But if she survived I didn't give a lot for his chances.

I said, therefore, hoping to needle her into careless driving,

"You set fire to Khartoum Cottage, I suppose? That was pretty pointless, wasn't it? Why did you do it? Out of sheer temper because Charles had shot your precious leopard?"

My childish taunt had no effect. She jerked on another ten m.p.h. but we were galloping along a straight stretch of main road; it didn't make any difference. I was discouraged to see, from one or two recognisable landmarks which flashed past : a church, a pair of lodge-gates, a section of beech forest; that we had worked round in a circle and were now aiming back towards our final destination.

After a minute she said coolly,

"I set fire to the cottage because that tiresome old woman wouldn't make over the money for my clinic. I get it in her will. Anyway it's high time she died; what use is she?"

"Oh? You must have been rather annoyed, then, to hear Charles had saved her?"

"It's very unlikely that she'll survive the shock at her age," Aspic said with the confidence of know-how.

"So you inherit the money and start a clinic with Maggie?"

It brought a bitter burning sickness into my mouth even to speak of Maggie's intelligence and integrity in association with this bottomless fount of venom. I went on with some satisfaction,

"Maybe there's one thing you don't know? Your eccentric aunt seems to have kept the bulk of her fortune in the form of five-pound notes as bookmarkers in her library. How many volumes did she have? A couple of thousand? Reckoning fifty pounds to a book, that seems to work out at quite a lot of cash gone up in smoke tonight. I think I saw some bearer bonds too. I hope for your sake that the cottage was insured."

For the second time Aspic turned to me a perfectly bloodless face. But she kept her driving under careful control.

"I do not believe you," she said. After a pause she repeated, "I don't believe you."

"Well, the matter is easily proved. Do you have access to her bank account? And I saved a dozen or so books, all stuffed with notes, and put them in the toolshed. It would be too much to credit, wouldn't it, that they had been the only ones with money in them."

For the next ten minutes Aspic clean forgot me. It was restful, really; I didn't feel inclined to keep up the conversation any longer. My leg was hurting like bloody murder, the effects of the chloral hydrate had quite worn off, and I was not optimistic about my immediate future.

Only one thing cheered me at all; the map pocket in the door beside me had a sharpish metal edge from which the protective aluminium strip had peeled away; it was not easy or comfortable but in what I hoped was an unobtrusive manner I kept rubbing the plaster that bound my wrists against this sharp edge.

Eleanor drove faster than ever, utterly concentrated on her objective. Every now and then she muttered to herself,

"*Surely* she can't have been such a fool? Even Aunt Julia can't have been quite as crazy as that?"

All too soon we turned off the main road and climbed the hill towards Khartoum Cottage. I looked hopefully for flames, fire-engines, activity, but the trampled garden was dark and deserted; a heavy black column of smoke rolled up from sodden ruins, nothing more. The peaceful moon swam overhead.

Eleanor brought her car briskly to a stop and jumped out. She took the Diabolino from under its covering.

"I'll come back for *you* in a moment," she said to me, and there was a note in her voice suggesting that, even in her present preoccupation, she hadn't forgotten the treat she intended to get from roasting me. I hoped the Diabolino's battery had run down but this didn't seem at all probable; Aspic was too good an organiser.

She hurried off, lugging the heavy thing, in the direction of the shed, and I went on sawing at the surgical tape, and speculating as to whether my hurt leg would take my weight, and how I would manage if it wouldn't. The firemen had torn up Aunt Julia's front fence and there were picket-posts lying strewn about. If I could only hop as far as one of them and use it for a crutch—

Then I heard voices.

Hope flooded my mouth with salt and chased the blood round my veins.

"What are you doing here? Why aren't you in the lock-up?" That was Eleanor, shrill with surprise and suspicion.

"Because I got out of the lock-up, that's why!"

A man's voice. Peter Lannick. But I didn't pay too much attention. At that moment the plaster on my wrists parted stickily. I wrenched it off, eased open the car door—luckily Eleanor was now out of sight round the ruined cottage—and more or less fell out into the road.

Getting my hurt foot to the ground wasn't as bad as I had expected; it was much, much worse. The pain was so excruciating that after one attempt I gave up that notion. I shuffled sideways along the car until I could lean over and grab one of the fence-posts.

Balancing with it wasn't too easy because I hadn't yet learned to make allowance for my weakness; a broken leg and a bang on the skull plus Eleanor's dose of sedation had left me both feeble and a bit light-headed; the cold night air brought me out in a sweat and I found it hard to judge distances correctly. I swayed from side to side, my eyes wouldn't focus properly, and remaining at right-angles to the ground seemed an almost insuperable problem.

It had to be done, though. I helped myself to a second stake and lurched off down the road. After six painful yards my decelerated brain came up with an objection : if I stayed on the road Eleanor, as soon as she discovered I was missing, would come cruising along in the car and chop me down like a thistle.

So, with the utmost reluctance, I turned aside to my left, along a footpath which skirted Aunt Julia's garden. God knows where it went but it must lead somewhere; perhaps I could get down to the Marlin lighthouse road and thumb a lift home. In my confused and feverish state it naturally didn't occur to me that a hospital or police station would be a more practical objective; I ached for Maggie who would, I knew, rise to this emergency, lavish concern and sympathy on me, and do all the proper things for my leg and head. Furthermore these injuries would show her, past all disbelief, the sort of thing friend Aspic could achieve when crossed. A savage satisfaction filled me at the latter thought; for the first time I worked up enough courage to glance down at my leg. What I saw was not reassuring : a long ragged flap of trouser hung down, clotted with blood, which had soaked my shoe as well; the leg itself was hugely swollen, and something stuck out where it had no business to. I looked away again, fast.

At this moment I heard two shots in quick succession and a yell from the direction of the cottage. That's good then, I thought vaguely, Peter Lannick must have brought a gun with him and he's shot Aspic. What could be more providential? Fate is giving me a break.

My break lasted about half a minute; then I heard more shouts and the sound of running footsteps; two lots of them. Whichever of the pair had been shot could not be letting it affect them seriously. Moreover the footsteps were coming my way.

I hadn't any wish to tangle with Peter Lannick; if he had shot at Eleanor I could think of no reason why he might not shoot at me. I looked stupidly up and down the footpath, which was well-worn and ran between sparse hedges; in the moonlight you could have seen a ladybird walk across it, spots and all. Miss Julia's garden lay to the left; on the right was a wood extending all the way down to the Lan river. Somewhere bisecting that wood, I knew, was the road that led out to Marlin Head.

The footsteps were drawing near, too near. By using one of my stakes as a lever and one as a prop I hoisted myself through a gap in the right-hand hedge, and so into the wood. It was a mysterious-looking place, part of the pleasure-grounds of the old Marlin estate, composed mainly of laurels and rhododendrons which had grown to giant height. They were planted far apart, there was no undergrowth, and moonlight, filtering through occasional gaps in the dense canopy of evergreen leaves which didn't begin till twenty feet up, made sinister, Lamia-like forms out of the scrawny, writhing, twisting trunks. The wood had one advantage as far as I was concerned; I could make my way between the trees without much difficulty on my improvised crutches. But conversely, as soon as one's eyes became accustomed to its dimmer light the place provided very little real cover. The first use I made of what cover it did afford was to vomit my heart up, until the trees reeled in an arabesque round me. While I was recovering from that, gagging and wiping my eyes, I suddenly heard Eleanor's voice from the footpath, so near that I would have cried out and betrayed myself if I'd had any breath left.

"Next time you steal a gun, Peter Lannick, better make sure it's one you won't jam," she called contemptuously. "Not that you're likely to have another chance—you realise it'll be Broadmoor for you after this—attempted murder and setting fire to Miss Foley's cottage?"

I could hear heavy breathing, then Peter's voice, a little farther away, growled, "Just wait till I get my hands on you, you devil. I'll slit your gullet. You know full well it's a lie about the cottage, just as it was about the pigs—Ah, would you, then—"

She had evidently made a dart forward, opening fire on him with the Diabolino; I heard its savage crackle, his yell as he leapt back to safety, and a crunch; something struck the hedge and I got a momentary glimpse of Peter, who had apparently abandoned the jammed gun, slashing out furiously with a lawn-scythe, but I judged that he must have missed Eleanor, for there came no cry.

Presently she said—I imagined them, like duellists in the narrow footway, watching one another warily, all set for a lunge or parry—"And the police will guess it's you who stole the gun. My old nurse knew it was missing when I rang her, so I told her to get straight on to them. Who else would take it but you?"

"What do I care? They'll be hunting for me out Watertown way, not here. I knew she told them. I was listening outside the window when she phoned, see? Soon's I heard about the fire I knew you'd come here, so I come too. I fooled 'em, I come across the viaduct..."

I stopped listening then. The viaduct! Why hadn't that occurred to me? A straight, flat, easy way home, spanning the two valleys in one smooth stride. Hardly a quarter of the distance round by road. Illegal to cross it, of course, but that worried me not a jot, I was past such minor considerations. Besides—I looked at my watch—the ten-thirty-five to Paddington was just due, and after that no train crossed the viaduct for an hour and a half. I hadn't lived all those weeks in Watertown cottage without acquiring an intimate knowledge of the timetable. Very likely I could get across between trains and nobody would spot me.

I started the journey downhill. My head had begun to pound like a pile-driver and by this time my arms and wrists were shaking and sore from the unaccustomed punishment they were receiving; in fact I felt so terrible, one way and another, that I was obliged to stop every few minutes. But I gave myself the shortest possible rest each time; as soon as I was at all better I hobbled off once more.

Peter Lannick and Eleanor seemed to be out of earshot now.

In a vague way I felt sorry for Peter, who was being used so ruthlessly as a scapegoat by Eleanor; what had he done to deserve it? And he was doing me a good turn by distracting her; I hoped both for my sake and his that he would be the victor or at least come out equal in their peculiar duel.

But I hoped in vain.

I was taking one of my rests, leaning against a tree, when I heard Peter let out a ghastly yell—a high-pitched, sobbing wail of physical pain mixed fifty-fifty with sheer terror. I saw him run down the path, which more or less paralleled my course, over to the left; probably it led to the railway. It was possible to see Peter quite clearly because his clothes were on fire; the smoke and flame showed through gaps in the hedge as he fled, for quite a long way, until at last his screams died out down the hill.

Eleanor did not follow him; she turned and went back.

Now it's my turn, I thought; as soon as she finds I'm missing the hide-and-seek will begin. I had better not waste any more time.

Dragging myself upright I ploughed on, vaguely wondering how many minutes it would take the clear-minded and intelligent Eleanor to work out my probable escape-route. A good poker-player would have chosen the road after all; but it was too late to think of getting back to the road now. I might as well have contemplated climbing Vesuvius on roller-skates.

Tread, lift, swing. Lift, tread, swing.

My hands were all splinters and cuts from the roughly lopped stakes, but the pain of that was mild, even enjoyable, compared with my leg. Sometimes I bumped it, landing clumsily. It was better not to do that. Tread, lift, swing.

I heard the whistle of a train, half a mile away, on the viaduct, and then its mild rumble, growing louder as it slowly approached, creeping along at the regulation speed. The noise, conducted over water, sounded as clear as if the train were directly below me. Then I realised that it *was* directly below me —my perceptions were becoming very slowed-up now.

Steering cautiously past a mound of rhododendrons which dropped pallid dead petals on the grass, I came out into the open and found a short steep drop straight ahead.

It was the embankment leading down to the railway, which here emerged from a cutting in the hill, just before the entrance to the viaduct. Two more steps forward and I could see the lines themselves, bright in the moonlight like four narrow silver ribbons laid along the dark base of the permanent way. On my left the ribbons vanished into a V cleft in the hill; on my right they ran off to infinity, straight as a brick-layer's rule, carried on Brunel's immensely high, noble, insubstantial-looking columns. And far below the mile-wide misty mudflats of the Lan river at low tide, smooth jet, pooled and pearled with silver, extended into the distance like a Japanese print. Beyond them, the opposite shore could be seen dimly as a black furred ridge of trees against the pale western sky.

Home was over there; Maggie sitting by the dead embers and her final brew of coffee; Charles, perhaps, back from the hospital with Claire and Nin fussing round him; over there was warmth, shelter, affection—only a mile away along a straight track.

But first I had to climb down to the track. And in front of me was a fence: a strong, solid, five-foot no-nonsense Great Western Railway fence, concrete posts supporting a thick wire mesh. Hard to climb in the best of health, impossible with a broken leg.

Then I remembered the path not far away to my left, and handed myself sideways along the wire, carrying the crutches and resting my arms from them. There was the path, sure enough, and a gate, guarded by a notice that said trespassers would be prosecuted. It was not locked, though. I hitched myself through, and down some shallow brick steps on to the well-trodden plate-layers' footpath which ran alongside the granite chips of the roadbed.

Beyond the cutting, half a mile or so to the east, lay a signal-box, Lanrith Station, the dried-milk factory, telephones, and people, but it never even occurred to me that I might go that way. I turned my face to the viaduct. Before starting my mile-long hobble, though, there were adjustments that had to be made. With exquisite care I tore off the bloodstained flap of trouser-leg which was tending to trip me. My armpits and the insides of my arms had been rubbed raw by the crutches, so, sitting on a mysterious little concrete box set on legs and filled with sand by the side of the track, with my hurt leg gingerly stuck out in front, I removed my anorak and wrapped it round one stake. There was nothing left for the other but my handker-chief and the sock from the good foot.

I thought I might change them over from time to time.

The word *thought* hardly gives a clear picture of my mental condition. I was long past inference or reasoning by now, reduced to what is, I suppose, the normal state of an intelligent animal : external percepts appeared to me in the form of simple images, to be accepted or rejected or ignored.

Some burnt scraps of black rag on the path I ignored; they had no relevance for me. The assaults of pain in its various forms I almost succeeded in ignoring. Lanrith station I rejected because it lay in the wrong direction. But the shape of the viaduct was familiar as my own handwriting and I accepted it wholeheartedly.

By the time I had struggled past a signal set at danger and as far as the two little pepperpot towers like chessmen, one on each side of the track, that guarded the entrance to the viaduct, another rest was urgently necessary. I took it leaning against the parapet, looking down with a sort of mindless amazement at the panorama below me. Close by, the wooded hill dropped to the river; I could see the white splash of a small tributary water-fall through the trees and hear its murmur. Far under my feet the Marlin lighthouse road threaded the first arch of the viaduct, down by the river's edge. Then the silvery mudflats began, veined with narrow dark channels, and dotted with motionless, reflective, night-fishing birds. I heard the lovely liquid haunting cry of a curlew.

The prospect was so familiar, and yet so utterly strange seen from this unusual viewpoint, and my physical state was so abnormal, that I drifted into a kind of trance, helplessly waiting to pick up some clue to my identity, which seemed to have slipped away from me. Gracious knows how long I stayed there, propped against the wall; it seemed as if I had always been on the viaduct in the moonlight, and, coincidently, that I had never been anywhere, anybody, ever before.

But at last I began to move.

The path, which lay between the parapet-wall and the track on its bed of granite chips, was narrow and very difficult for me to negotiate on my stakes. The granite, piled as high as my hip, tended to come shaling down and impede progress; I clambered up its slope and for a short time tried hopping along on the sleepers themselves but they were awkwardly spaced for me; I had to maintain a punishing pace in order to achieve enough momentum to get from one to the next. So back on to the path. There were drain-holes through the parapet every ten yards or so; at every drain-hole I rested. There were also regular gaps where the brick wall gave way to a six-foot stretch of iron railings, in case of floodwater on the track, I suppose. The railings were substantial enough, no doubt, but they didn't look it; I gave them plenty of clearance.

The distance ahead of me didn't seem to grow any less, although I was now well out over the channel; I looked back hopefully to see how much distance I had put behind me.

Aspic was there.

I saw her descend the steps—unmistakeable in her gleaming white PVC coat—stoop to pick something off the ground and examine it, then turn, see me, and start deliberately in my direction.

She paused for a moment when she reached the two pepper-pot towers, looking up and down the track. The White Queen between two rooks, I thought—and it was a queen's move from her to me, straight, unimpeded, the best pounce in the game. No way to interpose or retaliate; my only hope lay in retreat. King's move, slowed down by a hundred per cent. The hope of a snail in the middle of the M.1.

I did what I could. The sight of her had given me such an incentive to put my best foot forward that I even rashly tried putting my worst foot to the ground; which was a catastrophic mistake and cost precious minutes while I hung on my two sticks, sweating and shuddering with agony and trying to accumulate enough impetus to move again.

She gained on me, of course, fast. She didn't call out or say anything; beneath her dignity, maybe; just came quickly and purposefully along the track. I didn't look back much because of the risk to my balance, but soon I began to hear the thud of her feet on the sleepers. Sounds—her footsteps, my gasping breath—reverberated oddly out here, over the water.

The shout which came then had the shocking quality of total surprise; it was deep and hoarse and desperate, the cry of a man sinking in a morass. Halted by it, in spite of my urge to flee, I turned cumbrously on my crutches, in time to see a black figure clamber up on to the track from the bushes below the left-hand tower, and start along the path towards us.

Eleanor was now very close to me, hardly fifteen yards lay between us. She too had turned and was staring back at the approaching figure. He called out again, wordlessly, there was something petrifying about the mixture in his voice of triumph and mortal agony. His eyes were on Eleanor—I caught the flash of the whites as he stumbled along; the rest of him was black—black and dripping; he seemed like a creature escaped from the pit.

Peter Lannick.

He's wet, I thought. Why? Why is he wet?

Slowly it came back to me that his clothes had been on fire, he had run down towards the railway...and then, perhaps, on to the little stream that cascaded through the woods.

"Give me one of your sticks!" Eleanor said to me in a low, tense voice. "Quick—give it to me!"

She started towards me again, and I realised for the first time that she no longer had the Diabolino with her; she must have discarded it as too heavy to carry so far, or too hard to account for if she met anyone with legitimate business on the track. Instead she held something small and gleaming: a hypodermic.

I backed away desperately past one of the railed gaps; she came on, cursing me in the same low voice.

"You little fool, can't you see he's out of his mind? Give me that stick!"

My back was against the parapet now, beyond the gap; I sagged there, stupid with pain, and saw the calculation in her eyes as she gauged my state. In her right hand the needle was poised, ready. She reached out with her left for the stick.

I lifted the stick and whacked the needle out of her hand. Next minute Peter Lannick had come up with us.

He was muttering, whether to Eleanor or himself I did not know, a dull, continuous stream of words, unpunctuated save by labouring breaths:

"...get her now for sure like she got my mum poor old mum rest her soul shooting's too good a death for her so I'm glad it was t'other one got shot and not you thought you were clever didn't you letting her wear your bloody leopard-spot coat and so I shot her in it but now it's your turn my lady tried to burn me all up didn't you thought I was done for but you was wrong you've had it now—"

The hypodermic lay on a sleeper, midway between them. I don't know if he realised its potency, but he understood that she wanted it; they crouched tensely about four feet apart, their eyes at grips. She was calm, controlled, and strong, he was maimed and half delirious; none the less, they were well

209

matched; his fanatical will for revenge made up for any disparity in strength.

Eleanor feinted towards the needle, then sprang back and grasped one of my sticks, taking my by surprise, snatching it away. I fell, twisting my hurt leg and getting such a kingsize jolt of agony that for several minutes my whole attention was concentrated on not coming to pieces. Swamped by successive waves of ice-cold weakness, I dug my fingers among the granite stones. Let the others do what they would . . .

When I could raise my head from the ground again I saw that he had managed to knock the stick away from her but that she had got possession of the hypodermic; however, he held her gripped by both arms and was slowly pushing her nearer and nearer to the railings.

"If you can't be shot—you can bloody well drown," he grunted, "you can rot in the mud for the gulls to pick at—"

I tried to call out but my tongue was thick and heavy in my mouth; no words came.

By this time he had dragged her to the fence and was forcing her back over it, but in order to do so he had to lean far out himself; they writhed in silence, silhouetted like some grotesque pair of figureheads. At last she managed to drag one of her hands free and stab upwards at his face with the needle, but he had got his hands clamped round her neck now, and was slowly tightening them. With a violent effort she thrust his head backward, but the effect was to overbalance them both. He swayed in a half circle, clutching fiercely at her—for an instant they remained in equilibrium, struggling on the rail—then they were gone, still locked in that terminal embrace. I thought I heard her call out "Karl!" hoarsely; perhaps at the last minute she thought Peter was somebody else.

Presently I crawled to the parapet, dragged myself up, and looked over. There was nothing to be seen. The incoming tide moved steadily over the mudflats in smooth crescents of foam; it had already passed the viaduct and covered all the area beneath.

A salt, fresh wind fanned my face and far away, somewhere inland, I heard a cock crow out of turn, saluting midnight.

It took almost all the strength and resolution I had left to rescue my second stick, which was lying up on the track; then I turned my face again towards home, doggedly, like a wounded animal that can only drag on in the direction of its burrow.

Some words of Peter's had come back to haunt me.

"Letting her wear your bloody leopard-spot coat and so I shot her—"

Maggie. Sitting in the cottage with her back to the open door, still wearing Eleanor's coat. Maggie. But surely he couldn't—? He had the gun, though.

A dreadful vision came to me: Maggie, badly hurt in the cottage, with nobody near, no way of summoning aid.

I must find enough strength to get there; find out what has happened, help Maggie, summon Charles—

So I started off again. Lift, tread, swing. Tread, lift, swing. No matter what it cost me, I must reach the other side.

And it couldn't, surely, be very much farther now, I seemed to have been going for my whole lifetime . . .

But I am told that when the milk-train from Penzance came along, and the driver spotted my unconscious body by the side of the track, I was barely a third of the way across.

XXXIV

AFTER THAT I remember nurses, doctors, nurses, succeeding one another in a sterile, bothersome chain, asking questions, doing things to me, pushing me back into the body I would have been only too glad to leave. The police came, too; I became accustomed to the grizzled, puzzled face of Inspector Pollard persistently by my bedside.

"But what were you doing on the viaduct, miss?"

"It seemed the quickest way home . . ."

"And Dr Foley? And Peter Lannick?"

"He came after her . . ."

In the end they decided that he had set fire to Miss Foley's house, out of revenge for being sacked, somehow burning himself frightfully in the process; that he had stolen the gun at the same time as the Diabolino (it was a puzzle about the fingerprints, though; none on the firelighter due to Eleanor's obsession for wearing gloves); that he had killed Eleanor and tried to kill me. The bodies weren't recovered for two weeks because the outgoing tide carried them round Marlin Head; they were eventually located by an Air-Sea rescue helicopter.

I didn't trouble to contradict the police theories; that way seemed to do the least damage. Peter Lannick left no close relatives, but Eleanor had left Charles, who would have enough to bear as things were.

Claire came to see me; kind, reliable Claire, with her greying hair and shrewd, tired eyes. We found it hard to think up painless topics for conversation. Long, awkward silences tended to develop. I asked her about Maggie's funeral. (For some time the hospital staff, guessing from my delirious mutterings that Maggie was a close friend, had kindly tried to keep the news of her death from me, but of course Inspector Pollard had blown the gaff on that).

"She's buried at little St Monack church," Claire said. "Right by the river. It's a lovely place ... I'll take you, as soon as you're allowed out."

"Thank you," I said dully. They had told me my leg would take three months to mend; a month before I even left hospital. I thought of Maggie lying friendless and unvisited, in a foreign country, by a strange river. Oh well. Maggie never cared about her surroundings.

"Did she die at once?"

"Yes. He must have shot her at very close range, the police said."

I hoped Claire was speaking the truth. But she didn't meet my eyes.

"And Charles?" I asked. "How is he?"

"Back at home. Still a bit shocked, of course, but his arms are healing well."

"That's good..."

Charles had not been to visit me. Everyone had advised against it; we were both too ill, had suffered losses, we would only upset one another. He had stayed in the hospital three nights and then gone home to Nin's nursing. I was relieved, really, not to see him; indeed, I didn't know how I could ever face him again.

"Wasn't it an amazing thing about those five-pound notes?" I said presently. "Had Miss Foley any money in the bank at all?"

"About a hundred pounds. No fire insurance, of course."

"It's just as well Eleanor died," I said drily. Claire gave me a queer look; we hadn't exchanged any confidences, but she was no fool. And she never had liked Aspic.

"The odd thing is," she said, "that Eleanor was due to die anyway—did you know that?"

"Eh?" I tried to sit up in bed, jarred my broken leg, and groaned in pain and frustration. *"Eleanor* was due to die— what do you mean?"

"I've been doing various bits of family business for Charles," Claire explained, "as he couldn't use his hands. Sorting through Eleanor's personal papers. And I found a consultant's report; apparently she was suffering from Ischaemic heart disease which would have carried her off in seven years at the outside. I gather that was why she gave up her London practice and her job at the Ogham and moved down here."

"Then it was *she*—that explains a lot," I said. "Good heavens. Does Charles know?"

"I haven't told him, no," Claire said without expression. "It seemed—it seemed too complicated. And not much point in telling him really."

"I quite agree."

After she had gone I lay restlessly turning my head from side to side, thinking of Eleanor. What a rage must have filled her when she knew that she was doomed. Ambition, the will to get on, had been the dominating drive of her life—that and her hate for Charles. How she must have longed to transfer the death sentence to him. Perhaps she deserved pity. At least some of her efforts could be considered disinterested—aimed at getting Maggie established. But I was unable to pity her. A ruthless action is no less ruthless if it is committed in order to benefit another person. Besides it was obvious that for Eleanor Maggie was just an extension of herself, a continuation who would live after her. And Maggie couldn't have borne to profit by someone else's misfortune—let alone the murder of two perfectly harmless individuals. Why had Maggie never suspected the jungle that raged inside her friend, I wondered. Then I realised—of course Maggie must have known, or at least suspected, about Eleanor's heart disease—in fact I remembered her virtually alluding to it on at least one occasion. Of course she would have guessed, however hard Eleanor tried to keep it secret—Maggie had too good a diagnostic eye to be misled, particularly about someone she knew so well. That was why she had excused so much of Eleanor's behaviour, and why she had felt obliged to stay in Cornwall. And of course she had not suspected Charles's illness for the simple reason that he was not ill.

Irrelevantly at this point I remembered that first morning when I had nearly dropped the sheet of iron on Charles from the roof; how angry Eleanor had looked, not because I nearly hit him, I realised now, but because I had missed him. What a simple solution *that* would have been for her. How angry Maggie had been with me, too, for overtaxing my strength. That had been the day when Charles and I first began to make friends.

A nurse came in and I turned my face away from the light because the memory of that idle, carefree day had brought me dangerously low. I hadn't wept yet and didn't intend to; a hospital is no place for tears.

"Two letters!" she said. "Lucky, aren't we!" pleased for me, because I had been a cause of kindly pity to the hospital staff; no letters, no visitors, except for Claire and the police; evidently no friends; it all seemed sad and odd.

I took the letters with my usual irrepressible throb of hope. One of them had a Florida postmark and contained another great big get-well card from Wal, who must have seen some one-line news item about peculiar goings-on in Cornwall.

"Hope you're better now chickabiddy I still remember the cutest gal in Curzon Street," he had written inside. At another time I would have been touched to think of Wal remembering me all the way across the stormy Atlantic, but now I just dropped the card in my waste bin, touched wood, and looked at the second letter.

Not the one I'd hoped for. My heart slowly returned to its normal position. Vanessa's purple typing and a Greek stamp.

Darling Aulis I gather from the Continental Daily Mail that you have been in the wars ridiculous creature what have you been up to? Mustang was full of Commissars. Not at all what I expected so I left quick and intend to stay here till it grows too hot. Why don't you come out and recuperate in your birthplace? I have had a large advance from Athens University Press for Vol Thirteen so here is your fare. But come soon!

Vanessa

The letter was headed Vathi (Aulis) and folded round a cheque for £400. I nearly dropped that in the waste bin too.

Claire visited me again and told me that Charles had gone to Madeira for a fortnight; it seemed a sensible step. He sent me a postcard: Having nice time, hope you are better. I thought: the last time I saw that handwriting it was forged—most expertly—by Eleanor, in a suicide note. Good thing I didn't leave those for Claire to find. Well, now he's all set for a long and happy life.

I saw his writing once more. That was on the day I was due to leave hospital with a crutch and twenty-pounds-odd of plaster cast. Claire had offered to fetch me and take me to my train; I was going straight up to London and on to Greece. There seemed, after all, no reason to linger in Cornwall.

"I've brought you a note from Charles," she said, competently packing me and my scanty luggage into the Jaguar. "He got back last night but he thought you wouldn't want too many of us fussing around."

"No, of course not," I said meaninglessly, and read the note while she drove down the little road that petered out at St Monack church.

My dear Tuesday, Charles had written, *or do I call you Aulis? I couldn't let you go without wishing you a speedy recovery and the very greatest success and happiness in your future life.*

I am sure you guess how deeply I feel for you over the loss of your friend. She was a most remarkable person, someone it is a privilege to have known. I am afraid you will leave Cornwall with sad memories, but I hope that later on, looking back, you may remember some happy times too. I know I shall carry memories of Tuesday and her guitar to the end of my life. I think you will never know how much your friendship meant to me. Please give my kind regards to John Fitzroy when you next see him. I hope you will be very happy together.

Yours, Charles.

I folded the little stilted letter small, and tucked it into my bag. Fifteen lines. They, like the kiss, were going to have to last me a long time.

Presently I asked Claire about her future plans.

"I'm going to stay on at Watertown," she said, and added rather hesitantly, "perhaps I'll buy the cottage off Charles and do it up."

"Oh, that's good! I shall like to think of you there, keeping an eye on him. Does he—does he know yet that he's not going to die?"

That was one piece of information I had passed on to her.

"Not yet," said Claire. "He thinks old Trevelyan—who told him he has a slight heart murmur, no more—is just keeping him cheerful."

"You'll have to tell him the truth in the end. It'll be quite a shock for him."

"Yes," Claire said. "I'll tell him when he's ready to know. Not just yet.—Here we are."

It was a tiny church, with graveyard to match, tucked down on a slip of flat land by the Lan river. Two haystacks, a small sandy beach, and trees all round. No one could ask a better place to lie. I had been afraid that Eleanor and Peter Lannick might be here too, but they occupied family plots at Lanrith, so Maggie could sleep here undisturbed, save by curlews and gulls and the changing tides.

I was surprised to see fresh flowers on the grave, a bunch of the piercingly sweet semi-wild yellow azaleas in a jar. Then a figure down by the water caught my eye—Matyas Kormendi, tossing out some withered flowers to float away on the tide. He made us a sort of salute as he passed his countrywoman's grave, but didn't speak. I looked at the inscription on the little stone.

Magdo Erzebet Tassák, Aetat. 35. M.D., M.R.C.P. Rest in Peace.

We murdered her among us. Eleanor began it, I helped, and Peter finished her off.

I went down to the water, where Kormendi had stood, took out Maggie's little crystal bird from my pocket, and dropped it into the clear, fast-running river, so that she would have something to remind her of home.

Claire looked at her watch.

"Perhaps we ought to be moving, if we're to get you to your train in comfortable time."

Because we were west of the river she took me to Hellanport Station, which was nearer. This meant I'd have to cross the viaduct in the train, but it hadn't occurred to Claire that I might not want to. And it would be unreasonable to ask her to take me an extra nine miles to Lanrith.

She put me on the train with anxious solicitude for all my possible needs.

"Sandwiches? Got your pills? Paperbacks? Shall I alert the guard?"

"Honestly not, thanks, Claire. You've been marvellous. Please don't bother to wait.

But she insisted on buying me a *Times* and waving till the train had left.

XXXV

CHARLES, HAVING ELUDED Nin's vigilant fussing, was in the orchard when the eleven-fifteen London train ran across the viaduct. In fact he had been out ever since breakfast, not doing much, just wandering around, trying to make some sort of plan of work to occupy the next few months. He was not finding it easy; but perhaps it would be easier when the train had gone. He looked at his watch. The signal on the viaduct winked its eye. Here came the train now, dead on time; for a moment it was silhouetted on the nearer span of the bridge, between the two wings of wooded hill. He lifted a hand, just in case; then it disappeared past the little headland and he heard it rumble out over the Lan river. There goes my future, he thought, and walked indoors. The clock on the sittingroom mantelpiece said eleven-seventeen; another twelve hours before the day would end.

XXXVI

OF COURSE I couldn't stop myself looking out as the train ran across the viaduct. There it all lay in its eggcup of valley, neat and compact, like a toy: Watertown. The white square house, the orchards, the outbuildings, the cottage, the row of cypresses, the giant yew tree. In the upper orchard a tiny figure stood quite still, watching the train. Charles. Gentle, simple Charles. It would never have done. Not with the ghost of Eleanor between us, not with all I knew and all he didn't know. Besides—who could tell?—I might presently become bored with gulls and streams and daffodils. Much better leave now; much better make the cathartic journey to Greece, hoping that for once Vanessa will have stuck to her word and still be there.

The last of the cypresses vanished; now the house was out of sight.

Quickly opening Claire's *Times* I saw the heading *Gull Race Losses* :

> *All hope has now been abandoned for the crews of the three boats which were presumed lost in last week's severe Atlantic gales. The names of the competitors are now given as Mr J. Fitzroy, Mr Liam O'Donovan, Mr S. Mitchell . . .*

There didn't seem to be any point in reading further just then.

Instead, as the train rumbled on across the broader span of the viaduct, I sat looking out of my first-class window at a sea-mist which ran like tears over the pane, blurring the distant outlines of the Lan estuary.

218